Murder on the River

ALSO BY JANICE FROST

MURDER ON THE RIVER

JANICE FROST

JOFFE BOOKS

Joffe Books, London
www.joffebooks.com

First published in Great Britain in 2025

Cover art by Dee Dee Book Covers

ISBN: 978-1-80573-282-2

To the memory of my Mum and Dad. Thank you for all the love.

CHAPTER ONE

DI Steph Warwick was sitting at a window seat in the café of Waterstones bookshop. She'd spent the morning jostling with hordes of other Christmas shoppers on the high street. Now it was time for some much-needed refreshment.

While waiting for her order to arrive, she'd been keeping a watchful eye on a trio of young men on the street below. They were near the entrance to Primark, one of them astride a red-and-black mountain bike, the other two hovering shiftily either side. Steph was on a rare day off. She could just look the other way — whatever the lads were up to, it needn't concern her.

"Ham and cheese panini?"

A couple of seconds, that was all. In the time it took for Steph to glance at the young waiter with the topknot and give him a nod, two of the lads had already walked away, and the one on the bike was pedalling off down the high street. Again, not her concern. If a drug deal had gone down in the few moments when her attention had been diverted, so be it. Let them have the benefit of the doubt. Maybe the lads had merely stopped for a chinwag. *Yeah, right.*

Steph whipped a notebook out of her handbag, quickly jotted down a few descriptive details, and made a quick call to the control room. Then, she turned a new page and refocussed her attention on her Christmas list, pleased that, after a productive morning's shopping, she could now tick off a few more items. Not that she had much more shopping to do, but she was on a strict deadline. Her brother, Fraser, along with his wife, Alba, and their three children, had moved to Sydney two years ago. As Steph's parents were flying out to join them for Christmas in a week's time, presents needed to be bought and wrapped before they departed. If the afternoon went as well as the morning, Steph hoped she might be finished ahead of schedule.

Steph had just polished off her panini when her phone rang — Elias Harper, her sergeant. She gave a deep sigh. *The best laid plans . . .*

"Yes, Elias. What is it?"

"Sorry, boss. It's a body. On Waterside South. Suspicious circumstances. There's no one else available."

I'm not available. "Okay. I assume you've set the wheels in motion?"

"All sorted, boss. There's a couple of Initial Response Vehicles there already. They're securing the scene, and forensics are on their way."

"Okay. I'm on the high street. Can you pick me up outside the Central Library on Free School Lane?"

"On my way."

Steph took a last, regretful sip of her Yorkshire tea, reached for her jacket and left the bookshop in a hurry. She made her way to the arranged meeting place, a short walk away along Saltergate. The lunchtime traffic was brisk, but Elias arrived only a few minutes after Steph. She tossed her shopping bags in the boot of the car and slipped into the passenger seat. "Fill me in."

"The victim is white, male, early twenties. He was carrying a University of Lincoln student ID card, so we've been able to identify him as Max Barsby. Twenty-one years old."

Steph nodded. She couldn't help thinking back to a murder investigation she'd headed up nearly three years ago now, involving the death of another young man, also a student at the university. Steph had been in a difficult place with her mental health at that time. A dark place, and she shuddered at the memory.

"Sorry to interrupt your day off. Did you manage to get presents for your family — nieces and nephew all sorted?" Elias asked.

"Mostly. I've just been getting a few extras for my parents to take with them. It's hard to know what to get for the kids when I don't see them very often. I haven't actually met their youngest."

"When was the last time?"

"Two years ago. Before they left. They were only supposed to be staying out there for a year, but Fraser's contract was extended for two more."

"And you've never been over?" Elias said.

"No."

"You should go."

"Maybe. But a year isn't a long time. They'll be back soon enough." Steph turned her head to look out the side window, signalling to Elias that she didn't wish to discuss the matter further. He didn't pursue it.

With the assistance of the 'blues and twos', they made speedy progress to Waterside South, where the road ended abruptly at a car park serving a riverside office complex. Two IRVs were parked a short distance from the car park. A PC from one of the vehicles greeted them. His colleague stood a short distance away, next to the car, with a young man and woman. Both had blankets draped around their shoulders. Steph assumed that they had been the ones to stumble on the victim, an assumption that was confirmed by the PC who greeted them.

Steph spoke in a low voice. "I'll speak with them after we've seen the body."

"Yes, ma'am." He directed Steph and Elias to a patch of woodland lying between the River Witham and a watercourse known as the Sincil Dyke. The path leading into the wood formed part of the Water Rail Way, a purpose-built walking and cycling trail that followed the route of the former Lincoln to Boston rail line. Steph had cycled the trail quite recently. She recalled seemingly endless skies, wide expanses of open space and the haunting beauty of the fenlands. Today's business, she suspected, would be a grim contrast.

They walked into the woodland and met up with another two police constables. Steph noted, with approval, that the scene had been secured. One of the PCs came forward and waited while they donned gloves, overshoes and protective suits. Then, he led them to where Max Barsby's body lay, well off the path, in a tangle of woodland close to the River Witham.

Steph frowned, noting the young man's wet clothing and hair. It had not rained overnight. "He was in the river?"

"The couple who spotted his body pulled him out, ma'am," the PC informed them. "They thought they were doing the right thing. The body was caught in some low-hanging branches. They were worried it might work loose and be borne away by the current."

"He's just a kid," Elias remarked.

"First thoughts?" Steph asked.

"Blow to the back of his head, which might have been sustained before or after he went into the water." Elias looked uncertain. "If I had to make a guess, I'd say before."

"Agreed." Steph stood up from her hunkered position over Max's body and cast keen eyes over the surrounding area. She looked at the PC. "Did you ask what the couple were doing so close to the water?" There was no clear access from the trail to the river. The couple would have had to beat their way through the tangled undergrowth.

"Foraging, ma'am. They were looking for things to use to make Christmas decorations."

"Right," Steph said. "We'd better speak with them." She and Elias went through the slightly laborious process of removing their protective clothing, to avoid any cross-contamination of evidence, before making their way back to the young couple.

The PC waiting with them introduced the couple as Axel and Rayna Young. Steph began by acknowledging that it must have been quite a shock to find a body. Then, she said, "Can you tell me how you found him? I'm told you were gathering materials to make Christmas decorations with."

"That's right," Axel said. "Rayna's good at crafting. We've got some friends coming round for supper tomorrow evening, and she wanted to make a centrepiece for the table. We were looking for twigs and branches to decorate with lights or candles, and maybe some ivy and other evergreen leaves, a bit of holly, some berries and pinecones . . ."

He spoke with a quick, nervous energy, as if by listing these irrelevant details he could put off mentioning the body. He swallowed. "I bent to rake among some leaves near the water's edge, and something caught my eye. A movement."

"The body?" Steph said. "Moving in the current?"

Axel nodded. "It was caught in some branches, but . . . bobbing."

Rayna spoke up. "I heard Axel gasp and came over to see what he'd found. We couldn't be sure the man was dead. His head and shoulders were being held out of the water by a branch. Axel waded in and we pulled him onto the bank. I'm sorry if we ruined a crime scene, but we weren't thinking."

Steph was sorry too, but it was what it was. "The body might have remained undiscovered for much longer if you hadn't been there. We stand a much better chance of finding out what happened to that young man now."

"What do you think happened to him?" Rayna asked. She grimaced. "There was blood on the back of his head."

Steph's reply was swift and cautious. "We don't know. It's too soon to speculate. I'd be grateful if you would keep your discovery to yourselves for now. The young man's next of kin need to be informed before anything is made public."

"That's no problem, is it, Axel?" Rayna said.

"Of course not. We understand completely."

Steph and Elias left the PC to look after the couple. They walked back towards the crime scene. Steph blew on her fingers to warm them. It would be a while before they could leave the scene. If this turned out to be a murder, as she strongly suspected it would, Christmas would be cancelled.

CHAPTER TWO

Steph had confirmation within twenty-four hours that Max Barsby's death had not occurred by drowning. The absence of water in his lungs indicated that he had died before ever entering the Witham. Cause of death was most likely the catastrophic injury to the back of his head. The weapon, a heavy, blunt instrument. In short, he had been murdered.

Breaking the news to Max's family was a disheartening experience. As usual, Steph left it to her sergeant to handle the strong emotions of the grieving parents and the other close family members present — Max's aunt, Emma Wentworth, and her son, Seth, Max's cousin. It was practically impossible to conduct an interview with the parents due to their extreme distress. Steph all but gave up. She decided to request that a Family Liaison Officer interview Anne and Tom Barsby at a later date.

Seth Wentworth was able to provide a useful snapshot of Max's social world — his circle of friends, the activities he engaged in and the places he frequented, which included bars and restaurants, sports facilities at the university and a couple of nightclubs — all pretty standard for a young man his age. When asked if Max had had a girlfriend, Seth became a bit flustered. "Or a boyfriend?" Steph suggested, to which Seth had muttered that as far as he knew there had been no one special in Max's life.

Regarding Seth, the lad seemed to have been holding back. He appeared more nervous than he should be considering he had a solid alibi for the date and time of Max's murder. He'd been at his girlfriend's house, with her extended family, for a festive get-together.

Steph hadn't been alone in her suspicions. Elias had also picked up that Seth seemed uncomfortable being questioned. He commented almost as soon as they left the Barsby's house. "Seth was definitely hiding something."

Elias had managed to draw Seth aside for a moment, out of hearing of his mother, aunt and uncle, to give him an opportunity to confide in private. "You should have seen his face when I asked him if there was something he'd rather tell us in confidence. Talk about alarmed. You'd have thought I'd just told him I'd read his mind and knew all his secrets. I gave him my contact details, but I won't be holding my breath."

Back at Newport, Steph noted some priority lines of enquiry. Among the people who needed to be interviewed first were the names of Max's friends, supplied by Seth, and also the members of the university staff to whom Max had been known. Seth had also advised them that Max had been a second-year student of archaeology, so they had a starting point.

It wasn't a great time to be tracking people down. With only two weeks left before Christmas, the university campus would be a ghost town, staff and students alike having gone off for the holiday.

"At least most of the people on this list will have a sound alibi," Steph said. "They could have been elsewhere in the country, or even abroad, on the date Max was murdered."

She tasked the various members of her team with making a start on contacting the names on the list and checking alibis. They would also check out Max's favourite haunts. It would involve hours of interviewing and carrying out visits to gather information, which would need to be recorded and cross-checked in the coming days and weeks. Thankless, but absolutely vital work.

Turning to Elias, she said, "Let's start at the top. We'll speak with the head of the archaeology department first." She left it to Elias to make the necessary arrangements.

Fortunately, Dr Emilia Hogue, head of archaeology, was available to see them that afternoon. Steph and Elias drove to the university and made their way to Dr Hogue's office, which was located in the archaeology department on the top floor of a five-storey building.

Dr Hogue invited them into her office with an air of impatience. She was a tall woman, attractive and slimly built. Her perfect posture suggested that she would run in horror from a comfy chair. Steph noted the presence of one of those weird, backless kneeling chairs that thrust your body forwards onto your knees. They were supposed to be good for your back but looked more like a form of torture. The chair was tucked away in a corner of the room, so maybe Dr Hogue had come to the same conclusion.

Dr Hogue apologised for the view. "I'm on the wrong side of the building for a view of the cathedral. Alas! We're a new department at the university, so we're perched up here as a kind of afterthought. All I get is a view of the car park." She signalled to them to sit, waiting until they were seated to sit down herself.

We're not here for the view. A young man is dead. Murdered. One of your students. Steph kept the thought to herself, realising that Dr Hogue might be feeling nervous. Prattling on about the view was a delaying tactic, a way of avoiding launching immediately into a conversation she'd probably rather avoid.

"Well, I don't even have a window," Elias said in sympathy.

Steph cleared her throat, bringing the small talk to an end. "Dr Hogue, what can you tell us about Max Barsby?"

Emilia Hogue spent the next five minutes pretty much echoing what Max's family had already told them — Max had been a lovely young man, studious, hardworking, passionate about archaeology. Why would he have any enemies? She was less informative when it came to Max's social life, as her relationship with him hadn't extended beyond her role as one of his lecturers. All the time she was talking to them, Dr Hogue's eyes darted from their faces to her computer screen, to her phone, to some paperwork on her desk.

Nevertheless, she dealt with their questions in an efficient and thorough manner, although it became quite obvious that she had not really known Max Barsby at all well, a fact she admitted.

"Of course, much of what I've told you about Max was what my colleagues who knew him better have told me. I didn't know Max personally, as I told you when you rang to arrange to see me, DS Harper. I've made a list of the academic staff in the archaeology department who had most contact with Max through seminars and tutorials. Most of them are free this morning and are willing to speak with you. If I were you, I'd start with Dr Bianca Carr. Bianca was Max's academic personal tutor. She was very upset to hear about Max's death."

Dr Hogue's next words confirmed that the only upset she had suffered was the inconvenience of having to deal with the fallout from Max's murder. "I'm just hoping it'll be possible to manage the negative impact all this is having on the department's image. Being a new department, we don't need any bad publicity." She looked at her watch. "I'm sure Dr Carr will be ready to see you now."

"Right. Thanks," Steph said. She stood up.

Dr Hogue seemed to ponder a moment. "DI Warwick. My colleagues are extremely hardworking. They have been deeply affected by the news of Max's death. I hope you won't cause them further upset by insinuating that you believe one of them might have been responsible."

Steph raised an eyebrow. "One of them *might* have been responsible. I'll do my job, Dr Hogue. Max and his family deserve nothing less than that I conduct a thorough investigation. And that means interviewing the people who knew him, including members of your staff."

"Of course. I didn't mean—"

Steph cut her off. "We'll stay in touch, Professor Hogue." She and Elias left the office before Hogue had a chance to reply. Outside, in the corridor, Steph counted off the seconds before Elias made a comment. Exactly four.

"Was it just me or did you get the impression that she doesn't give two hoots about poor Max?"

"It wasn't just you. She made it pretty obvious she didn't have time for so trivial a matter as the murder of one of her students. As for that comment about 'managing the department's image' . . ." Steph frowned. "Am I like her? I know I can come across as aloof, uncaring. I can't deny that there have been times when I've regarded a murder victim as a body, not a person."

"I've never known you to treat a victim with disrespect," Elias said. "Professor Hogue did just that when she kept looking at her computer and her phone while talking to us. As you just said, she didn't consider Max's death important enough to give it her full attention. So, no, you're not like her."

"Thanks, Elias." Navigating emotional territory was still tricky for Steph. As a young woman in her early twenties, she'd witnessed her violent ex-partner take his own life after admitting to murdering her best friend. The traumatic experience had caused Steph to shut down emotionally for years, until things had come to a head almost three years ago now. Save for the intervention of Elias, and a special constable named Jane Bell, Steph would have lost her job. Elias and Bell had insisted that Steph seek out counselling. She had come to rely on Elias's opinions, which she trusted unreservedly.

They walked along the corridor to Dr Carr's office. The door was ajar. A welcoming voice invited them inside. Dr Carr came out from behind her desk to greet them. In her late twenties, or early thirties, she had brown hair pulled back in a messy ponytail, and a pretty, expressive face. Intelligent, sympathetic eyes observed them from behind heavy-rimmed black glasses that made her look slightly geeky.

"I was expecting you. Professor Hogue just called to say you were on your way." Her voice was warm, the tone rich and slightly husky. Everything about her seemed to speak of compassion and sincerity. A refreshing change from Professor Hogue's hurried, dispassionate manner.

"Please, sit down. Would you like some coffee? I was about to make one for myself. I doubt Professor Hogue would have thought to offer you some."

Was Dr Carr communicating her opinion of Dr Hogue in that comment? Steph suspected she was. She consulted Elias with a glance, before accepting for both of them.

As she prepared their drinks, Dr Carr talked incessantly about Max. "I can't say how much the death of this young man has affected me." A clatter of mugs as she selected two from a small cupboard that seemed to be full of files and books. "Only twenty-one years old. A tragic loss. I can't stop thinking about his poor family, how they must be feeling. Max was so full of promise. Such an able student." She poured the coffee. "And a kind, caring boy too."

She walked towards them, steaming mug of coffee in each hand. Elias stood up to take them from her.

"Oops. I forgot coasters. One moment." Dr Carr searched in the drawers of her desk and produced two coffee-stained coasters, each bearing an image of Lincoln Cathedral. She placed them in front of Steph and Elias. Then, she sat down opposite them and asked how she could be of help.

"Professor Hogue told us that as Max's academic personal tutor, you probably knew him better than many other members of staff," Steph said.

"Yes, yes, of course. That's probably true. Although I should point out that I'm not, strictly speaking, responsible for the welfare of the students for whom I act as personal tutor. It's an academic role, although students often do come to me with their personal problems. I help if I can, but I also direct students to more appropriate support as required." Dr Carr passed Steph the sugar. "I hope the coffee isn't too strong for you. I like it like tar, with plenty of sugar."

"It's fine," Steph said. "Dr Carr, did you ever get the impression that Max was worried about something in the weeks leading up to his death? Did he approach you with any concerns he had that were unrelated to his work?"

Dr Carr sat back in her chair frowning. Several moments passed. Dr Carr gave the impression of being deep in thought, which raised Steph's hopes that she had something worthwhile to relate. So she was disappointed when Dr Carr, finally, shook her head.

"No. He didn't mention anything. Perhaps that's why the news of his death came as such a shock."

Steph had hoped for something more, but as Carr was not forthcoming, she asked how well Max got on with his fellow students.

"Max was well liked, I think. He was generous with his time in helping students less able than himself. He seemed to get on with everyone." Here, she paused. "With one notable exception."

"Who was that?" Steph asked.

"Harry Scott. I'd better tell you about the field trip to Vindolanda." Dr Carr inhaled deeply before beginning, as though she needed something to sustain her. "In October, I accompanied a group of students, which included Max and Harry, on a field trip to Vindolanda." She paused and looked at them enquiringly. "Have you heard of it?"

Steph shook her head. Beside her, Elias nodded enthusiastically.

"It's the site of a Roman fort in Northumberland," he explained to Steph. "Archaeologists have made some wonderful finds there, most notably, wooden writing tablets that give real insights into the day-to-day lives of ordinary Romans living on the northern frontier of Britain."

Steph listened patiently while her sergeant and Dr Carr jabbered on about the amazing writing tablets and the rather mundane — in Steph's opinion — content they contained. One, about a mother inviting another mother and her child to her child's birthday party, was especially dull, but the way

Elias and Dr Carr enthused about it, you'd have thought it was the best thing since sliced bread. Maybe she was missing something.

Elias began rabbiting on about a trip he'd made to this magical Vindolanda, and how wonderful it had been to see the writing tablets at the British Museum. Steph stifled a yawn.

"So sorry," Dr Carr said. "To return to Max and Harry Scott, and a particularly ugly incident that occurred on the Vindolanda trip. There had been tension between the two of them for some time prior to the trip. Max never mentioned it, but I found out from another student that Max believed Harry wasn't pulling his weight in preparing for seminars. Max and the other two students in the group were doing all the work. Unfortunate, because marks were being awarded for group work, and if one student doesn't contribute much, the others have to contribute more, or risk being marked down."

"That seems unfair," Steph commented.

Dr Carr shrugged. "Group marking isn't popular with a lot of the students. Except the lazy ones, of course."

"So, what happened on the field trip?" Steph asked.

Dr Carr seemed embarrassed. "Actually, a fight broke out between Max and Harry."

Steph looked at Elias. Here, at last, might be something to get their teeth into. She waited for Dr Carr to elaborate. After a prolonged silence, Dr Carr sighed deeply and continued. "It was on the evening of our last day there. The staff had organised a barbecue. There was a campfire, and the students were relaxing, having a few drinks and singing songs around the fire while the staff were busy preparing and cooking the food.

"I was preparing some salad to go with the burgers when I became aware that the singing had stopped, and that loud shouting and screaming had taken its place. I looked over to the campfire and saw Harry and Max fighting. Some of the other students were trying to pull them apart, and they eventually succeeded in doing so, but as soon as they let go of Harry, he went for Max again. He rammed right into him."

Dr Carr closed her eyes as if deeply troubled at the memory. "Max was taken off guard. He stumbled backwards onto the fire."

"How badly was Max hurt?" Steph asked. It was clear that this was much more serious than the 'tension' between the students that Dr Carr had first alluded to.

"Well, he was injured, but not as badly as he might have been, thanks to some fast action on the part of my colleagues, and Max's fellow students. Two of my colleagues pulled him off the fire, and some students used the blankets they'd been wearing around their shoulders to beat at the flames and smother them. Luckily, Max was wearing a thick coat. He escaped with minor burns, mostly to his hands."

It must have been a shocking scene after a long day spent working companionably at the dig, followed by the camaraderie around the campfire. "Was the incident reported to the police?" Steph asked, suspecting she knew the answer.

Dr Carr shook her head. "Harry showed remorse for what he'd done — he said he hadn't meant to push Max onto the fire. He'd drunk too much and lost control."

Steph nodded. "What was their fight about? Surely not just over Max accusing Harry of not pulling his weight with seminar work?"

"It was partly that, but also, before the field trip, a student had sent an anonymous note reporting Harry to the seminar group tutor. Students don't usually do this because they don't want to be seen telling tales. Harry thought that Max had been the one to send the anonymous complaint. He confronted him about it."

Dr Carr paused for a moment. "But of course, there was more to it than that. Harry accused Max of 'stealing' his girlfriend."

"Ah. Was the young woman in question also at the barbecue?" Steph asked.

"Yes. Her name is Sophie Egan. I don't know if it was true that she was two-timing Harry with Max. Anyway, Harry faced disciplinary action for injuring a fellow student and was probably looking at expulsion. Then, he left of his own accord. To be honest, I think if Harry hadn't left, he would most likely have been obliged to leave at the end of the year anyway. His grades were so low it was obvious he was going to fail his course."

"Right," Steph said. "Did the identity of the person who sent the anonymous tip-off ever come to light?"

Dr Carr shook her head. "Not that I know of. It might have been Max, or it might just as easily have been one of the other disgruntled members of the seminar group. It was a handwritten note, not an email, and the tutor threw it in the bin after speaking with Harry, so there's no way of tracing who wrote it."

"Pity," Steph said.

"As far as they were concerned, the matter had been dealt with," Dr Carr said. "There was no reason to hang on to it. I can't believe any of this has anything to do with Max's murder though. I just thought I'd mention it as you're bound to hear about it from someone else."

Steph asked Dr Carr a few more standard questions. She also requested information on the students and members of staff who had witnessed the campfire incident. Carr assured her that she would compile a list and contact her as soon as possible. Steph drew the interview to a close, and Dr Carr accompanied them to the door of her office.

"Max Barsby will live on in my mind, and in my heart," she said. It would have sounded mawkish were it not for the fact that Bianca Carr came across as one hundred per cent sincere.

"What did you make of all that?" Steph asked Elias. They had left the building and were making their way to the car park, through a campus almost devoid of students.

"Well, I guess we now have a potential suspect in Harry Scott," Elias said. "He's obviously got a fiery temper — excuse the pun. But murder is a big step up from a fist fight."

"Sexual jealousy can provoke strong emotions — and can result in murder," Steph said. "We've seen it often enough.

Let's bump Harry Scott up to the top of our list of interview-ees for tomorrow. It's going to be a long day of interviewing dusty academics for the rest of today, I'm afraid."

"I wouldn't describe Dr Bianca Carr as dusty," Elias said.

Steph gave him an amused look. "Yes, well, you can run off to Vindowhatsit with her when we've solved this case. For now, I need your mind on the job."

Elias sighed. "Always, boss."

CHAPTER THREE

"Special Constable Jane Bell?"

Jane looked up at the mention of her name. She was in the shift briefing room, uniform on, ready to start an afternoon stint. A man with gingery blonde hair who looked to be in his late twenties, with shoulders like girders and an air of knowing where he was going, stuck out his hand.

"PC Seb Kirk. We've been posted together tonight."

Jane shook hands with him. "Nice to meet you, Seb." She noticed his gaze flick to her right hand as he shook it, and she felt slightly self-conscious about the scars crisscrossing her fingers, the legacy of having acid hurled at her almost a year ago. If PC Kirk noticed, he didn't comment.

Jane was used to being partnered with lots of different colleagues, but she missed PC Tim Sterne, whom she'd worked with more than most. Tim was currently convalescing, having suffered a heart attack just over a month ago. The last time she'd spoken with him, he'd told her he was going to take early retirement. All that experience lost to the Force. Still, she didn't blame Tim for wanting to go. He'd been looking forward to retiring for a long time, and his brush with mortality had merely acted as a spur.

Jane left the station with Seb Kirk, practically jogging to keep pace with his long stride. They walked together to the

Incident Response Vehicle, or IRV — police acronyms rolled off Jane's tongue like liquid silver these days — parked in the yard outside. Seb seemed eager to drive. Jane was happy to let him, and so they set off.

"How long have you been a special?"

"How long have you been in the Force?" Their questions collided.

"You first," Jane said.

"Six months," Seb said. "It's a career change for me. I used to be a farmer."

"That's quite the career change."

"I never wanted to be a farmer. I just did it to help my parents out. My younger brother was keen, and when he was old enough to take it on, I went off to do a degree in criminology. Then I joined the police force, something I'd always wanted to do. I want to be a detective. How about you? What's the day job?"

"Teaching," Jane said. "I worked as an English teacher for over twenty years, then when my husband died, I sold his business and became a part-time tutor instead. It meant I could be my own boss, work the hours I wanted to work, and have time to volunteer as a special. I've been doing it for about two years now."

Eyes on the road ahead, Seb nodded. He seemed like a serious young man. And dutiful — he'd worked the farm until his younger brother was in a position to take over, delaying his own career plans. Jane wondered why he'd chosen to join the Force as a police constable instead of following the Police Now National Detective Training Programme for graduates. By doing so, he could have bypassed the requirement of having to spend two years as a PC before applying to be a detective constable. Seb pre-empted her question.

"I joined as a PC instead of taking one of the graduate fast-track routes into policing because I didn't want to miss out on the opportunity to work at grassroots level with experienced officers like you. I want to know policing inside out and from the bottom up before I get to a level where I'm telling other people what to do."

"That's very admirable," Jane said, feeling flattered that he regarded her as an experienced officer. Still, she considered Seb's attitude a bit old-fashioned. Jane had witnessed new graduates straight out of university in her own profession of teaching doing a better job than those with years of experience. It was all about the ability to do the job.

Her train of thought was interrupted by a transmission from Control. And so began a series of call-outs to minor incidents, breaches of the peace mostly, requiring tact and careful handling from Jane and Seb, but no arrests. Then a quiet spell, followed by a request for them to investigate a report of a burglary at an address just north of Lincoln Cathedral.

"Challenge accepted," Seb said enthusiastically, making Jane smile.

The call handler advised that a Dr Linus Crow had reported returning home from work early to find a burglary in progress. The offender had bolted. As there was a chance he was still in the vicinity, a second unit had been requested to respond, to assist in carrying out a search of the local area. Unfortunately, none was available. Hopes of giving pursuit when they arrived at the address were further dashed by the heavier than usual mid-afternoon traffic, which held them up for a good ten minutes, despite their flashing lights.

When they finally arrived at the address, a man dressed in jeans and a Barbour jacket stood at the open door. "Dr Linus Crow? Are you injured, sir?" Seb asked.

The man looked confused. "What? Yes, I'm Linus Crow. No, I'm not injured." He gave a grunt of exasperation. "And you've got no chance of catching him now. It's nearly fifteen minutes since he made his getaway. What's taken you so long?"

Seb ignored Crow's criticism. "Did you see which direction he went in?" Crow pointed towards Nettleham Road, one of the main roads leading into the city centre. If he was nifty on his feet, the burglar would be in the Bailgate by now, mingling with afternoon shoppers and pedestrians.

Jane updated the Force Control Room, informing them that they'd arrived at the property, and that pursuit of the offender had been ruled out. "May we come in?" she asked Crow when she'd finished giving the sitrep.

Crow gave a weary shrug. "Be my guest." He led them into the front room of the house, which, despite some untidiness — a couple of misplaced cushions on the sofa, a sideboard with its drawers pulled out, all of them empty by the look of it — didn't exactly look like it had been ransacked.

"Not too much mess, is there?" Seb said, echoing Jane's thoughts.

"That's because I don't have many possessions here. I'm renting this house temporarily while I'm working in Lincoln," Dr Crow said.

"Do you think anything's been taken, Dr Crow?" Jane asked.

"I'd left some cash in a bowl on the kitchen table — not much, probably around fifteen pounds in total. That's gone. I don't know if anything else is missing. I haven't had time to check properly. I also left my laptop on the dining room table. It's still there, thank goodness. The doors and drawers to the cabinets in the kitchen have been pulled out, but because this is a rental property, the only things in them are basic crockery, cutlery, pots and pans.

"He'd have been able to see at a glance that there was nothing worth stealing. He must have got in through the back door leading into the kitchen. He didn't even need to use force. I stupidly forgot to lock it." Crow rolled his eyes. He'd been talking fast, a sign that he was agitated and nervous. Understandably so. His space had been violated. He led them to the kitchen and showed them the evidence.

"What about the bedrooms? Did the burglar go upstairs?" Seb asked.

"I haven't been upstairs yet. I've been looking out for you arriving. And I didn't feel like going up there on my own."

Jane understood. Coming home to find an intruder in your house was an unsettling experience. "Talk us through what happened when you got here."

"I wouldn't normally be here at this time of day. I came back to get some notes I'd left behind. He must have heard me when I came in and waited until I made for the kitchen before coming downstairs. I heard the sound of footsteps on the stairs and reached the hallway just in time to see him slip through the front door."

Crow had already described the intruder to the call handler when he rang 999, but Jane went over the description with him again. "And you didn't get much of a look at him, our call handler said."

"He was tall, gangly almost, with a bit of a stoop — no youngster, I'd say. As well as the stoop, I think I caught a glimpse of white hair. He was wearing black trousers and a black padded winter jacket of the sort nearly everyone wears at this time of year. Black gloves, I think. He had the hood of his coat up, so I've no idea what he looked like. Not much to go on, is it?"

"How did you know it was a man?" Seb asked.

"I could just tell. His shape. His gait. I suppose I can't say for absolute certain, but I'm as sure as I can be."

"Would it be all right for us to take a look upstairs, Dr Crow? It would help if you would accompany us, so that you can tell us if anything's missing or out of place," Jane said gently.

Crow nodded. "Of course." They went upstairs. Crow showed them two empty bedrooms, both at the back of the house. One was very small. It would have been obvious to the burglar that both rooms were unoccupied. The beds were made up. There were no knick-knacks of any sort on display. The large room had a wardrobe — the doors stood open — and a chest of drawers. The drawers had been pulled out, revealing nothing inside. The smaller room was just big enough to fit a single bed and a bedside table, but it did have a built-in cupboard, empty, save for a rolled-up spare duvet and a couple of pillows.

Crow gasped when they entered the master bedroom. The intruder had been more thorough here. The mattress

21

was half off the bed, the wardrobe doors were open wide, drawers were pulled out, clothes and other belongings strewn across the floor. Jane had seen a lot worse, probably because there wasn't a lot for the burglar to rifle through, only what Crow had packed for his trip.

Crow inspected everything. Looking perplexed, he said, "As far as I can see, there's nothing missing. Nothing at all." He sighed, then let out a cry. "Wait a minute." He crossed to the bedside table and picked something up. A Rolex watch. "I just remembered I left in a rush this morning and forgot to put my watch on. You'd think he'd have lifted this at least." He frowned. "Do you think he was looking for something specific?"

"What do you do for a living, Dr Crow?" Seb asked. "Could this be connected with your work in some way?"

Jane thought of Crow's laptop lying untouched on the downstairs table and doubted it.

"I'm an archaeologist. I run my own archaeology consultancy firm," Crow said. "My firm was contracted to do an archaeological survey on a site just west of the university. We started a couple of weeks ago, but I don't see how that could have any bearing on my house being burgled. It's a routine dig on a site that's going to be developed into a wellness centre by a firm called Roadknight Construction. In a nutshell, my brief is to carry out preliminary surveys to check the site for any important archaeological remains, and carry out excavations, as necessary, prior to and alongside the construction work."

Jane nodded. "That sounds exciting."

"Yes, well, even if I'd found a hoard of buried treasure, I'd hardly be storing it here, would I? So, no, in answer to your question, I don't think the burglary has anything to do with my work."

"It was most likely an opportunistic crime," Jane said. "The house looked empty, the street quiet, no one around. The burglar saw an opportunity and acted on it. He found the cash in the kitchen, grabbed it, and decided to check for other valuables. My guess is you disturbed him before he saw your watch."

Crow looked unconvinced. He gazed at his Rolex, now safely strapped around his wrist. "Yes, you're right. That's probably what happened."

They checked the upstairs bathroom, and finding nothing amiss, went back downstairs to the kitchen, where Jane took down some further details of the incident from Crow to assist in preparing her report of the crime. She and Seb then left Crow in the kitchen and went outside to check for any evidence left by the offender. Jane checked the back and front of the house, while Seb knocked on the doors of nearby residents to find out if any had surveillance cameras, or had seen someone approaching Crow's house.

They reconvened at the front door when they'd completed their tasks. Seb hadn't had much luck. "No reply from the nearest neighbours. We'll have to follow up when we can get hold of them. Negative response from the others. No one noticed anyone hanging about. Did you find anything?"

Jane hadn't been particularly successful either. "Not so much as a footprint. Let's go back inside."

Linus Crow was in the dining room sitting at the table, his laptop open in front of him. He looked up expectantly at their arrival. "Anything?"

"Your near neighbours weren't at home, but they will be contacted. I'm afraid no one else in the surrounding area was able to provide us with information to help identify the intruder."

"Well, most people don't sit by their window all day looking out for trouble, so that's hardly surprising." Crow's irritability was understandable. Jane always felt disheartened at the scene of a burglary when there was little evidential material to act on. She couldn't offer Crow much in the way of reassurance. He'd been lucky that so little had been taken — if only because he'd had few possessions at the house to take, but she wasn't about to say that to him. Crow echoed her thoughts.

"Thank goodness I didn't bring anything valuable with me." He touched the strap of his Rolex again.

It did niggle Jane a little that it had been left behind — why take fifteen quid in cash and leave an expensive watch? She sighed. The explanation had to be as she'd surmised earlier — the burglar had been disturbed before he noticed it. She advised Crow that a CSI would call later to check for forensic evidence, which seemed to cheer him slightly. They left him at the door to his rented home, looking slightly concerned at being left alone.

Jane and Seb attended another couple of minor incidents before their shift ended and they returned to Newport. "A quiet shift," Seb remarked as they parked up outside the station. He sounded disappointed.

Jane thought of Dr Crow standing forlorn at the door of his house as they were leaving, and thought that, for him, the day had been anything but quiet. Maybe, if she found herself on a shift with Seb again, she could help him work on his empathy skills.

CHAPTER FOUR

After her shift, Jane just had time to shoot home and change before going out again to meet her son, Patrick, at the train station. She stood waiting on St Mary's Street within clear sight of the exit. The last time she'd seen Patrick was at the beginning of October when she'd stayed overnight at his flat in Balham. A long time ago, as far as Jane was concerned.

Patrick's upcoming visit of two weeks was as unexpected as it was welcome. Jane suspected it might have been curtailed had Patrick not broken up with his partner, Jorge, a few weeks ago. Previously there had been some talk of the pair of them spending Christmas skiing in Colorado. Was it evil of her to be secretly glad those plans had fallen through? It wasn't as if the relationship would have gone anywhere, with Jorge returning to Spain in January when his visa ran out. Jane had never met Jorge — he always seemed to be somewhere else when she visited Patrick. She'd sensed that the relationship had cooled off as far back as October, when Patrick had confided that Jorge wasn't really his type.

An announcement boomed from within the station: *The train arriving on platform three is the fifteen thirty from London Kings Cross.* Minutes later, Patrick appeared on the square outside the station exit. He gave her a wave and a big, Patrick-sized grin.

Jane rushed over to hug him, and Patrick squashed her back. "Hi, Mum." He looked around. "No Norah?"

"She's at work," Jane said. "Finishes at seven. I've booked a table at Veganbites for quarter past, so there's time for us to drop off your bags, have a cuppa and walk down to meet her. She's excited about seeing you. Here, give me one of those bags." Jane reached for a padded briefcase.

"Okay, but be careful. That's my laptop," Patrick said.

They walked along Sincil Street to City Square, then crossed the footbridge over the River Witham. From there, it was a short walk to Jane's end-of-terrace cottage on Danesgate.

Jane made a pot of tea while Patrick lugged his bags upstairs to the first floor, to the bedroom that doubled up as a snug when no one was staying over. Jane's bedroom was next to this. Norah was currently occupying the largest bedroom on the second floor, which had been Jane's when she'd first bought the house. She'd assumed the property would be adequate for herself and occasional visits from the children. Now she was wondering whether downsizing had been such a good idea. The cottage's rooms were small, the snug especially so. At a squeeze, there was room for a sofa bed, a bookcase and a coffee table. Handily, it had quite a deep cupboard that Patrick could keep his clothes in, now that Jane had had a big sort out.

Jane had spent much of November living in her partner Ed's much roomier house in the village of Doveby in the Lincolnshire Wolds. She had been helping out in a murder investigation, working undercover — a word that Steph Warwick, the detective inspector conducting the investigation, would have frowned upon. As far as she was concerned, Jane's role had been to seek out and listen to local gossip.

Jane knew that Ed would have liked nothing more than for her temporary residence at his place to become permanent. Being Ed, he would never press her on this, and he'd only once remarked how lovely it was, the two of them living together instead of in separate houses.

Jane had been a widow for five years when she met Ed. She'd had one or two relationships after the death of her husband, Sam, but until Ed there'd been no one for whom she'd had feelings other than a faint sexual attraction.

"Is that a nice cup of tea?" Patrick's voice boomed from the door. His hulking figure seemed to crowd the small kitchen, but, in spite of his size, Patrick was as soft as a teddy bear.

Jane smiled. She handed him his mug — the same one he'd used at home since he was ten years old. He glanced at it in amusement. "I see Tigger's still going strong. Has Norah still got Eeyore?"

"Of course, and I've still got Owl," Jane said. There was no need to mention the Winnie-the-Pooh mug that had belonged to Patrick's dad, still hanging from a hook in one of the kitchen cabinets.

They moved into the living room. Patrick looked around. "The tree looks nice."

Jane had collected her Christmas tree from a nursery a few miles outside Lincoln the previous weekend. She liked to put it up early. It was modest in size compared to the ones they'd had in their old family home, but it fitted the proportions of the room.

"And the decorations," Patrick added. "A very tasteful blend of the old and the new."

"I'm glad you approve," Jane said. Last year, Norah had criticised her mother for recycling the Christmas decorations that they'd been using for years. This year, Jane had had a sort out and thrown away the tatty and the torn. She'd kept some of the tree decorations — the ones that the children had made, and the ones that had sentimental value, such as the glittery baubles that she and Sam had bought for their first Christmas tree.

Patrick got up and inspected the tree. He lovingly touched one or two of the familiar decorations hanging from its branches. Jane felt a lump in her throat, aware he was trying to anchor himself in this house, where he had not grown up and which held no memories for him. When she sold the old family home, Jane hadn't really considered the impact it might have on the kids. She'd needed a new start, but she'd sold Patrick and Norah's biggest link to their dad.

"Patrick . . ."

"It's okay, Mum. Really."

Darling boy. He could always read her mind like an open book.

They drank their tea and by then it was time to go. Veganbites was owned by two of Jane's closest friends, Frieda and Karun Arya. It specialised in vegan and vegetarian dishes. Patrick liked his meat, but he'd been won over by Karun's cooking on previous visits, and Jane knew that he wouldn't be disappointed this evening. When Karun heard Patrick was coming, he'd announced that Patrick's favourite butternut squash and sweet potato curry would be on the menu.

They walked up Steep Hill to Castle Square, where they paused to look at the Christmas decorations. The central arch of the Exchequer Gate offered a glimpse of the shimmering, silver-lit Christmas tree in the cathedral precinct.

As they approached the tree, Jane directed Patrick to one of the many memorial tags hanging from its branches. Jane and Norah had placed one there in memory of Sam the previous week. Patrick touched the card and read what they'd written. Then, he and Jane nodded at each other. Both had tears in their eyes. After a few more moments of silent contemplation, they moved on.

A warm welcome awaited them at Veganbites. Karun and Patrick high-fived and patted each other on the back. Patrick bowed low to allow Frieda to kiss him on both cheeks. Soon after, Norah arrived. Patrick swept her off her feet into a crushing bear hug, making her shriek with delight.

Jane looked around and saw Ed already seated. He rose to his feet to greet everyone. Ed and Patrick had met only a couple of times before, but they clasped hands and hugged like old friends.

Halfway through the meal, and without warning, Patrick made a big announcement. "So, I've quit my job." They all stared at him.

Norah was the first to recover. "Seriously?"

"Yep. Seriously."

Jane cleared her throat. "Have you got another job?"

Patrick's reply was not reassuring. "Nope."

"Uh huh," Jane said. Great. Another child she'd thought was settled was now unemployed. Norah had quit her job with the BBC in London earlier that year, and was now working in Lincoln as a temp.

Patrick must have registered her concern. "Don't panic, Mum. I'm a qualified, experienced finance manager. I don't intend to be out of work for long. I've already submitted some applications, and I've got a few interviews lined up in the early New Year. In the meantime, I'd quite like to stay at yours until I get sorted. If that's okay?"

Jane beamed. It was more than okay. She'd be seeing her son for longer than a few days snatched here and there. "Of course it's okay. It's fantastic."

"That's a relief. Save me travelling all the way up from London to attend my interviews."

Jane and Norah exchanged a look that Patrick noticed. He turned to Norah. "Yep. I've decided London isn't for me either, Sis. The jobs I've applied for are all in Lincolnshire and Nottinghamshire, so, with luck, you'll be seeing a lot more of me in the future. Aren't you lucky?"

No one disagreed. "Only problem is," Patrick continued, "it'll take me a bit of time to readjust to the pace in this part of the world after the thrills of the big city. I just hope I'm not going to be bored."

Jane didn't comment. Since becoming a special constable, she'd had her share of thrills, if that's what you'd call being mixed up with fraudsters, kidnappers, rapists and murderers. She raised a glass and proposed a toast. "To a quiet life in the provinces."

When they were home, Jane sat up with Patrick for a couple of hours after Norah had gone to bed. Patrick had always tended to be a bit of a nightbird. Jane was tired but reluctant to leave him alone on his first night at home.

Besides, she sensed that he had something on his mind. She was right.

"So, I had a call from Seth Wentworth last night," Patrick said.

Patrick had met Seth in reception class, and they'd remained friends throughout their schooldays and beyond. Jane always enjoyed hearing how Patrick's friends were getting on. After all, she'd known some of them as long as he had.

"Great." Jane, who was making them both a cup of hot chocolate, spoke loudly over the roiling kettle. "Did you tell him your big news?"

"Yep."

"I see." Jane tried not to feel peeved at not being the first to know about Patrick's career move. "And how was Seth?"

Patrick took the mug Jane handed him and gave a loud sigh. "Not so good. His cousin Max was murdered."

Jane's eyes widened. "What happened to him?"

"I'm not sure exactly. His body was found a few days ago. It had been in the river, but the couple who found him hauled him out. The police have told his family that he was dead before he went in."

"That's terrible," Jane said. "His poor family. When did it happen exactly?"

"Well, his body was found on Wednesday morning near the start of the Waterway path on Waterside South. I don't know if they know exactly when he died yet."

Jane empathised with the family. Max's parents would need answers quickly to help them process their loss, but all too often in murder investigations, answers were hard won. "I do remember it being reported on the radio, but I didn't know the victim was Seth's cousin. How sad."

"I don't suppose you could ask that DI you know about it?" Patrick said, his voice hesitant. "Only, I might have said to Seth that I'd ask you if you could ask some questions, find out if Max's death is being properly investigated."

Jane was taken by surprise. "Er . . . I don't know DI Warwick that well. I mean, we get along better than we did in the beginning, but we're not exactly best buddies. Plus, I don't think she'd appreciate me asking if a case is being 'properly investigated'. Particularly if she's the lead officer."

Patrick looked at her pleadingly. "But you've worked on loads of investigations with her now, haven't you, Mum? You even went undercover for her just recently."

Jane began to object. "That's going a bit far . . ." She thought again of Warwick's disdain of the word *undercover*. Jane's role had been rather vague and unofficial. "Basically, she asked me to pass on village gossip."

Patrick shrugged. "Same thing. Anyway, you're friends with Elias Harper, the DS she works with, aren't you? Maybe you could have a word with him, and he could have a word with DI Warwick."

That might be a better idea. Jane did consider Elias a friend, and he was certainly more approachable than Warwick. "I suppose I could speak with Elias about it." She added a cautionary note. "But don't expect much. Even if it is DI Warwick's case — actually, especially if it's DI Warwick's case — the chances of her talking to me about an investigation are very slim."

Patrick gave her his best smile. "I knew you wouldn't let me down."

Jane hoped she could live up to his trust in her.

CHAPTER FIVE

Elias picked Steph up at eight o'clock on Friday morning. Steph had been up early having tossed and turned half the night, but she'd spent the extra time taking a leisurely shower, and then catching up on some online banking — always a chore — over a decent breakfast.

Her tiredness caught up with her as she was strapping herself into the passenger seat next to Elias. Her voice grumpy, she complained, "Harry Scott and Sophie Egan couldn't have lived near one another, or at least in the same direction, could they? Save us driving up and down the country."

"Won't take long to get to Gainsborough," Elias said. "Unless there's a lot of traffic about."

Harry Scott lived in Gainsborough, Sophie Egan in Hull. They were hardly at opposite ends of the country, but it still involved spending valuable time travelling.

As Harry lived on a newish housing development to the west of Gainsborough town centre, Elias headed northwards on the A15, which took them past RAF Scampton, home of the legendary 613 Squadron, which had flown the famous Dambuster raids during World War Two, destroying dams in the Ruhr Valley in Germany. On catching sight of the air-base, Steph, unconsciously, began to hum the theme tune to the 1950s film about the raids, which she'd watched count-less times with her grandfather growing up.

"Great movie," Elias said. Elias was a bit of a film buff. "Great cast." He rattled off the names of the key actors. Elias was an amateur actor who regularly took part in productions — mostly Shakespeare — put on by a local theatre group. Prior to joining the police, he'd toured the country with a well-respected national theatre company before deciding he didn't want to pursue a career in acting. Steph had seen him in a number of roles now. She knew that he could have made a success of acting. As he was making a success of being a detective. Theatre's loss was the police's gain.

It was a short but unexciting journey. Flat fields, brown and furrowed at this time of year, flashed by, stretching as far as the eye could see against a broad, never-ending sky. Only the occasional white fingerpost, bearing the name of some village or other and pointing along narrow roads winding between the fields, gave a hint that anything other than a vast emptiness lay either side of the A15.

On the outskirts of Gainsborough, they swung past a large industrial estate and, soon afterwards, took a left to arrive at the estate where Harry Scott lived with his parents. Elias parked up outside the small front garden, which was crowded with outdoor Christmas decorations, dominated by a five-foot-tall inflatable gingerbread man.

"If that thing was made of real gingerbread, I'd be tucking into one of its arms right now," Steph said. Despite her hearty breakfast, she was already feeling hungry. She looked to see if anyone was watching out for them and noticed that the win-dows were dotted all over with little gingerbread men stickers.

A boy of around eight, dressed in a gingerbread man onesie, answered the door. Without taking his eyes off them, he called over his shoulder. "Harry, the police are here."

A figure appeared at the top of the stairs. Harry Scott, presumably —dressed in normal clothes, thank goodness. Steph didn't fancy conducting a serious interview with a man dressed as a ginger biscuit.

"Yeah. So, I'm Harry Scott," the young man said. He'd reached the bottom step and hovered there, holding on to the newel post.

Steph introduced herself and Elias, holding up her police ID for him to see, but Harry barely glanced at it. He spoke to the boy, presumably his younger brother. "Go upstairs, Lewis. Remember what Mum and Dad said about not getting in the way when the police are here."

Protesting that he wasn't getting in the way, Lewis brushed past his brother and disappeared upstairs. "You'd better come in," Harry said. He pointed to a door. "The lounge is through there. Can you just give me five?" Before Steph could answer, he'd bounded back up the stairs.

Steph and Elias moved into the lounge. Elias shunted a large crocheted gingerbread man further along the sofa to make room for them to sit down. He gazed around. "What is it with this family and gingerbread men? It's like some kind of cult."

Steph nodded. It was impossible to miss them — one was even impaled on top of the Christmas tree, replacing the traditional fairy. "They're creepy little beggars when they're all around you like this."

Harry Scott walked into the room. Presumably, he'd heard. "Excuse the gingerbread men. My mum likes to have a theme for the Christmas decs. No prize for guessing what it is this year. She's even bought us all gingerbread men pyjamas to wear on Christmas morning. As you saw, Lewis actually seems to like his — he's been brainwashed. Dad and I are thinking of staging an intervention."

Steph gave a brief smile. "You know why we're here, don't you, Mr Scott?"

"Harry. Mr Scott's my dad. And, yes. Whoever phoned yesterday said it was about Max Barsby. Not sure why you want to talk to me about him. I didn't know him much out of class, though as you're here, I assume someone's been telling tales about what happened at Vindolanda. I suppose I'm a suspect because I gave Max a bit of a push, and he lost his balance and managed to stagger backwards all the way to the campfire and fall right on it. Miraculous the way he managed to escape with minor injuries, while I nearly suffered a broken nose. Barsby punches me in the face, turns a little shove into a big, staged drama, gets some minor burns, and I'm the one who gets the blame." Harry's speech was punctuated with dramatic gestures and flourishes, including punching the air and stumbling backwards.

"There were witnesses," Steph said. She gave Elias a nod.

Without consulting any notes, Elias quoted the accounts of two of the witnesses with whom one of their colleagues had spoken the previous afternoon.

"*Harry Scott barrelled into poor Max with all the speed and force of a bullet train.* Dr. Lily Bunting, archaeology lecturer. *I couldn't believe the force with which Harry shoved Max Barsby. He put his whole body weight into it and sent Max hurtling backwards like a rocket in reverse straight onto the campfire.* Dr Sean Brogan."

"Thank you, Sergeant," Steph said. "You're a big lad, Harry. Looks like you work out. Max was shorter, slighter, and was probably not well acquainted with the gym. He was more the cerebral type."

Harry shrugged. "Yeah, well. I was there too and I don't remember pushing him with that much force. Max hammed it up and milked it for all it was worth."

What had Dr Carr said about Harry showing remorse? Not a lot of that in evidence today. Since Harry had his own version of the event, and was unlikely to change it, Steph moved on. "What did you fight over?"

"I expect your witnesses have filled you in. Max had accused me of not pulling my weight in the seminar group we were in," Harry said.

"Was his accusation justified?" Steph asked.

"I contributed as much as most people would have done, but that wasn't good enough for Max. Personally, I thought he was a control freak. Nothing I did was up to his standard. I reckon he preferred to do the work himself. It was a waste of time doing anything when Max would just criticise your contribution, or overlook it altogether. Might as well do nothing and let him get on with it."

"As far as we've been informed, Max didn't accuse anyone else of not contributing enough."

Harry looked sullen. "You know what, even if I didn't work as hard as I might have done, it's not exactly a crime to miss a deadline, is it?"

"You accused Max of reporting you to your seminar group tutor, didn't you?" Steph said.

This only elicited another shrug from Harry. He ran his fingers through his dark brown hair, which was styled longish at the nape, with textured layers and a fringe parted in the middle sweeping outwards and downwards. PC Joey Fairbairn, a regular on Steph's team, sported a similar style. He called it a Korean mullet. It was, Steph conceded, a flattering style on both men. But she wasn't here to admire Harry Scott's hair.

"Can you tell us where you were on the evening of the eighth of December, Harry?"

"Of course I can," Harry said. "First thing I checked when I heard you were coming here to see if I could 'help you with your enquiries' was think back and make sure I knew what I was doing on that date. I was with my girlfriend. We were at her place. I'm sure she'll vouch for me."

"You're talking about Sophie Egan? We're seeing her later today."

"Sophie!" Harry gave a fake laugh. "We split up right after the Vindolanda trip. I'm with someone else now. Not sure what I ever saw in Sophie. She was right all along — we weren't a good match."

He didn't sound entirely convincing. "Right," Steph said. "I believe the fight between you and Max was really about you being convinced that Sophie was cheating on you with Max Barsby?"

Harry gave his signature shrug. "With good reason. Sophie was always going on about how clever Max was, how he was good-looking but didn't even seem to know it, how he was so generous and blah, blah, blah."

Harry paused. He sat back in his chair as if deflated. "Okay, so I guess I was jealous. I really liked Sophie. She was different from other girls I'd dated, and, to be honest, I thought she might be the one. You know?"

Steph raised an eyebrow. Harry sounded wistful. He'd obviously cared about Sophie.

"I was the one who wanted to talk about our future together — you know, getting engaged, marriage, kids, and all that kind of stuff. Sophie wasn't interested. She didn't even want to be exclusive for a long time."

Harry seemed to wrestle with his thoughts for a moment. "Look, it was Sophie who dobbed me in to our tutor, would you believe? Said she felt sorry for Max. That just made me even more suspicious that she was two-timing me with him."

"Did you accuse Max Barsby of seeing Sophie behind your back?"

"Yeah. He denied it. Said he was seeing someone else."

"Did he say who?" Steph asked.

"No."

"But you didn't believe him?"

"No."

"Did you ever see Max Barsby after you left the university?" Steph said.

"No. Why would I? I haven't even been back to Lincoln since, except when my dad took me there in the van to help me collect my stuff from my flat."

"Can you think of anyone who would want to kill Max?"

Harry laughed. "Besides me, you mean? I didn't have anything against Max until he started whining about me not pulling my weight with the seminar work. And until Sophie started going on about what a bloody saint he was. I didn't even know him until we got assigned to the same seminar group. I'd seen him around, of course, but he wasn't very memorable. He was geeky, probably not that much fun to hang out with — unless you were really into history and archaeology. But no, I can't think of any reason why someone would have wanted him dead."

"Weren't you into archaeology, then? You chose to study it at university," Steph pointed out.

"Yeah, well. For me, doing a degree was a means to an end. I only went to university in the first place because teachers at school kept banging on about it being a way into a better job, but I know kids I was at school with who are earning great money without a degree. I only chose archaeology because I like to be doing stuff. I didn't think there'd be so much studying involved. I thought I'd be out on a dig most of the time getting my hands dirty."

"What are you doing now, Harry?" Elias asked.

Harry's face brightened. "What I should have done in the first place. Learning to be a plumbing and heating engineer like my dad. We're going into business together when I qualify."

Elias nodded. "I hope that works out for you."

Steph glanced at the clock on the mantelpiece, squinting to see the face which was partially hidden behind a ceramic gingerbread man ornament. Time to move on.

"Thanks for your time, Harry," Steph said. "Get in touch if there's anything else you want to tell us. People don't always remember everything first time around."

"Sure," Harry said. "But I'm pretty certain I've told you everything." He accompanied them to the door. The sudden movement downstairs must have alerted his younger brother, who appeared at the top of the stairs, still in his gingerbread man onesie. He came down to join his brother. Harry ruffled Lewis's hair affectionately. "Lewie's the clever one in the family. He'll fit right in at uni, won't you, Brains?"

"My teacher says I'm gifted and talented," Lewis said. "I want to be a hotshot lawyer." Everyone smiled.

"Good for you," Elias said.

Back in the car and heading back along the A15, Steph was quiet.

"What are you thinking?" Elias said.

"I'm thinking that Harry Scott isn't the sort of person I expected him to be."

"You were expecting more of a bully, I bet," Elias said. "Same here. But he came across as a pretty ordinary lad. Not the kind to shove someone onto a fire. Unless—"

Steph completed his sentence. "Unless severely provoked, or his passions were aroused. Sexual jealousy can do that. It's a common motive for murder. They're all nice, ordinary lads — until they're not." A slight pause. Then, "It was a bit strange, Sophie Egan going to Harry's tutor about Max's complaint. You'd think she'd at least have had a word with Harry first, and not gone behind his back."

"You can see how it would have fuelled Harry's suspicions that there was something going on between them," Elias said.

Steph agreed. "Yes. Well, he has an alibi, but only the word of his current girlfriend. If it checks out, he still won't be off the hook. It'll be interesting to hear what Sophie Egan has to say about him."

The journey to Hull would take just over an hour, but hunger drove Steph to instruct Elias to pull in at a pub in the market town of Brigg on the way so that she could stock up on calories.

The pub menu offered some compensation for the inconvenience of the two separate journeys, offering a good selection of the hearty and the healthy. Steph went with the steak and ale pie, while Elias chose Hunter's chicken with a jacket potato and salad.

Refreshed, they took to the road again, quickly covering the rest of the distance to the Humber Bridge, beneath which lurked the wide Humber estuary, murky with churned-up sediment.

As they neared the end of the bridge, Elias informed Steph that when the structure opened in 1981, it was the longest single-span suspension bridge in the world, a record that it held until 1998. "Even now," he added, "it's the twelfth longest."

"Admit it," Steph said. "You've been bursting to tell me that since we first drove onto it."

"Guilty as charged, ma'am."

Steph smiled. She didn't let on that she knew these statistics already. The satnav guided them to a quiet, residential area north-west of the city centre, and close to the university, where the Egans lived. They parked on the wide, paved drive and walked up to the front door.

Sophie Egan's mother, Beatrice, answered their knock. She invited them in, offered them tea and called her daughter downstairs. When the tea arrived and there was still no sign of Sophie, Beatrice gave a sigh. "She'll be on her laptop with her headphones on. I'll go up and give her a tap on the shoulder."

Beatrice went off to find her daughter. Both appeared a few minutes later, Sophie with a small French bulldog in her arms. "Sorry, I didn't hear Mum calling me down. I had my headphones on."

Sophie's mother did the introductions, which included the dog. "This is Ferdinand. Ferdy for short. We showed him at Crufts last year. He was third best in his breed."

Dressed in a little brown coat, the dog reminded Steph of the Ninja Turtle action figures her brother used to play with. She appraised Sophie Egan as the young woman made her way across the room to a spare armchair in the window bay. She was around five six in height with an athletic build, and had a pretty, if unremarkable, face and dark brown hair. Her olive-coloured yoga pants and cap-sleeved crop top showed off a tightly toned body.

"Mum said you wanted to ask me some questions about poor Max." Sophie's bottom lip quivered.

Beatrice, who had been hovering protectively near her daughter, now leaned over and pressed her arm. "Sophie was very upset when she heard about Max. Still is."

Sophie dabbed at her eyes. "Max was a dear, sweet friend. I miss him every single day."

It's barely been two. Still, Steph gave Sophie a few moments to recover before beginning. "Maybe you could start by telling us how you got to know Max Barsby."

Sophie sniffed. "I met him on my course. We were both studying archaeology." She looked at Steph, but didn't say any more. At Steph's nod of encouragement, she continued. "I didn't really talk to Max much in my first year. We weren't in any seminar groups together, but I did see him around and knew him to say 'hi' to. Then, one afternoon, near the start of our second year, I was at a pub in Lincoln with my boyfriend, Harry Scott. You've been to see him this morning, haven't you?"

Another nod from Steph. If Sophie intended to seek reassurance after everything she said, they'd be here until the middle of next week.

"Max was there with his cousin, Seth. Harry was talking to his mates, and I was feeling a bit left out. So, I started chatting to Max and Seth."

Again, Beatrice interrupted. "What young man wouldn't talk to a looker like Sophie?" Steph gave her a tolerant, if strained, smile.

Sophie blushed. "Muum. Don't embarrass me. It was hard work at first. Max wasn't a big talker. Fortunately, I can chat enough for two. But, after a while, he started to relax, and the conversation flowed more easily. Max knew a lot about a lot of things. He was really interesting. That's the thing with shy people — other people dismiss them because they don't contribute enough but, given the opportunity, they can shine."

"And Sophie always gives people that opportunity. She's such a generous girl," Beatrice said, sounding proud. Steph bit her lip. She looked at Elias and saw an amused smile playing on his lips. No doubt he was thinking — and with justification — that not so long ago, Steph would have told Beatrice to shut up by now.

Sophie took her mother in hand. "Mum, they haven't come to hear you praising your darling daughter, however justified that might be. Maybe just sit quietly and let me do the talking? The officers have got a long journey back to Lincoln after this interview."

"Don't I know it," Beatrice said. "Sophie's dad and I drive backwards and forwards to visit Sophie in Lincoln in term time. There's always some sort of hold-up on those roads—"

"Not to appear rude, Mrs Egan, but your daughter is right." Steph had had enough. At least she remembered to have some tact. "We are a bit pushed for time. We need to crack on and speak to Sophie with no more interruptions."

Beatrice looked suitably slighted. Now it was Sophie who leaned over and pressed her mother's arm. "I'm fine, Mum. You don't really need to babysit me."

Beatrice stood up and smoothed her dress. "Right, I'll get on with making the roast, then." She bent and gave her daughter a kiss on the cheek. "I'm just in the kitchen if you need me, darling."

When she was out of earshot, Sophie whispered, "She means well. She's just overprotective, and a proud mum. I'm an only child." Her eyes misted up again. "Max was too. I can't begin to understand how his poor parents must be feeling."

"They're devastated," Steph said, speaking straight. "That's why it's so important for us to speak with you. Nothing will compensate for the loss of their son. The least we can give them is justice by finding his killer."

"Well said," Sophie agreed, rallying. "What else do you need to know?"

"How well did your ex-boyfriend, Harry Scott, know Max?"

"Hardly at all," Sophie said immediately. "Max wasn't the sort of person who'd be on Harry's radar. He was quiet, academic, geeky. Harry was one of the popular kids. Good-looking, good at sports. He made friends easily. All the girls fancied him." She winked. "'Cept me, of course." Sophie waited a moment for her comment to sink in, then smiled. "I think that's what attracted him to me. He couldn't twist me around his little finger, or disarm me with his dazzling smile."

That made sense. Harry wouldn't have been the first — or the last — man to chase after a girl who seemed impervious to his charms. Still, it wasn't the whole story. If Harry had just wanted to prove that he could have Sophie, he would have dumped her soon after getting her. His fondness for her had seemed sincere. He'd genuinely wanted to make the relationship work, even take it to the next level. Sophie had been the one to resist — or so he'd told them.

"I'm not sure what Harry told you about our relationship. He was really in love with me and wanted us to get engaged. We'd only been together for six months when he asked me. I was nowhere near ready for that level of commitment."

"Harry did mention that you 'wanted different things'," Steph said.

Sophie laughed. "You can say that again."

"Harry also told us that he suspected you of having a relationship with Max Barsby."

"Well, he was right about that. I did have a relationship with Max, though it wasn't what Harry thought. It wasn't a sexual relationship, if that's what you're wondering, although Max and I were very compatible in many ways. Kindred spirits, and I wouldn't have ruled out a romantic relationship, given time."

"Right," Steph said. "You and Max were good friends."

"I suppose. We trusted each other completely. I felt really comfortable with him."

"So, you said Harry didn't know Max well. They were in the same seminar group for one of their archaeology modules. Harry told us that Max accused him of not pulling his weight with the workload. This led to soured feelings between them. Things came to a head on a field trip to Vindolanda in November. He—"

Sophie jumped in. "So, I'm guessing that Harry also told you that I dobbed him in to his seminar tutor? That's true, I did."

"May I ask why?" Steph said.

"Max had mentioned to me a couple of times that the quality of Harry's work was so poor that he had to re-research and rewrite everything Harry produced. Eventually, Harry just stopped doing the work altogether. Bless him, Harry was no scholar. He was convinced it was Max who dobbed him in."

"And you didn't set him right on that?" Steph asked.

"I did. Just not immediately. I knew Harry was jealous of my friendship with Max, and I thought it would make him even more jealous to hear I'd taken Max's side."

"You must have known Harry would assume it was Max who had reported him to his tutor, and that it would lead to a build-up of resentment between them."

Sophie shrugged. "I should have told him it was me sooner, I guess. I would have done if I'd realised Harry would blow up over it. I only reported him to his tutor in the first place to teach him a lesson. You know, make him see he couldn't just treat poor Max like that and get away with it. And I felt sorry for Max. He always got top marks. He was working hard enough without having to do Harry's share as well.

"When I told Harry it was me, predictably, it made things ten times worse. I never thought he'd get so wound up about it as to pick a fight with Max and push him onto the campfire. I didn't think he had it in him to do that, however jealous he might get."

"That was a bit short-sighted of you," Steph said. *To say the least*.

Sophie sighed. "On reflection, I should have had words with Harry about his laziness with the seminar prep. Or I should have encouraged Max to report him, except I knew Max would never do that. Max was a very honourable person."

Steph got the impression that Sophie had enjoyed winding Harry up. Had Max shown any interest in her? "Did Max have a girlfriend?" she asked.

Sophie seemed to recoil from the question. "I . . . Harry said Max told him he had a girlfriend. Maybe that's why—" She bit her lip.

Maybe that's why Max didn't show any romantic interest in you.

"You and Harry broke up after Vindolanda. Had your relationship been on shaky ground even before the incident there?" Steph asked.

"Yes. Harry was getting more and more jealous of my relationship with Max. And, I suppose, if I'm being honest, I didn't do much to discourage his suspicions. I might even have encouraged them by going on about how wonderful Max was. I think I was just trying to get Harry to see that our relationship wasn't going anywhere. He was always so sure of himself around women. It must have been a blow to his ego to be the one about to be dumped."

"Did Harry blame Max for the break-up of your relationship?"

"Yes, I think so." Sophie's lip trembled. "If it turns out that Harry murdered Max over me, I won't be able to live with myself."

Elias reassured her. "You shouldn't feel like that, Sophie. Harry must have been able to read the signs that his relationship with you wasn't going anywhere, even before Max entered the equation. You're not responsible for the actions of other people."

Steph allowed a moment for Elias's words to sink in. Then, she pressed on. "Where were you on the night Max was murdered?"

"I was here with Mum and Dad."

"When was the last time you saw Max?" Steph asked.

"I saw him a week before he was . . . murdered," Sophie said. "I work a couple of nights a week in a bar at the uni. Max was there with his cousin, Seth Wentworth."

"How did Max seem?"

Sophie shrugged. "He seemed preoccupied. Not that interested in talking. I assumed he had a lot on his mind with work and all. I thought after Harry and I broke up—"

"You thought that Max would make a move on you?" Steph said. "Even though Harry had told you Max was seeing someone else? Didn't you believe Harry?"

Sophie shrugged. "Doesn't matter now, does it?"

Steph wound the interview to a close. As soon as she and Elias stood up to leave, Beatrice appeared in the doorway, holding a transparent plastic tub. Steph got the impression she had been close by, listening all along. Her suspicions were confirmed.

"I couldn't help overhearing. The walls are so thin in this house. What Sophie said about being here the night that poor boy died is the truth. I can vouch for her personally. As could my husband and Ferdy. Though why on earth you'd have to ask someone like Sophie for an actual alibi, I've no idea." Smiling, she thrust the plastic tub on Elias. "For your journey."

Elias held it up. Steph examined the contents. Gingerbread men biscuits. She and Elias exchanged a look before thanking Beatrice for her gift.

Back on the road again, they discussed what they'd learned from the interview with Sophie Egan.

"I can't help believing that Sophie was being disingenuous when she described her reasons for holding back on telling Harry that she'd been the one to report him to his tutor. Maybe she just enjoyed the idea of having two men in thrall to her," Steph said.

Elias agreed. "I reckon Harry was more in thrall than Max. In fact, it sounds like Max wasn't attracted to Sophie in a romantic way, although, I agree, she was probably interested in him, and probably didn't see that at first."

Steph considered for a moment. "Hmm. I don't feel I have a handle on Sophie. Harry's much easier to pin down. He's more the what-you-see-is-what-you-get type."

"She did seem genuinely distressed at the idea she might have pushed Harry into killing Max."

"As well she might." Steph opened the tub of gingerbread men biscuits, selected one, and bit off its head. "Nice," she said, munching. "Just the right amount of spice."

CHAPTER SIX

When Jane promised Patrick she'd approach DS Elias Harper to sound him out about the murder of Max Barsby, she hadn't expected an opportunity to speak directly with his boss to arise the very next day.

Jane had called at Veganbites first thing on Saturday morning to return a book that she'd borrowed from her friend, Frieda Arya. The minute she walked into the café, she clocked DI Steph Warwick sitting alone by the window.

Warwick acknowledged Jane with a nod and the ghost of a smile.

"So, are you all ready for Christmas, then?" Jane asked. She spoke in a breezy, friendly tone, although she was still not quite sure what kind of footing the two of them were on. Their relationship tended to blow hot and cold.

Warwick shrugged. "Yes. I suppose so. Are you?"

"Getting there. So much to do at this time of year, isn't there? Have you got some time off over the holiday?"

"Christmas day, officially. But I'll probably end up working. I'm knee-deep in a new investigation."

"Oh." Jane felt sorry for Warwick. It occurred to her that she had no idea if she had any family.

Warwick must have guessed what she was thinking. "My parents decided to spend Christmas in Australia with my brother and sister-in-law, and the grandkids, so I don't have family to visit this year."

Jane didn't like to ask if Warwick would be spending Christmas alone. Instead, she told her what she would be doing. "I'll be spending the big day in Doveby. With Ed and my kids. My son Patrick's home for the holidays. Actually, not just the holidays. He's quit his job in London, and he's looking for work in this area."

"That's nice for you," Warwick said.

Was it a bit sad that Jane's first thought was that Warwick was being sarcastic? But that wasn't how her comment had come across. In fact, Warwick seemed to be in a good mood, for her.

Jane decided to seize the moment. "Er . . . Do you mind if I join you? I was just going to grab a quick coffee."

For a moment she thought Warwick would refuse. They were off duty, but Jane was always conscious of the difference in their status.

To her surprise, Warwick accepted. True, she did make it sound like she had nothing better to do, but Jane took it as a win.

"Sure. Why not? I'm just taking a break from boring paperwork."

Jane ordered her coffee and, after returning Frieda's book and telling her friend that she wanted some time alone to speak to Warwick, she joined the DI at her table. For a few minutes, they indulged in small talk, mostly about the weather, and the chore of Christmas shopping. Then, Jane jumped straight in.

"So, this new case you mentioned. Would it be the murder of that young man who was found on Waterside South last week?"

Warwick gave Jane a sideways look as she blew on her coffee. "Max Barsby. What's your interest in this case, Bell?"

Busted. "My son, Patrick, is friends with Max's cousin, Seth Wentworth. Seth told him about the murder. My heart goes out to the young man's family, especially at this time of the year." Jane bowed her head and blew on her coffee.

Warwick was silent for a moment. Her eyes narrowed with suspicion. "Is that why you wanted to join me for coffee? So you could pump me for information to satisfy your curiosity about the murder?"

Jane swallowed. "Of course not. Patrick was very upset about Max—"

"Did Patrick prompt you to ask me about the investigation?"

"Er . . . No. Actually, he prompted me to ask Elias."

Warwick laughed. Jane wasn't skilled at reading the DI, so she wasn't sure how to interpret the laugh. It seemed best to err on the side of caution and assume that Warwick wasn't actually amused. "I really only mentioned it because it sort of came up in the conversation. It was a sort of segue—"

"Using fancy words won't let you off the hook, Bell."

"No, ma'am."

"But, to answer your question, yes, I am involved in the investigation into Max Barsby's death. In fact, I'm the Senior Investigating Officer." Warwick picked up the Biscoff accompanying her coffee. She dunked it in her latte. Her gaze fell on Jane's saucer, where her biscuit lay untouched. "You planning on eating that?"

Jane handed her the biscuit. "No. I'm not keen on them."

"It's my lucky day."

"I wouldn't have put you down as a dunker."

"That's not the only thing you don't know about me, Bell," Warwick said. She licked her fingers — another action that seemed out-of-character — and then unwrapped and ate the second biscuit. Finished, she looked at Jane and cleared her throat. "You did some good work on my investigation into the murders of Susan Gedney and Bree Fawcett. Elias tells me that he mentioned the graduate fast-track scheme to you, and that you weren't interested. I'd have thought you'd be keen."

Jane gave a small start. Praise from Warwick followed by her actually suggesting detective work as a career. "Er . . .

Thank you. I enjoyed the experience of working—" Jane checked herself. She'd been about to say 'undercover'. Safer to opt for 'incognito'. She sipped her flat white to give her some thinking time before explaining. "As for beginning a new career at my age, I don't know—"

"You're not too old," Warwick said. "True, there was a time when people your age were looking at retiring in a few years, but that's not the case these days."

"I won't lie," Jane said, "it's quite an attractive proposition in some ways."

"But?"

Jane was reluctant to reveal what she'd learned about herself with all the soul-searching she'd done since that conversation with Elias. Plus, she felt like she was under forensic scrutiny.

Warwick didn't wait for a reply. "Not for you? You know what, Bell, correct me if I'm wrong, but I suspect you enjoy the challenge of investigative work. The thing is, you want to do it in your own way, and on your own terms."

Jane raised an eyebrow. She hadn't had Warwick down as a great reader of people, but her observation was spot on.

"Ha!" Warwick's tone was triumphant. "I'm right, am I not?"

The truth was that Jane would find it hard to give up the sense of freedom she enjoyed working for herself as a part-time tutor and volunteer police officer. Of course, she still had to put the hours in but, in the case of her tutoring, these were of her own choosing. She had committed to only sixteen hours of volunteer police work a month — again, any extra hours she worked were determined by her alone. Joining the police would mean stepping back on the treadmill of the daily grind. Reporting for duty first thing in the morning. Having to be there and be answerable to the powers that be. Investigating cases that didn't have some sort of pull for her. All the excitement that working as a detective seemed to offer would be swallowed up by it's becoming the day job. How long before it lost its sparkle?

She opted for honesty. "Guilty as charged."

Warwick nodded. "I get it."

"Still," Jane said, "it was frustrating to find a dead body, like I did that time on my first ever shift as a special, and have to just walk away." Jane was referring not just to her first shift, but also to her first meeting with DI Warwick, which had not gone well.

"As I recall, you didn't just walk away."

Jane braced herself for a caustic reminder of how much she'd 'meddled' in that particular investigation. To her astonishment, Warwick passed on the opportunity.

"I thought maybe you'd fit in well as a staff investigator," Warwick said.

Jane nodded to show that she was familiar with the term.

"These days, civilian staff can work alongside experienced detectives to the extent that the lines between them start to blur. But, as I suspected, and you've all but confirmed, you want the thrill of being a detective without the day job, and without the restrictions posed by those with authority over you. Maybe you should set up as a private investigator, Bell."

Jane could tell that Warwick wasn't being entirely serious. Or entirely flippant. "And spend my days on boring stakeouts trying to catch out unfaithful spouses? No thanks."

"Right," Warwick said. "I sense you won't let this Max Barsby thing lie, Bell. Am I right?"

Jane couldn't deny it. "I—"

"I'm right," Warwick interrupted. "I know you by now. So, I also know that nothing I say will stop you from doing your own digging. Therefore, I'm not going to waste my breath trying. And, to be perfectly honest, I can't actually stop you, as a member of the public, from talking to people. So, go ahead, do your thing, use your connections and talk to people. Indulge your hobby of amateur sleuthing, or whatever you want to call it. Just . . . don't get in my way, Bell, and if you find anything out, I want to know about it. Work with me, not against me."

Was Warwick acknowledging that they could work along-side each other? Had she just hinted that their different roles — senior detective and ordinary member of the public — could work to their mutual advantage? "Er . . . yes. Ma'am."

"For heavens' sake, Bell, we're not at work now. Call me Steph."

Jane smiled. She didn't point out that Warwick had just used her surname. It wasn't the first time that Warwick had invited her to drop the formality when they weren't at work, but for both of them, it seemed an elusive goal.

"I've been invited to a party here, on New Year's Eve," Warwick said in an abrupt change of subject. "I take it you'll be there?"

"Yes," Jane said. "I wouldn't dare miss it. Ed, Patrick and Norah will be there too, although I'm not sure how long the kids will hang around. You have accepted, haven't you? Frieda will be disappointed if you don't come."

"I'm hoping to show my face for a bit, work permitting, and as long as nothing urgent turns up for me to deal with." Warwick reached for her coat. "I need to get on."

"Of course. Don't let me hold you up. Let's do it again sometime." Jane spoke as casually as she would to any other friend.

"Er . . . yes. In the meantime, remember what I said about you and detective work."

"Indulge my hobby. Keep you in the loop," Jane said. She noticed Warwick reach for her bag. "Please, let me pay. This was my suggestion."

Warwick nodded. "Right. Thanks. I'll pay next time." And with that, she slipped her cross-body bag over her shoulder and headed for the door.

"Nice to see you two getting along so well," Frieda said when Jane went to pay.

Jane agreed, although she wouldn't bet on it lasting too long.

CHAPTER SEVEN

As soon as she arrived home, Jane filled Patrick in on what she had learned from her conversation with DI Warwick at Veganbites.

"So, does this mean you're invested in the case now, Mum?" Patrick asked. "Warwick certainly seems to think so."

There was no sense in fighting it. Max Barsby's death had been playing on Jane's mind more and more since Patrick had told her about it. She sighed. "Tell me about Max."

"I met him a few times when I was out with Seth. He was friendly, serious," Patrick began. Then he surprised Jane by saying, "You met him once, Mum. He was at my twenty-first. Same sort of height as Seth, but slighter. Fairish hair, glasses."

Jane frowned. A lot of people had been at Patrick's twenty-first birthday party, and she had left early. Despite Patrick's description, she couldn't summon an image of Max to mind.

"He had a pot on his arm."

"Oh," Jane said. Now she could picture him. Standing with his cousin, his arm in a sling, the plaster cast covered in graffiti. "I remember. Oh dear." It seemed worse to put a face to the name, knowing what had become of poor Max.

"Listen, Mum, why don't you talk to Seth, or better still, to Max's family? You're good at talking to people."

"Well . . ." Jane considered Patrick's words for all of three seconds. Subconsciously, maybe she was hoping he'd make the suggestion. "I suppose I could. It's nice that you have so much faith in my abilities."

Patrick gave a sigh, perhaps of relief that his unsubtle tactic of flattery had worked. "I'll text Seth now, ask when would be a good time to visit."

Sooner rather than later, as it turned out. Max's parents were keen to speak with Jane straight away. Jane hoped Patrick hadn't built up unrealistic expectations by exaggerating her involvement in previous murder investigations.

In the late afternoon, the two of them headed out to a pretty village only a few miles north of Lincoln. They drove through the heart of the village with its picturesque church, and winding beck overcrowded with ducks, to arrive at the Barsbys' mid-century-style house, situated in a quiet cul-de-sac on the outskirts of the village. Jane parked the car on the long drive and they walked to the front door, where they waited under an open-sided porch. The festive brightness of a string of icicle-shaped Christmas lights suspended from the roofline of the house seemed at odds with the unhappy reason for Jane and Patrick's visit.

The door was answered by an elderly man wearing only his pyjama bottoms. He looked confused to see two strangers standing on his doorstep.

"Dad!" A woman's voice called out. A moment later, she appeared in the hallway looking dishevelled and flustered. She took the man's arm and led him gently away from the door, then gestured to Jane and Patrick to come inside.

Patrick closed the door behind him. "Tom," the woman called, "Seth's friends are here. Can you see to them while I sort Dad out?" She guided the man down the hall, and both disappeared through a door at the end. Tom, who had answered her plea, immediately took over.

"Sorry about that. Anne's dad has dementia. He was expecting Anne's sister, Emma — Seth's mum. Emma's coming round to sit with him while we talk with you."

"No problem," Jane said.

Tom led them into a living room that looked as though it could do with a bit of TLC. He began to apologise. "Excuse the mess. No one's felt much like housework since . . ." His voice faltered.

"Please don't apologise," Jane said at once. "I can't begin to know how you must be feeling. Please accept my sincere condolences for your loss."

Patrick mumbled something that sounded like what Jane had just said. He was probably uncomfortable with the situation. Like Jane, he tended to soak up the emotion in a room. Also, Jane suspected, all this was bringing back painful memories of the days following his father's death, when the house had been filled with well-intentioned callers expressing their condolences.

"Anne will be back in a minute, soon as she's got Alec settled in the conservatory. He likes to sit in there in the late afternoon and watch TV. In the meantime, can I get you both a drink?"

Jane understood Tom's need to keep busy. She accepted the offer. In the days after a loved one's death, downtime is a formidable enemy to be battled with constant activity. "Tea would be nice. Same for you, Patrick?" Patrick nodded.

As soon as Tom left the room, Patrick sighed, long and hard, as though he'd been holding his breath. "That was intense," he said. "Seth told me his aunt and uncle are finding it hard to keep it together."

"Did Max have any brothers or sisters?" Jane asked.

Patrick shook his head, whispering, "Only child."

That shouldn't make it worse, but somehow it did. Jane's gaze fell upon the Christmas tree in the bay window, on the array of presents wrapped up and arranged underneath, and she felt a lump in her throat. Her heart ached for Tom and Anne Barsby. At that moment, she resolved to do everything in her power to help them.

There was a knock at the door. A woman's voice called from the hallway. "It's only me."

Patrick whispered to Jane, "That's Seth's mum."

A moment later, Emma Wentworth walked into the room. She smiled at Patrick. Jane had met Emma before — when Patrick and Seth were still at school — at fundraisers and parents' evenings, mostly. It must have been at least five or six years since they'd last met, not long enough for either of them to have changed much. Emma's red hair showed no sign of grey, and her manner was as open and friendly as ever.

"Lovely to see you both. I'm just sorry it's under such sad circumstances."

Before Jane could agree, Anne entered the room, and Emma rushed over to embrace her. Before long Alec's voice could be heard calling for Emma, and she excused herself to go and tend to their father.

Jane and Patrick offered Anne their condolences. Anne nodded. She was quite unlike her sister in looks, being older, with short grey-brown hair and a more restrained manner. "He was our one and only. Our miracle baby. I was forty-four when he was born. Tom and I had accepted that we weren't destined to have a family, and were resigned to it, when lo and behold, I fell pregnant. I was already starting the change."

The change. It was an oddly old-fashioned way to refer to the peri-menopause. Anne must have become aware that she was wringing her hands, for she prised them apart and smoothed them against her dress. "Tom's offered you a drink, I take it?"

"Yes, he's got it all in hand," Jane said. Seeing that Anne was at a complete loss what to say or do, she stood up and took her arm. Just as Anne had led her bewildered father, Jane guided the grieving mother over to the sofa. "Why don't you sit down for a bit? You look all in."

Anne's eyes welled up. "Thank you. I am. I don't know what to do with myself. It's nearly Christmas. I'm usually rushed off my feet at this time of year, and here I am, at a complete standstill in more ways than one." She looked at the Christmas tree then abruptly away, as though the sight of it distressed her.

She began to cry. "What's the point of anything?"

"Oh, love." It was Tom. He was standing in the doorway, holding a laden tea tray. Patrick stood up and took it from him. Jane stood up too, moving aside to allow Tom to sit beside his distressed wife. For a few moments, she and Patrick looked away.

Jane was beginning to think it had been a bad idea to come, when the couple drew apart and Anne said, "We can't even bury our son. Did you know that? His body is evidence. That's how that woman detective put it when she was here."

The woman detective. DI Warwick, no doubt. Again, Jane was struck by Anne's slightly old-fashioned way of speaking. She probably still used phrases like 'lady doctor', as though nothing had changed since the middle of the twentieth century.

"I'm sorry. I know that must have been hard to hear. It's not how we want to think of a loved one."

Tom Barsby spoke up. "Our nephew, Seth, tells us you're good at solving mysteries. The police don't tell us anything, and we don't feel confident they can find out what happened to our son. Anne and I were hoping you could help us."

"Have you been visited by a Family Liaison Officer?" Jane asked. "They're supposed to support you, keep you up-to-date with what's happening in the investigation."

"Yes, someone came round, but we don't want a stranger in the house at a time like this," Tom said. "She said she'd come back again, but Anne and I don't see the point. Will you help us, Jane?"

Jane considered his question. It was a big ask, and a big responsibility to take on. Once more, she hoped that Patrick hadn't overstated her abilities. She looked again at the Christmas tree and thought of how much the Barsbys had to contend with — a father with dementia, a murdered son. It was a no-brainer, emotionally. "I would like to help you if I can." Jane still felt a need to manage their expectations. "But you must understand that I'm limited in what I can do. The police have far more resources at their disposal. Given time, I'm sure they'll find out what happened to Max."

"We understand," Tom said. "We just need to know that we're doing everything we can. And more."

The sense of desperation they gave off made Jane's heart sink. She was anxious not to disappoint them. Tom said he understood that she was limited in resources, but did he really? True, she could take a different approach from the official investigation, operate under the radar and pick up leads that might be closed to Warwick. But would any of it make a difference? She wasn't so sure she could add value in the way the Barsbys hoped. Still, she found herself saying, "I've pieced together some facts about Max from what Seth and Patrick have told me. Maybe you can help fill in some of the gaps?"

Tom and Anne exchanged a look and sighed in unison, as if relieved that Jane had accepted their plea for help. It was as though they hadn't heard any of her cautions.

Jane continued. "So, what I know is this: Max was in his second year at Lincoln University studying archaeology. He was living at home to save money and was in the habit of coming back at around the same time every day." Jane looked at Tom and Anne to check they were in agreement.

Anne nodded. "Max came home around six thirty most nights, unless he was meeting friends, or working late at the library. He'd always let us know his plans."

"And he called on the day that he died to say he would be home late?"

"Yes. He phoned at around five to say he was meeting someone that evening. I was a bit surprised because he hadn't mentioned it before — it must have been arranged last minute. He said he'd get an Uber home, and that he'd probably be back around eleven."

After a pause, Anne added, "I didn't mention this to the policewoman. I wasn't able to think straight the day she was here. When Max called, he sounded excited. I wondered if he was going on a date, but he didn't say, and I didn't want to pry."

"Do you know if Max had been seeing anyone?" Jane asked.

Anne looked at Tom, who gave a shrug that seemed to suggest he would have been the last to know. Anne shook her head. "No. He went out with a lovely lass when he was at school, but she went off to university in Manchester, and their relationship fizzled out. If he'd been seeing someone recently, he didn't tell us. He's been working so hard since he went to university, what with having a part-time job as well as all the studying, I doubt he'd have much time for meeting people. Or for leisure activities, although he got involved in that dig, recently, didn't he, Tom?"

Anne switched, unconsciously, between past and present tense when talking about her son. It would be a while before she adjusted. At the mention of the dig, Jane's interest was aroused. "The dig near the university?"

"Yes. Max volunteered as soon as he heard about it from his tutor. He's loved history and archaeology since he was a boy and we took him on a trip to Hadrian's Wall during a holiday in Northumberland. So, you've heard of the dig. Are you interested in archaeology, Jane?" Anne said.

"No, it's just that I came across the man who was in charge of the dig quite recently," Jane said. She didn't mention the circumstances.

"Dr Linus Crow? He was one of the reasons Max wanted to study archaeology. Max read a book written by him when he was a child. He was so thrilled about meeting him."

It was surprising to learn that Max had a connection with Linus Crow. Jane wondered what it meant, if anything. It was also interesting that Anne thought Max sounded excited when he called her on the day he died. Where had he been going and whom did he meet? Anne and Tom had no explanations, other than Anne's theory that it might have been a date.

When Jane asked what else Max might have got excited about, if not a date, Anne said, "The dig, of course. Archaeology is his passion. He was hoping that some exciting finds would be made while he was working there. He would have been delighted to have been a part of that."

"Perhaps I could get in touch with Dr Crow. See what he can tell me about Max and his time at the dig," Jane said.

"There's someone else you could talk to," Tom said. "A man called John Headley. Max spoke about him quite a lot. He's a local man with a keen interest in history and archaeology. Max met him at a talk on local history. Max sometimes worked at Headley's house instead of at the university library. I suppose we should have mentioned Headley to the detectives."

"Thank you. I'll certainly speak with him," Jane said. "Could this John Headley have been the person Max was meeting that night?" Her words were met by a sudden chill in the room. She added, hastily, "Not to suggest that Headley had anything to do with what happened to Max. I was just considering that he might have some information for us."

"The woman detective—"

"DI Warwick," Jane said, interrupting Anne.

"Yes. She said they'd check all the CCTV cameras to see if they could pick up Max's movements. They asked if he knew anyone who lived near the spot where . . . *it* . . . happened. Tom and I couldn't think of anyone. When he was younger, we always used to know where he was and what he was doing . . ."

Anne didn't finish her sentence, but Jane nodded in understanding. She exchanged a look with Patrick, remembering the conversation they'd had after he'd gone off to university. She'd been in the habit of quizzing him on his every move, until he pointed out that he was an adult and did not need to report to her. It was the moment Jane had realised her children had a right to their own private lives, and that she had no right to interfere as she had done when they were younger. It was hard, but she'd taken a step back.

"I mentioned just now that the police have resources I don't have," Jane said. "Having access to CCTV cameras is one of them."

Tom Barsby spoke up. "We get it, Jane. We know you're limited, but it doesn't matter. In our minds, you have an emotional tie to Max through Patrick's friendship with Seth. Having you on the case makes us feel there's someone who cares about our son as a person. And, of course, you're a parent yourself."

Tom's gaze travelled to Patrick and, despite the compassion she felt for this family, Jane couldn't help feeling that she was being manipulated — emotionally blackmailed even, in a not very subtle manner. Nevertheless, she couldn't find it in her heart to hold it against the grieving father.

At that moment, Emma Wentworth reappeared in the doorway to say that Alec was asleep. She immediately began tidying up — straightening cushions, collecting the empty mugs, and stacking together what looked like a few days' worth of unopened mail, including, if Jane wasn't mistaken, a number of white envelopes that probably contained a poignant mixture of Christmas and bereavement cards.

Jane had already been wondering how to take leave of the Barsbys. Emma's return offered the perfect cue. She signalled to Patrick, and they rose as one from their respective chairs. Emma offered to see them out. The Barsbys remained on the sofa, pressed tightly against one another.

"I'm so worried about them both," Emma whispered in the hallway. "They're clearly not coping. I'm going to suggest that Dad goes into respite care for a bit. I'd have him, but I work full time, and he needs constant watching."

Jane agreed. As Emma said, the Barsbys were scarcely managing to look after themselves, never mind Anne's father.

Patrick was quiet as they walked back to the car. "You okay?" Jane asked.

"Yeah. I guess. It's just — you know — a bit full-on, is all." He seemed about to say something more, but didn't, and Jane didn't press him, assuming he was thinking about his dad. When they arrived home, out of the blue, Patrick said, "Mum, I feel even more invested in all this now. I'd like to help in any way I can. I mean, like, help you investigate, but first, there's something I need to tell you. Something not even Max's parents knew."

CHAPTER EIGHT

"A secret? What sort of secret?"

"It's complicated," Patrick said. His hesitant tone reminded Jane of when he'd used those exact words to describe his first date. He was seventeen years old, and he had no idea Jane had suspected for years that he was gay. He'd been bowled over when she expressed only delight when he told her that his date was a boy.

"Complicated how?"

Patrick sighed. "If I tell you, you'll have to swear you won't tell anyone."

Jane placed her car keys in a bowl on the kitchen table. "You know I can't make a promise like that, Patrick. Especially if it might have some bearing on the investigation into Max's murder."

"Oh God, I knew you were going to say that." Patrick put his head in his hands in a dramatic gesture. "It's something that only Max's trusted friends know about."

"Then how do you know? You didn't know Max that well, did you? So how do you qualify as one of his most trusted confidantes?"

Patrick sighed again. "So, Seth told me, right? He swore me to secrecy. If it becomes common knowledge, he'll know who's responsible. That's why I need you to promise you won't tell anyone."

"You do appreciate the irony of asking me to keep a secret of Seth's that he couldn't keep from you, don't you?" Jane said, perplexed.

"Yes," Patrick said with a shake of his head. "Oh God, why did I even mention it?"

"You wouldn't have mentioned it if it hadn't been playing on your mind. And I suspect you won't find much peace unless you share whatever this secret of Max's was with me."

"Aargh! Why are you always right? It's sooo annoying."

"I'm not always right. Except when it comes to knowing my children," Jane said. "You're like me. This sort of thing will gnaw away at you until you get it off your chest."

Patrick threw his hands in the air. He was a demonstrative person. Usually Jane loved this about him, but right now it was irritating.

"All right. All right," Patrick said. "But, first, let me make us both some coffee? I really need one."

Jane worried that Patrick might change his mind while he fixed their drinks, but to give him his due, after accepting he must tell her about Max's secret, he didn't waver. They sat down in the cosy living room to have a heart-to-heart. The lights of the Christmas tree twinkled in the darkened room, seeming to add a further layer of mystery to the sense of intrigue evoked by Patrick's allusion to a closely kept secret.

Patrick took a breath and began. "Remember, this is about Max's private life, and I'm only telling you because, like you said, it might be relevant to the investigation."

Jane was truly puzzled. She had no idea what Patrick might be about to tell her.

Patrick continued, "And the last thing I want is for the person Max was closest to, to get into trouble because of me. God knows, being gay, I understand how some people think. The ridiculous and hateful accusations they throw out."

Jane nodded, conscious that Patrick had encountered prejudice from narrow-minded and bigoted individuals on numerous occasions. "You can trust me, Patrick."

"Okay. Thanks, Mum." Patrick seemed to relax a little. "So, Max had a girlfriend who was in the country illegally."

Whatever Jane had expected Patrick to tell her, it wasn't that. Before she could say anything, Patrick continued. "Her name is Maryam. She's from Iran. She arrived in this country in the back of a lorry, and is currently staying in Lincoln, where she has a family connection — an aunt, her mother's sister, Darya."

Jane nodded. "I'm sure she must have felt desperate to take the brave step of leaving her own country." Knowing that Patrick was not going to like her next words, she waited a couple of seconds before adding, "Patrick, you know I have to tell DI Warwick about this, don't you? She needs to be aware of all the people who were close to Max."

"So that they can become suspects," Patrick said.

Jane corrected him. "So that they can be eliminated as suspects. But I don't need to tell you this, do I? You knew I'd have to tell DI Warwick about it."

Patrick looked downcast. "I was kind of hoping that you could talk to Maryam and her aunt first. Then, if you were satisfied they had nothing at all to do with Max's murder — and I know for certain they didn't — there'd be no need to tell DI Warwick."

"Patrick, I get why you want me to withhold this from DI Warwick for now, I really do, but that would put me in the difficult position of potentially withholding information from the police, which could get me into trouble. I have a duty to inform Warwick." Jane thought for a moment. "But I'll do my best to ensure that it's handled sensitively. I'm sure Maryam could apply for asylum, and that she would be treated sympathetically—"

Patrick exploded. "And how are you going to do that, Mum? As you said yourself, you and DI Warwick aren't exactly bosom buddies. Do you really think she'll listen to you when you ask her to handle things sensitively? Not to mention that the police don't exactly have a glowing record when it comes to dealing with marginalised groups."

Not for the first time since becoming a special, Jane felt conflicted about having to balance her duties as a police officer against her personal life. And it didn't get any more personal than when it involved upsetting a member of your own family. Still, she'd made her position clear to Patrick from the outset.

Jane reiterated what she'd said before, both to Patrick and the Barsbys. "The beginning of a murder investigation is very much focussed on building up a picture of the victim's life — it's important to uncover all the different people and groups of people they interacted with—"

"I know, I know. So, what now? You going to get straight on the hotline to DI Warwick?" Patrick said.

Jane thought for a few moments before reaching a decision that went against all her better judgement. "Thinking about it, I suppose I could do a little preliminary work, just so that when I do contact DI Warwick, she has the right information. What if you get in touch with Seth and tell him that you've told me about Max's secret?"

At the sight of Patrick's now horror-stricken face, she added, "I know that will be hard for you, but it's better that you tell him than that he finds out some other way. I'll hang fire on approaching Warwick until you've had a chance to contact Seth and ask him for more information about Maryam and her aunt. Also, can you ask Seth to arrange for us to visit Maryam and Darya? And don't leave it too long."

A short delay in informing Warwick about Max's secret wouldn't do any harm. Jane told herself this to offset her feelings of doubt — and guilt — but the truth was, she was worried. Still, there was the hope that, if Warwick was worth her salt, she would probably have uncovered this information already.

At some point, also, Jane would have to tell Warwick about Max being involved with the dig. Again, Warwick was probably already aware of this, but if she wasn't, it would appear to her as though Jane's promise to keep her in the loop had gone out the window.

The sound of a key turning in the lock announced that Ed had arrived. He had been in Lincoln for a meet-up with some fellow blacksmiths and was staying the night. Relieved, Jane jumped up to greet him. Ed's presence would put an end to any further discussion on the subject of Max's secret for the rest of the evening.

CHAPTER NINE

Jane had the house to herself for the morning. Not that she didn't enjoy having Norah and Patrick around. It was just nice to have a few hours' peace and quiet — and a bit of time to do a spot of housework. Nothing too onerous. A flick round with the duster and some vacuuming downstairs followed by a speedy tidy-up in the kitchen was all that was needed. Then, Jane planned to put her feet up with a coffee, a slice of cake and a good book. There was a stack of books in her 'To Be Read' pile and, as she'd requested more books for Christmas, it was only going to get bigger. Immediate action was required.

Patrick and Norah had nipped into town to have a look at the sales. They planned to have lunch together in one of the new restaurants that had opened in the Cornhill Quarter and weren't expected back until the early afternoon.

Ed had driven off to his house in Doveby first thing in the morning. He had an order to finish for the new owners of Thornally Hall, a country house on the outskirts of his village.

The house had a slightly dark association. The body of a murdered young woman had been discovered dumped in the grounds back in October, and everyone was surprised at how quickly the sale had gone through. The order, which was for ornamental railings and garden sculptures, among other things, had been placed by the previous owner. When the new owners saw what had been planned, they approached Ed and asked if he would do the work for them. Ed had been delighted not to lose such a big order.

Jane's phone pinged. A text from Patrick. He'd received a message from Seth giving him John Headley's contact details. Did she want to pay him a visit that afternoon? Would three o'clock be okay, if it could be arranged at such short notice?

Jane's thoughts had been so full of Max's secret girlfriend that she'd almost forgotten about John Headley. He was the man Max had befriended after attending one of his history talks. Jane texted back that this would be fine. Ten minutes later, she received another text from Patrick confirming the arrangement.

Jane completed her chores in record time and moved on to phase two of her plan for the morning. Coffee. Cake. Book. Nothing short of an earthquake would keep her from her reading until Patrick and Norah returned from their shopping expedition. Or so she thought. Her conversation with Patrick the previous evening — and its implications — kept distracting her, and she had only managed to read a couple of chapters by the time the kids returned.

Jane and Patrick set off at two forty-five. John Headley lived about fifteen minutes' walk from Danesgate. When they turned into his drive, Jane saw a man standing at the front window looking out for them, his face half in shadow. There was no need to knock, for he had opened the door before they reached the doorstep.

To her surprise, Jane recognised him. A slight start from Headley confirmed it was mutual. "You work in the second-hand bookshop near Newport Arch."

Her comment brought a smile to Headley's face. "You have a fondness for crime fiction, I think."

Jane smiled back. "I do, among other things. I'm an eclectic reader."

"I only work in the shop on Monday afternoons and Wednesday mornings. It's owned by some friends of mine, and I do it to help them out."

"That explains why I've only seen you there a couple of times," Jane said. "Say 'hi' to Bill and Louisa for me, next time you see them." Jane had got to know the owners on her frequent visits.

"Of course." Headley led them into a sitting room with a bay window, in which stood a tastefully decorated Christmas tree, its coloured lights matching the top lights of the windows which were glazed with pretty stained glass, a feature of houses of this period. "Welcome to my humble abode. Can I offer you a glass of sherry as it's the festive season? Or a brandy if you'd prefer. Otherwise, tea or coffee is also possible."

Jane and Patrick both requested a glass of sherry. Headley disappeared for a couple of minutes and returned with three glasses that were much bigger than the standard size. "Can't be doing with those dainty little glasses," he said as he handed one to Jane. "One sip and you need a refill." He handed Patrick a glass. "You are mother and son, I take it?"

Patrick nodded. "I look like my dad, but I've got my mum's eyes — and her nature — or so I've been told."

"It was the eyes that gave it away," Headley said. "And you're a friend of Max Barsby's?"

"Yes. I knew Max. I'm a good friend of his cousin, Seth Wentworth. Mum and I went to see Max's parents yesterday, and they suggested speaking to you because you knew Max quite well."

"Yes. Tom Barsby was in touch just after your visit to ask if I minded. I've been waiting for you to get in touch." Headley rubbed his chin. "I was upset to hear about Max's death, even more so given the circumstances." He took a sip of his sherry. "I met Max when he came to a talk I gave last year. He's also a frequent visitor to the bookshop. Max approached me after the talk to ask me some questions on the topic, and we got talking. He told me he was study-ing archaeology at the university, and I told him I'd studied history many moons ago, and that I had a particular interest in antiquity. Max was remarkably well-informed about his subject. I wish the students I lectured had been more like him."

"Are you a retired professor?" Jane asked.

"Er, no. Just a humble teacher. I worked at an FE college for a couple of years before I retired. I'm something of a failed academic, I'm afraid. As I said, I did a degree in history in the distant past. I'd hoped to go on to further study, but . . ." He sighed deeply. "Life, you know, getting in the way, as it has a habit of doing. I met my wife-to-be, Joan, in my final year at university, and she fell pregnant . . . I was a father at twenty-three. Anyway, I never lost my enthusiasm for my subject."

Headley regarded them over the top of a pair of wire-rimmed spectacles perched on his nose. His brushed-back white hair seemed to elongate an already deep forehead. Dressed in brown corduroy trousers and an Arran cardigan with suede patches at the elbows, he looked every inch the stereotypical academic of bygone days, a look which Jane felt sure he cultivated.

"Anyway," Headley continued, "Max kept coming into the bookshop asking for recommendations. He was reading far more widely than just the books on his course list. I saw a lot of my younger self in him. I hope I'm not being vain in saying that he regarded me as a mentor, a father figure even. We struck up an unlikely friendship. Unlikely, given our respective ages, I mean. Intellectually, we were well matched."

"Did you meet Max on a regular basis, Mr Headley? Outside of the bookshop, I mean?" Jane said.

Headley nodded. "Oh, yes. He came here frequently. We whiled away many an hour discussing everything from the origins of the Peloponnesian War to the fall of the Roman Empire. Max had a particular interest in Roman Lincoln."

Patrick nodded along. "Seth told me his cousin was a bit of a boffin."

"I like to think that I was of some benefit to Max in the capacity of intellectual mentor. I tried to structure our discussions to challenge him and extend his knowledge." He looked from Patrick to Jane as if seeking their approval.

"Max worked here at the house too. He told me one day that it was difficult for him to work at the university library because it wasn't always as quiet as it might be. So, I offered him the use of my library. It's my dining room, really, but I converted it after my wife died four years ago. I put an extra desk in there, and he and I would sit in companionable silence, deep in our respective studies."

Headley's gaze drifted to his sherry glass and, for a moment, he looked as though he was lost in nostalgia for the recent past, conjuring up the images he'd just described.

"You must miss him," Jane said.

Headley looked up from contemplating the bottom of his glass. "Yes, yes. I do. Since Joan died, I've been alone in this house. It was nice to have a bit of companionship. And, of course, I'd grown fond of Max. I almost thought of him as a son." He removed his glasses and pinched his nose. His eyes had teared up. Headley pulled a grubby-looking hand-kerchief from his pocket and blew his nose.

"I'm sorry for your loss," Jane said.

"Thank you. That's kind of you."

Jane wondered if Headley had family of his own. He must have read her mind, for he said, "I have two daughters and two granddaughters. One of my granddaughters, Pippa, is Max's age. Silly old fool that I am, I harboured hopes that they'd get married one day, and Max would be part of the family."

"That's not silly. Most parents and grandparents indulge in a bit of matchmaking where their offspring are concerned."

Jane caught Patrick's eye. She knew that he, too, must be thinking of Maryam. So, she asked, "Were Max and Pippa dating?"

"Oh no. Pippa's at university in Exeter. I just hoped that maybe one time when she was home for the holidays . . . Foolish of me, as I said." The glasses came off again, and again, he blew his nose to hide his tears. Jane waited, thinking about what she should ask him next, but Patrick got in first.

"How did Max seem the last time you saw him, Mr Headley? Was he worrying about anything, or did he seem the same as usual?"

Headley stuffed his handkerchief up his sleeve and took another sip of sherry before answering. He rubbed the suede patch on the elbow of his cardigan and looked down at the floor as if trying to remember. "As I recall, he was in good spirits the last time he was here."

"Which was when?" Jane asked.

There was a long pause. "I . . . It was a few days before . . . you know."

Not wishing to distress him again, Jane moved on. "Max's mum told us that he was excited to be working on a dig, here in Lincoln, with an archaeologist that he admired, Dr Linus Crow. Apparently, Dr Crow wrote a children's book, years ago, that Max read as a boy. The book inspired his interest in the subject."

Headley looked up abruptly. He stiffened. Something had upskittled him, but was it the mention of the dig? Linus Crow?

"Did Max tell you about the dig?" Jane asked.

No answer. Puzzling. Surely Max would have mentioned it to him, given their shared passion for history. According to Anne Barsby, Max had been full of talk about the excavation. Jane looked at Headley and was alarmed to see that he was red in the face with what looked like anger.

"Mr Headley? Are you all right?"

Finally, Headley broke his silence. "Max did mention the dig to me, yes." The muscles in his face tensed as if he were struggling to suppress some strong emotion. Jane glanced at Patrick, who was frowning. He too had noticed the shift in Headley's mood.

"You didn't approve of Max working there?" Jane asked.

Headley sighed. "Did I make it that obvious?"

"It's just you seemed a bit . . . put out when I mentioned it. I thought you'd be all for it."

"Ah. My lack of enthusiasm gave me away, did it? All right, might as well admit it. I wasn't over the moon about

Max being involved with the dig or with" — he paused — "that man."

"Oh," said Jane. Again, her eyes slid to where Patrick was sitting. He looked as puzzled as she felt.

Finally, Headley uttered a strangulated exclamation. "That man ruined my life."

CHAPTER TEN

There was silence for a moment following Headley's out-
burst. Patrick looked to Jane. She shook her head slightly
to indicate that they should wait for Headley to explain. In
the meantime, Jane studied Headley as discreetly as possible,
over the rim of her sherry glass.

"Excuse me," Headley said at last. "As you've probably
guessed, I'm not a big fan of Linus Crow's. I didn't tell Max
that, of course. He was so excited to be working alongside the
man who wrote his favourite childhood book that I didn't
have the heart to tell him what kind of a man Crow is."

"You know Dr Crow?" Jane asked.

"*Knew.* Back in my university days," Headley said. "We
were undergraduates together at Nottingham University.
We were good friends back then. Both of us studying history. Both due to start our master's degrees at the same time.
Unfortunately, due to Joan's pregnancy, and my financial
commitments, I was unable to proceed. I had hoped to
resume my studies at a later date, and I did carry on doing
research when I could, and discussing this with Crow. Little
did I think that he would put paid to my dreams."

Headley knocked back his remaining drink. He glared at
the glass as if angry at it for being empty. "To cut a long story

short, Crow and I had been in the habit of discussing our ideas and our research with each other. We were researching a similar area of scholarship, but our areas of interest had quite a different focus. Or so I thought. Never did I imagine that my best friend would commit the vile crime of plagiarism and steal my best ideas. I didn't know the extent of his treachery until he presented me with a copy of his PhD thesis."

Jane was sympathetic, but she suspected this kind of thing must go on all the time in academia. There must be more to it than that.

Headley was on a roll. "All the more galling because his intellect was inferior to mine. His work was of mediocre quality, but he was awarded his doctorate on the strength and quality of my ideas, and the research sources I'd shared with him to support my theories. Shameful.

"I wouldn't have minded, but Crow wasn't interested in pursuing a career in academia, as I was. After completing his PhD, he started an archaeology firm."

Jane understood why John Headley was upset. If what he said was true, Crow had done the dirty on him. But she couldn't help thinking that if there had been an interchange of ideas between the two men on a topic they were both researching, there was bound to be some overlap.

Headley's resentment of Crow seemed a tad over the top. It also seemed to highlight some negative aspects of his own personality — vanity and arrogance among them. It was obvious that he blamed Crow for his failed academic career, not to mention also blaming his future wife for getting pregnant, as though he'd had no part in that himself.

It was hard to know what to say. Jane felt that they'd veered way off topic, and that, given the chance, Headley would rant on about Linus Crow for the rest of the afternoon. It was Patrick who came to the rescue with a comment to help steer them back on course.

"That's a terrible story, Mr Headley. It must have been so difficult to keep your feelings about Linus Crow from Max."

"It was a strain. Especially when I had to listen to Max singing Crow's praises 'til the cows came home. But I couldn't shatter the boy's illusions."

Jane silently thanked Patrick for getting the conversation back on track. "So, you said you didn't notice any change in Max in the weeks leading up to his death?"

"Not really." Headley was slightly hesitant. "He was excited about the dig, of course. Even though the finds they were making weren't earth-shattering, Max was just thrilled to see traces of Roman settlement. Even finding some commonplace pieces of greyware or Samian pottery was thrilling for the lad. It's one thing seeing these common items in a museum, quite another digging them out of the earth with your own hands. I kept hoping something really big would turn up, just to see the excitement on Max's face."

Jane thought carefully before making her next comment. "Actually, I heard about the sort of finds that were being unearthed right from the horse's mouth, so to speak."

Headley regarded her questioningly. "From Max? Did you know him?"

"No, not from Max. From Dr Crow."

"You've spoken with Crow?"

"I'm a volunteer special police officer," Jane said. "A couple of days ago, I was called out to investigate a burglary at the house Dr Crow is renting during his stay in Lincoln."

Headley had refilled his glass. He spluttered over his first sip. Jane observed him as he took out his handkerchief again and wiped, first the glass, then his long, bony fingers. He stood up, briefly, to wipe the front of his cardigan, then sat down again, crossing his long legs.

It was Jane's turn to give a start as she flashed back to the description Dr Crow had given her of the man he'd seen running from his house. He'd described an older man, white hair, tall, gangly, with long legs. No! Could it be that Crow's burglar was sitting right in front of her? She caught Headley's eye. He looked away, seemingly reluctant to hold her gaze. Jane wasn't about to accuse him, but she felt in her bones that she was right.

"Excuse my clumsiness," Headley said, flustered. "Is there anything else I can help you with?" His abrupt question seemed to signal that he was suddenly anxious for their conversation to be over. For them to depart.

"Just one more question, if you don't mind, Mr Headley. Did Max ever discuss any of his friends with you?"

Headley frowned and picked at the pilling on the sleeve of his jumper. "I can't really remember. Only his cousin, Seth, comes to mind. Our conversations tended to be cerebral rather than personal in nature."

"I understand. That's quite all right, Mr Headley."

Headley shifted stiffly in his chair. "I've been sitting still too long. Am I likely to get a visit from the police? Tom Barsby said he hadn't mentioned my friendship with Max to them, but you're a special constable. Will you be telling the detective in charge of the investigation that they need to pay me a call?"

"I will have to inform Detective Inspector Stephanie Warwick — she's the DI heading up the investigation into Max's murder — about your relationship with Max. I can tell her what you've told me today. It will be up to her to decide whether she needs to interview you personally."

"I hope someone finds out what happened to Max soon," Headley said. "The one thing I was expecting you to ask was whether I could think of anyone who could have had a reason to hurt him. The answer's no. I can't begin to understand why anyone would harm a lovely, intelligent young lad like Max."

You've been very helpful." Jane looked at Patrick. They both stood up at the same time. Headley accompanied them to the door. "It seems a little inappropriate to say it under the circumstances," Jane said, "but I hope you have a happy Christmas when it comes."

"Yes, well, life goes on," Headley muttered. "Same to you when it comes."

Patrick didn't speak until they turned out of Headley's drive. "Phew. What did you make of all that? If it had been

Linus Crow who was murdered, I know who'd be topping my list of suspects."

"Same here," Jane said. "So strange that John Headley and Linus Crow knew each other." She thought for a moment before taking Patrick into her confidence. "Not a word of this to anyone, Patrick, but you know that burglary at Dr Crow's house I told you about?" Patrick nodded. "I'd bet money that John Headley was the culprit. He matches the description Crow gave us exactly."

Patrick let out a low whistle of surprise. "Now that is weird. Why didn't you mention something to Headley about it?"

"No proof," Jane said. "I can't just go throwing out an accusation like that without the evidence to back it up. He'd only have denied it. Not to mention the timing. I wanted Headley to remain cooperative. There was something off about that burglary. Nothing of any value was taken, except for a small sum of cash in a bowl on the kitchen table. A valuable gold watch was left untouched. We assumed that the burglar heard Dr Crow open the door and panicked before he'd spotted the watch. But if the burglar was John Headley, then it stands to reason that he was there looking for something. The sixty-four-thousand-dollar question being—"

"Dun, dun, dun," Patrick hummed dramatically. "What was he looking for?"

CHAPTER ELEVEN

Jane and Patrick returned from their visit to John Headley's house to find Norah stretched out on the sofa reading. Her temp job had come to an end and she wasn't due to start the next one until after the New Year. Jane was slightly worried about her daughter's current job insecurity. While temping was keeping Norah in work, it was meant to be a stopgap while she considered her career options. Jane worried she was drifting too long.

As the antidote to Norah's career-change crisis, Ed had come up with the idea of Norah becoming his apprentice. She could attend college to learn the blacksmithing trade and work with him at the same time.

Norah, who had once considered studying art at university, was initially delighted at the suggestion, but had ultimately decided that it wasn't for her. She'd been more interested in Ed's other craft of silversmithing, and was now looking into jewellery-making as a potential occupation. But Jane suspected that idea, too, would soon be abandoned. All Jane wished was for her daughter to be happy — but financial security was also a consideration.

Norah set the slim-looking volume she'd been reading aside and asked if they would like a cup of tea. "Put your feet up for a bit, Mum. I'll make us all a brew. No need for you to cook tonight either. I've made chilli. Hope you like it hot." She gave Jane a peck on the cheek and went off to the kitchen.

Jane sat down in the armchair Norah had vacated. She picked up the abandoned book and noted the title and author with some surprise. *The Magic Ring* by Linus Crow. "Where did you get this?" she called to Norah.

It was Patrick who answered. "I ordered it online last night. I was curious after the Barsbys mentioned the influence it had had on Max. It arrived this morning. It wasn't easy to find. Been out of print for donkey's years."

Jane turned the book over in her hand, careful not to dislodge the scrap of paper that Norah was using as a bookmark. "So, this is the book that so inspired Max Barsby." She gave a slight shudder. "I hope the choices it led him to make in his life didn't have anything to do with his death."

"That's a bit morbid, Mother," Norah said.

Jane read the blurb on the back of the slightly tattered paperback. The story was about a nine-year-old boy who, while holidaying near Hadrian's Wall, discovers a Roman military ring, believed to have been worn by a Roman centurion. The ring has magical properties. When the boy slips it on his finger, he's transported back to Roman times. As soon as he removes the ring from his finger, he's returned to his own time at the exact moment he departed. Not a particularly original concept, but it was written nearly forty years ago. Jane could appreciate how it would fire the imagination of a young child. She read a couple of chapters while she waited for her cup of tea.

Norah returned with the tea and a packet of hobnobs. Jane eyed the packet, noting that only half remained. Patrick had munched his way through three packs in as many days. He was eating her out of house and home.

"What do you think?" Patrick asked her, nodding at the book. "It wouldn't be sophisticated enough for your average nine-year-old of today, would it?"

"It was probably written with a younger age group in mind," Jane said. "The protagonists of children's books are usually a bit older than the intended readership. I think it's quite charming."

"It's out of print. I paid quite a bit for it second-hand," Patrick said.

Jane thumbed through the pages for a couple of moments. "Archaeology was Max's passion, his whole life, really. As I said, I hope it doesn't turn out to have played some role in his death too."

"So, what? Are you thinking Max might have been murdered by one of his professors, or someone on his archaeology course, or John Headley, or" — Patrick nodded at the book in Jane's hand — "Linus Crow?"

Norah interrupted. "Pass the hobnobs, Patrick, before you scoff the lot."

"Catch." Patrick threw the pack.

Norah caught it deftly. She took two biscuits from the pack, then handed it to Jane, who took one and handed it back to Patrick, who complained, "You've only left me four." He ate two before continuing. "So, is that what you were thinking? Max was killed by someone linked to the world of archaeology?"

"I don't have any better ideas at the moment. Unless he was murdered by someone in his . . . wider circle of friends." Jane saw Patrick's eyes narrow at the unstated suggestion that she might be referring to Maryam and her aunt. Which she wasn't.

Norah yawned and stretched. She stood up. "I'm going to have a nice, relaxing bath. I'll warm the chilli up when I get back."

As soon as she was out the door, Patrick spoke, quietly. "I was waiting for Norah to leave the room before telling you that I've just had a reply from my text to Seth. He got in touch with Maryam and she's agreed to see us. He's suggesting tomorrow evening."

"Good," Jane said. "I'm pleased that a meeting's been sorted so quickly."

Patrick joined Jane on the sofa. He pushed the coffee table away so that he could stretch his long legs out in front of him. "I've got some more news. I've been in contact with Dr Linus Crow about volunteering on that dig Max was working on. I want to see what I can find out. What do you think?" Before Jane could voice her opinion, he added, "Of course, I'm not really asking your permission, Mum. I meant it when I said I wanted to help Seth and his family find out what happened to Max."

"Okaaay," Jane said. She could see that Patrick had his mind set on this. She must have looked worried, for he asked what she was thinking. "I don't like you doing something that might put you in danger. I'm also wondering what DI Warwick will say when she finds out we've been interfering in her case without telling her. I mean, she did say she expects it of me now, but I sort of promised to keep her informed of what I was up to, and what I find out."

"So, that's exactly what you'll be doing. Whatever I find out at the dig I'll pass on to you, and you can pass it on to her. Imagine how pleased she'll be when we present her with information that helps crack her case," Patrick said.

"Not sure it works like that. And what if we don't discover anything of substance?"

Patrick threw up his arms in a gesture of exasperation. "Then she'll have nothing to get annoyed about."

Jane could see she was fighting a losing battle. She looked at him with a feeling of frustration. "Does it matter what I think? It sounds as though your mind's made up."

"That's right. It is." Patrick leaned over and kissed her on the cheek. "I start tomorrow. Are you impressed with how I talked my way into it? They're a man down with Max being murdered, so that helped, but I spun a good yarn — finance manager suffers existential crisis and decides to reinvent himself as an archaeologist. Thinking of applying for a place at the local uni and wants a bit of practical experience. Seemed to swing it." He jumped up. "Norah's taking her time over her bath. I'll put some rice on and warm up the chilli." A moment later he called from the kitchen, "I hope you're as hungry as I am. She's made enough to feed a Roman legion."

Patrick returned a moment later and handed Jane a glass of red wine. "Cheers," he said. "Here's to Bell and Son, Inc., the hottest new detective duo on the block." Jane smiled, rather liking the image his words evoked.

While her son busied himself in the kitchen, Jane sat in quiet contemplation. She'd forgotten how obstinate Patrick could be when he set his mind on something. Her late husband, Sam, had always claimed that Patrick took after his mother. Was her concern about Patrick volunteering at the dig bothering her because he'd somehow taken control of the investigation? *Oh my God!* A voice boomed inside Jane's head — DI Warwick's, smug and satisfied, saying, "Now you know what it feels like, Bell."

CHAPTER TWELVE

To take her mind off the meeting with Maryam that evening, Jane decided to do some sleuthing of her own. She toyed with the idea of turning up on Linus Crow's doorstep in her police uniform to lend a bit of authority to her presence there, but dismissed the idea immediately. It would be a blatant misuse of her powers, and would be certain to put Warwick's back up if she found out. Pity.

Turning up at Crow's house at all was risky. He was sure to think she was there in her official capacity, and if she didn't correct that assumption, she would be misleading him. The sensible thing would be for her to approach Warwick and tell her about Crow's connection with Max through the dig, and about John Headley's bitter enmity towards Crow, and let her investigate. But a rebellious little voice in Jane's head urged her to go ahead with her present plan, and so, here she was.

It was a quarter to eight on Monday morning. Jane was hoping Crow wouldn't be at work. She took a calming breath and rang his doorbell. Crow answered within seconds. He squinted at her from the other side of the threshold. "Oh. It's you. I didn't recognise you out of uniform."

Jane cleared her throat. "I was just wondering how you were feeling after your rather traumatic experience? I'm sorry to say that I have no new information on your burglar." This, at least, was true. Jane had checked, and although the case remained open, it was unlikely that a suspect would be found. Unless she raised her suspicions about John Headley, which she wasn't about to do before she'd had a chance to speak with Headley again. It would be useful to have some leverage when she did.

"Yes. I had a follow-up visit from a detective constable, but nothing's come of it so far. I think he lost interest when I said that nothing much had been taken."

Crow didn't ask her in. Jane hovered on the doorstep. "I wonder if I could have a few minutes of your time, Dr Crow? I just have some quick questions." She was careful to avoid mentioning that she wasn't there as a police officer, while knowing that Crow would assume she was.

"I can only spare you ten minutes or so. I've got to be at the dig this morning."

"Ten minutes is ample," Jane said.

Finally, he asked her to enter the house, and she followed him into the lounge, where he invited her to sit down.

"Do you remember on my last visit I asked you if you thought the burglary might have something to do with your work, Dr Crow?"

"Yes. I do remember that. I also recall telling you that I doubted it very much."

"That's right. Er . . . I take it you've heard about the murder of a young man — Max Barsby, an archaeology student at Lincoln University. Max was working on your dig."

There was the slightest pause. "Yes. A terrible tragedy," Crow said. "Max was an intelligent young man. I was saddened at the news of his death, even though I hadn't known him long. He was remarkably well-informed about his subject for someone of his tender years, and very enthusiastic about the dig."

Crow gave a sad smile. "He seemed quite excited at meeting me. Turned out, he'd read a children's book I wrote back in the eighties. He told me it inspired him to study archaeology when he grew up. I didn't think the book was even in circulation anymore. Max's mother picked it up in a second-hand bookshop. He even brought the book to the dig for me to sign for him."

"You didn't write any more books?" Jane asked.

Crow shook his head. "Didn't have the time — or the inclination, to be honest. It was just something I did to amuse myself. And the sales were disappointing, so it didn't seem worth pursuing a career as an author — not that I'd ever intended to. Once I got into archaeological consultancy work, I knew that it was the right career path for me. I've always been passionate about the historic environment, and about preserving our heritage."

"You work for the developer, not the planning authority, don't you?" Jane said.

"I'm employed by the developer, yes, to advise on historic matters and to carry out surveys and draw up specifications for any archaeological work. However, my role also includes liaising closely with the local planning archaeologist.

"Contrary to what a lot of people might think, it's actually quite rare for an archaeological excavation to be carried out as part of the planning process. Usually, other methods such as surveys and assessments will resolve how to proceed to lessen the effects of development on a site of interest. Sometimes, remains are preserved in situ to mitigate the effects of the development."

Crow paused a moment, seeming to check whether he still held Jane's interest. Jane gave an encouraging nod, and he continued. "The site I'm currently working on was predicted to be of interest because of pre-existing knowledge of the area. There had been previous finds nearby."

"Roman remains?" Jane said.

Crow gave what Jane interpreted as an indulgent smile. "Yes. Lincoln was a Roman settlement, but artefacts from other eras have been found here."

Jane was pleased that her tactic of getting Crow to talk about his job was working. He seemed at ease and had quite forgotten that he only had ten minutes to spare. Even so, he now seemed to catch on that something wasn't right. "Why are you asking me about Max Barsby? His death has nothing to do with the burglary, has it?" His eyes sparked with suspicion.

"Just crossing the t's and dotting the i's," Jane said. "The fact that both you and Max worked on the dig, and both of you were victims of a crime — admittedly very different ones — makes me wonder if there's any sort of connection. Of course, it's very unlikely. I'm just — you know — exercising an abundance of caution."

Jane was aware that she was rambling and becoming less convincing by the second. "Er, I don't know if you were aware, but Max was friends with a local man who has a keen interest in archaeology. His name is John Headley. I think you knew him at university?"

"Good grief! John Headley. That's a name I haven't heard in a very long time. Thank God."

"So, you do remember Mr Headley?"

From the way Crow was frowning, Jane could tell that he was wondering where all this was going. And what it had to do with his house being burgled.

"Yes, as you just said, we were undergraduates together." Crow's eyes narrowed. "Have you been speaking with Headley? What's he been saying about me? Not still accusing me of plagiarising his ideas, is he? As if the man ever had an original thought worth stealing."

"Er . . . He did mention it, yes," Jane said.

"Good God. What's it been? Forty-odd years and he's still banging on about my alleged betrayal. Beggars belief. Just to set the record straight, Headley and I were interested in the same area of research, and we often discussed our thoughts and shared our findings. Happens all the time. Two people hit on the same idea simultaneously, but one of them has the application and the intelligence to get it down on paper first.

"Headley's problem was that his reach exceeded his grasp. Mostly, the ideas originated with me, but Headley never acknowledged that. His intellectual lightness was matched only by his insufferable arrogance. The man had — and clearly still has — a vastly overinflated opinion of his own worth."

Perhaps aware that he'd been ranting on, Crow apologised. Then, a thought seemed to occur to him. "Hang on. Headley's not trying to say I had something to do with that poor lad's murder?" He looked about the room, as if in a panic. Surprisingly, he reached the same conclusion as Jane about the identity of his burglar, only Crow took it a step further. "Struth! I wouldn't be at all surprised to learn Headley was my burglar. What if he broke into my house to plant some damning evidence on me to frame me for Max's murder?"

Even Jane hadn't thought of that one. It wasn't as nutty as it sounded. What was that saying? Revenge is a dish best served cold. But forty-years' cold? It wasn't beyond the realms of possibility. Still, Jane sought to reassure Crow. "I don't think that at all, Dr Crow. Admittedly, John Headley still has a big chip on his shoulder, but I doubt he would try to get you sent down for murder."

Crow had calmed himself. "Right. Bit far-fetched, I suppose. Still, at least I stopped short of suggesting he killed the boy himself just to frame me."

Crow should have been a detective, Jane decided. Or maybe he shouldn't have been so hasty in abandoning his career as a writer of fiction. He wasn't lacking in ideas or imagination.

To be honest, what he'd just said did make her pause for thought. Had Headley hated Crow enough to kill Max, then plant evidence in his house in an attempt to pin the murder on Crow, all because of an ancient wrong he believed Crow had committed against him? Sounded outlandish, but . . .

"How did Max get on with the other people on the dig?" Jane asked in an attempt to divert Crow from Headley.

Crow shrugged. "All right, as far as I know. Max wasn't there that much really. He had his studies and a part-time job, which didn't leave him much time for working on the dig. A couple of other students from the university were also helping out. I can give you their names, and the names of my team. There aren't many of them — my team, I mean. Bit of a skeleton crew for this job, due to a number of factors like sickness and annual leave. Not to mention that Christmas is coming."

"That would be very helpful, Dr Crow. Are you able to do that now?"

"I suppose so. Let me just get pen and paper."

He left the room for a few moments, returning with the required items. Jane sat patiently while he compiled the list. She noticed him look up at the clock above the mantelpiece, a reminder that she needed to press on with the rest of her questions before he decided it was time to get to work.

"It's come to light that Max had arranged to meet someone at short notice on the night that he was murdered," Jane said. "Do you have any idea who that might have been? Someone on the list you're making, maybe?"

Crow seemed to be running out of patience. "How would I know?" he said irritably. "I hardly knew the boy, as I've told you already."

"Can you remember what you were doing that night, Dr Crow?" As soon as the words were out, Jane realised she'd gone a step too far. Crow looked up, sharply.

"Look, what is this? A bloody inquisition? Come to think of it, why are you really here? Because it's plain you haven't come about the burglary. And you're not a detective, are you? You're some kind of amateur police officer, if I remember correctly. Do you even have the right to be questioning me in this manner?" Crow set aside the list he'd been working on and stood up. "I think you've taken up enough of my time."

"I do beg your pardon, Dr Crow. I really did come here to check up on you after the burglary."

"Check up on me is right, but not out of concern for my welfare."

Jane knew it was time to beat a hasty retreat. "Er . . . thanks so much for your time, Dr Crow." She held out her hand. "If I could just have that list, I'll be on my way." For a moment she was sure he was going to refuse to hand it over.

"Here," Crow said, all but throwing it at her.

"That's very kind, thank you." Jane moved towards the door.

Crow followed her into the hallway. Just as she got to the front door, he called out, "You've been checking up on me, Jane Bell. Just so you know, I'm going to be checking up on you too. I intend to speak with your superiors."

Ouch! His words rang in Jane's ears all the way down the path to the gate. She knew she'd messed up big time, yet the encounter with Crow had been worthwhile. She and Patrick had speculated that Headley might have been looking for something at Crow's house. Had he been looking for evidence that would connect Crow with Max's murder? Or was it the far more sinister possibility — the one Crow claimed to have 'stopped short of suggesting' — that Headley might have been trying to set him up for Max's murder?

Jane couldn't wait to see Patrick's face when she told him the most interesting fact she'd learned that day — that each man believed the other to be capable of murder.

CHAPTER THIRTEEN

Patrick went shopping to buy some gear to wear on the dig. Cargo trousers seemed the way to go. It was what everyone wore on those archaeology programmes on TV. You needed pockets, and the more, the better. He wasn't sure what he needed them for, but it was better to be prepared.

He'd been assured when he'd spoken with Dr Linus Crow that all the equipment he'd require would be provided, so there was no need to go looking for tools. Still, he needed a waterproof jacket — he'd left his old one back in Balham — and a hat might be useful. A baseball cap would have done, but Patrick decided to go full Indiana Jones and purchase a ridiculously expensive, but seriously cool, fedora. He'd wear it again, wouldn't he?

When he arrived at the dig, he reported to the site office — a twelve-by-three-metre portacabin in a shade of gunmetal grey. Here, he met Dr Linus Crow, and a man called Jerry Roadknight, who was the CEO of Roadknight Construction, the company developing the land on which the dig was currently based. Patrick shook hands with Roadknight, noting that they were nose to nose and eye to eye. He wondered if Roadknight found that strange too. Patrick rarely encountered anyone who matched him in height.

Patrick had bent the truth slightly when he approached Dr Crow about becoming a volunteer. He'd claimed to have had a bit of experience, which was just about true. He and his sister Norah had gone on a one-day dig experience as children, and Patrick had also volunteered to work on a dig in Provence when he was a student. He'd left out the bit about abandoning the French dig after a week when a better offer had come along to spend the summer with a friend from university, house- and pet-sitting in Miami.

Patrick was using his mother's maiden name of King, in case Crow connected him with the special constable who had investigated his burglary. Fortunately, Crow hadn't asked for ID. Patrick was around six foot four. His mother was five four, so he wasn't worried about a physical resemblance.

"I don't often take on people with so little experience," Crow said. "I have my own team, and I often have a couple of archaeology students. But we're short-handed at the moment for various reasons, so I've made an exception since you've had a bit of experience, albeit some time ago."

Various reasons, including murder. "I'm very grateful for the opportunity, Dr Crow. As I explained when I first contacted you, I'm contemplating a career change. Accountant to archaeologist." Patrick tipped his fedora. "Staying within the same area of the alphabet. It'll be great to get my hands dirty on a real dig before I apply to the university."

Crow smiled. "Yes, well, it's hard work, but most of our volunteers find it very rewarding."

"Sounds perfect. I'm not afraid of hard work, and I'm here to learn."

Dr Crow smiled. "Good. Right, let's get you started. Boring stuff first, I'm afraid." Crow handed Patrick a booklet that he'd taken from the drawer of his desk. "Health and safety manual. Park yourself over there for the next hour and read it from cover to cover." He pointed to an unoccupied desk next to his.

"Sure," Patrick said, keeping the boyish enthusiasm in his tone, despite his distinct lack of fervour for the task.

Crow and Roadknight left him to it. They stood outside the portacabin talking. Their voices drifted through the open window, but Patrick couldn't quite make out what they were saying, so he moved from his desk to stand closer. That was better. Roadknight was talking about his construction project.

"I hope this murder isn't going to interfere with the timescale for my project, Linus. I know you don't need reminding, but time's money in this business, and the dig's already playing havoc with my schedule, but I suppose it was inevitable the police would eventually get wind of the Barsby lad having been a volunteer here."

"You don't need to worry, Jerry. They'll ask some routine questions and conclude that the lad's work here was nothing to do with his murder. Then hopefully, they'll go away."

"What about this special policewoman, and whatshisname, John Headley, that you were just telling me about?"

Crow reassured him again. "She's an irritant. Got ideas above her station and fancies herself as a detective, I think. I've dealt with her by reporting her for harassment. As for Headley, he's just a bitter and twisted loser with a big chip on his shoulder."

"He knew Max Barsby. He broke into your house. The police like joining dots even where none exist. That sounds like a problem to me."

"Believe me, it's not. Trust me, Jerry. It's a storm in a teacup. There's no reason for the police to bother us for long."

"I hope you're right, Linus because . . ."

At that point, their voices faded. Patrick risked a glance out of the window and saw them walking off in the direction of their parked cars.

Frustrated at not hearing the rest of their conversation, Patrick returned to his desk and opened the health and safety manual. Moments later, he got up and crossed to Linus Crow's desk. Unlike the other three desks in the room, it looked 'busy', with papers, books and framed photographs spread out around a desktop monitor and keyboard.

The computer screen was password protected, so nothing to gain there. Unsurprisingly, the books were all about archaeology or planning, and the papers seemed to relate to the construction project.

Patrick tried the drawers of Crow's desk. They were unlocked, meaning there was unlikely to be anything interesting inside. A quick rake through the top drawer revealed a plastic lunch box, an assortment of snack bars and a banana. The remaining three drawers were empty. Disappointed, Patrick returned to his desk and devoured his reading material, not because it was an unputdownable read, but because the alternative of twiddling his thumbs was only a marginally more entertaining prospect.

A woman popped her head around the door an hour later. She addressed Patrick in a broad Yorkshire accent. "Hi, Patrick, I'm Sue Sellars, one of Linus's team. Linus asked me to look after you. He's gone to a meeting with the planning people at the council along with Jerry Roadknight, whom I believe you've met."

Sue grimaced at the health and safety manual. "Right, I expect you've had enough of that. Let's get you started on some real work. Don't get me wrong, health and safety is our highest priority on the dig, but it's mostly common sense."

"Scouts honour, I've read it from cover to cover," Patrick said. "I'll never look at a retractable tape measure in the same way again."

Sue gave a hearty laugh. "Glad to hear you've got a good sense of humour. It's not a requirement of the job, but it definitely helps."

Patrick followed Sue Sellars across the site to where a small group of people were occupied in various tasks. One, a young man, held a wooden-sided screen into which a young woman was emptying the contents — soil and debris, mostly — of a small bucket. When the bucket was empty, the young man holding the screen gave it a vigorous shake. Sue explained that they were sifting for small artefacts. "Anything they come across will be bagged up and labelled for later examination."

Patrick peered into the screen and saw only stones and rubble. He hoped he would develop a more practised eye.

A few feet away, in a trench marked off with stakes, an older man was scraping away with a trowel. He looked up and gave Patrick a nod.

Sue introduced Patrick to the small team. The older man, possibly in his late thirties or early forties, was wearing aviator-style glasses. His name was Iain MacDonald and he spoke with a Scottish accent. His face had a weathered look, presumably from working outdoors a lot.

The young people were Jacob Abbot and Grace Toyne, both undergraduate archaeology students from the university. They all smiled and shook hands with Patrick. Jacob complimented him on his hat, with a grin that made Patrick wonder if it looked a bit naff.

Sue had been charged with showing Patrick the ropes. She began by demonstrating the various types of tools used for excavation work — trowels and spades — plus an array of brushes with different uses, including one that looked like a toothbrush, which she explained was used to clean small objects.

"Like teeth?" Patrick said.

"Sometimes," Sue said, deadly serious.

Patrick was then let loose on the dig to do some proper excavation work — under supervision, of course. It was absorbing work, and he was surprised at how quickly he took to it. He enjoyed the thoroughness it required, the delicacy and attention to detail. It would have been easy to surrender to the slow pace and work in a trance-like state, completely in the flow. Except Patrick wasn't there for any of that. He was there to find out as much as he could about Max Barsby.

It wouldn't do to launch right into the topic of Max's murder. That might make him look suspicious. Probably best to hold back for a bit and hope that someone else would bring it up.

Patrick worked steadily — and harmoniously — throughout the morning, discovering that, although the work required a certain amount of concentration, it didn't require silence. His companions on the dig were a chatty bunch, and he'd learned quite a bit about all of them before they broke for lunch.

Iain was forty-three, currently single following a divorce. Until recently, he'd worked at Leicester University. Sue was thirty-four. She was from Barnsley, and had an open, friendly personality. She had been working with Linus Crow for longer than Iain, and was an experienced field archaeologist. The students, Grace and Jacob, were first-year undergraduates. They had both spent their gap year working on digs — Jacob in Egypt, Grace in southern Italy.

Patrick felt a bit deceitful recounting his legend — as he liked to think of it — of a burnt-out 'big four' accountant rediscovering his childhood enthusiasm for archaeology. "I'm lucky I got the chance of working this dig. Linus explained that it was because you were short-handed." He wasn't fishing, but hoped, all the same, that someone would take the bait. Grace was the one to bite.

"There was another student working here," she said. "His name was Max. Max Barsby."

Patrick looked up from brushing some debris away from what Sue had assured him was a pottery sherd, possibly Roman in origin. "That name sounds vaguely familiar for some reason."

"Max was murdered. It's been in the news," Grace said.

Patrick stopped working and looked at her. "Oh my God. Really?"

"It's true," Jacob said. "You probably read about it somewhere."

"That's so sad," Patrick said, with genuine feeling. He thought of Seth and his family. "Was Max studying archaeology too?"

"Yes," Grace said, "but he was a second-year, so we didn't see too much of him before we all started at the dig."

Jacob nodded. "He was nice. A bit intense. Really looked up to Linus. He read a kid's book Linus wrote years ago, which inspired him to study archaeology."

"Linus wrote a book? That's pretty cool," Patrick said. "Hey, are you all okay? I mean, what a terrible thing to happen."

"It was pretty tough," Grace said. She sniffed and wiped away a tear.

Sue patted Grace on the arm, saying, "Look, why don't we break for lunch now? Have you brought a pack-up, Patrick?"

Patrick nodded. "I've come prepared."

"Good." She winked. "Important to keep your strength up. You'll be spending the afternoon with Jacob and Grace washing the morning's finds. We usually eat in the site office, or sometimes we go off to a local café, or just for a walk. It's up to you."

Patrick was slightly peeved that the conversation about Max had been brought to an end so abruptly, but it was obvious that Grace had found it distressing. Jacob, too, had looked upset. Sue had merely picked up on this and called a timely break. Patrick followed the others back to the portacabin where Sue put the kettle on and everyone retrieved their packed lunches from the fridge. They settled on some chairs arranged around a long table to eat.

As he munched on his cheese and pickle sandwich, Patrick tried to appraise his teammates objectively, in the way that he believed a detective might. None of them struck him as murderers. Grace and Jacob had seemed genuinely upset speaking about Max. Sue seemed like likeable person, but of course, she could be harbouring dark secrets for all Patrick knew. Iain appeared less sociable than the others, but that might simply be his personality. Then there was Linus Crow and Roadknight.

His thoughts were interrupted by a question from Sue. "So, Linus told me you'd had some experience of working a dig in France, Patrick. How did this morning compare?"

"Er . . . This morning was . . . colder," Patrick said, caught on the hop. "To be honest, I don't remember a lot about the French dig. It was quite a while ago now, and I was only there for a short time. I do remember finding a fragment of pottery that was part of some bigger bits that were eventually put together, like a jigsaw puzzle, to make a vase. That was pretty cool."

Sue stirred a sweetener into her tea. "We archaeologists get a buzz out of anything old. It's that thrill of holding something in your hand that no human being has touched in a long, long time."

Thinking back to the conversation he'd heard between Crow and Roadknight, Patrick asked, "I don't suppose the contractor is happy about this dig. Won't it mean a costly delay to his construction project?"

"Yes, but contractors are aware of their responsibilities towards the historical environment these days. It's something they have to think about even before they approach the planning authority for permission to develop a site," Sue said.

"Only good thing Maggie Thatcher's government ever did," Iain MacDonald growled through a mouthful of crisps.

"What was that?" Patrick asked.

"Ancient Monuments and Archaeological Areas Act," Iain said. When he didn't expand, Sue took over.

"It was — and still is — a major piece of legislation that provided for the protection of archaeological sites and ancient monuments in England. It's been amended since 1979, and further important legislation has been passed to help protect our heritage and preserve sites of archaeological importance. Thank goodness."

Grace piped up. "It basically stops people building what they want where they want with no thought for preserving the past for the future."

Sue nodded. "Developers now work with archaeological consultants like Linus, Iain and me to help them navigate and comply with legislation affecting planning decisions. We can advise on the likely impact of building works on sites of archaeological interest, and offer solutions to mitigate any potential damage."

"So, you're on the side of the developer?" Patrick said.

Sue frowned, as if disapproving. "It's not like that. We're employed by the developer, but the only 'side' we're on is that of protecting and preserving our national heritage. As archaeologists, we're passionate about protecting the historical environment. We work with builders and planners to ensure that's what happens."

Patrick sensed that the mood in the room had changed subtly and was unsure whether it was because Max's ghost had been raised and was still permeating everyone's thoughts, or because he had called into question the integrity of what Linus, Sue and Iain did for a living. Looking around, he could see that everyone was avoiding looking at him — except for Iain MacDonald, who glowered at him as he bit down on a chunky bar of chocolate.

Patrick apologised. "Okay. Sorry if I caused any offence."

"None taken," Sue said. "But you're right in saying that the dig will cause delays to Jerry Roadknight's schedule, and delays can be costly. That's why we need to be sure that the archaeological work is justified. Sometimes, it's a question of balancing the potential value of a site and its interest to the public, and our national heritage, against the costs of holding up a development. In this case, it is entirely justified as other important finds have been made near here, and our surveys have revealed evidence of a potentially important settlement."

Patrick was quiet for much of the rest of his lunch break, his mind constantly straying back to the conversation he'd overheard outside the portacabin between Linus Crow and Jerry Roadknight — Roadknight's concerns over further delays, and Crow's reassurances.

'Time is money,' Roadknight had said.

Despite Sue's assurances, Patrick couldn't help running a scenario in his mind in which Max had somehow got in the way of Roadknight's plans, and the contractor had — with or without assistance from Linus Crow — done Max in.

CHAPTER FOURTEEN

On Monday evening, Jane and Patrick brought each other up-to-date on what they had both discovered on their separate missions that day. Jane listened as Patrick recounted his day at the dig.

"Dr Crow described you as an irritant with ideas above your station who fancies herself as a detective," Patrick said.

Jane raised an eyebrow. "Rude, but he got some of it right."

"Oh, and by the way, he's reported you for harassment."

Jane groaned. So, Crow hadn't simply been making an empty threat, then. Not that she'd considered for a moment that he would. "He said he would. Man of his word, obviously. Go on."

Patrick's account of the conversation he'd overheard between the construction company owner, Jerry Roadknight, and Linus Crow was particularly interesting. Patrick's theory about Max stumbling on some information that might have got him killed by one or both of them was believable. "Good theory, Patrick. Definitely worth looking into, but I'm even less sure I like you being at that dig now."

Ignoring Patrick's protestations that he was big enough to take care of himself — there was certainly no arguing with that — Jane then launched into an account of her interview with

Linus Crow. "He was surprised to hear that John Headley still bore him a grudge. He called Headley arrogant, and basically accused him of being an intellectual lightweight. Crow also denied that he stole Headley's ideas, although he did concede that they were researching much the same topic."

Jane moved on to Crow's remarkable intuition about Headley being his burglar. "Not only did he clock that Headley might have burgled his house, he came up with the outlandish idea that Headley might have been planting something there to frame him for Max's murder. Then, believe it or not, Crow went almost as far as saying that he believed Headley himself capable of murdering Max, if only to frame his old rival for betraying him all those years ago."

"Wow," Patrick said. "Those two are like a pair of comic book villains."

At that point, Seth turned up, and they had to park further discussion for the time being.

Seth stood in Jane's doorway looking morose. "I'm feeling bad. I promised Max I wouldn't tell anyone about Maryam."

Jane thanked him for arranging the visit. She offered some words of comfort. "Max couldn't have foreseen the circumstances that you now find yourself in, so please don't be hard on yourself, Seth."

"I guess." He didn't sound convinced.

They got into Jane's car. Seth gave Jane directions to where Maryam was living with her aunt in a quiet residential street north-west of the city centre.

Outside the front door, as they waited for someone to answer, Jane tried to imagine how Maryam must be feeling about meeting them. Her heart went out to the young woman who had fled her own country in fear, only to find herself embroiled in murder here, in Lincoln, where she'd hoped she would be safe.

The woman who greeted them and invited them inside looked to be in her sixties. Her thick, slightly greying hair was arranged in a messy bun, and she wore large tortoiseshell glasses attached to a gold chain around her neck. She put the glasses on to scrutinise the strangers Seth had brought to her home. Then she introduced herself as Darya Shirvani and listened, smiling at Jane and Patrick in turn as Seth introduced them.

They stood in the hallway. A Persian-style runner ran all along its length. Framed photographs of smiling dark-haired men and women adorned the walls — Darya's family, presumably. Darya moved further down the hall and pushed open the second door on her right. A young woman, who could only be Maryam Bandari, sat at a table in a dining room that obviously doubled up as a library.

Bookshelves were magnets to Jane's eyes. She scanned them instinctively, taking in titles that she recognised, and many more that were unfamiliar. History and fiction domi-nated, but there were also books on art and literature. Darya Shirvani had eclectic tastes.

Darya was smiling at Jane now. "Please sit down. I see my books interest you, although I know there is another pur-pose to your visit."

Jane was embarrassed to realise that she'd been caught being nosey. Now her eyes travelled to the young woman. Maryam was dressed in jeans and a navy hoody. Her arms were crossed. She appeared to be appraising Jane and Patrick in a way that was not friendly.

"Seth has explained that you are police, but not proper police," Darya said.

"That's one way of describing a special constable," Jane said. "But I'm not here as a police officer today. I'm here because I've agreed to help Max's family discover the truth about their son's death."

At the mention of Max's name, Maryam let out a small gasp. Darya, who had sat down beside her, slipped an arm around the young woman's shoulder.

Darya introduced Jane and Patrick. "They are here as friends, Maryam," she said. "Your secret is safe with them."

Dark eyes examined Jane from under a fringe of brown-black hair. "She is police," Maryam said, her tone distrustful, bordering on hostile.

"I'm a volunteer police officer, but like I said, I'm not here as a police officer this evening."

"Not this evening perhaps, but what about tomorrow?" Maryam said.

Jane hesitated. She could not promise Maryam that she would keep her secret, and she would not lie to her. "That depends," she said.

To her surprise, Maryam nodded. "I understand. You will do what you have to do." Her eyes took on a resigned look now.

Jane wondered what was going through Maryam's head. There was no reason why she should trust someone who was connected with the police. In her country the police were not her friends. Seth had told Patrick they had arrested and beaten her for no crime other than being herself.

"I want justice for Max," Jane said. "I think you do too. It's for you to decide what you are prepared to risk to help make that happen."

Patrick glared at her. "Mum, surely—"

Maryam intervened. "It's all right, Patrick. Your mother is being honest with me, and that makes me want to trust her more. She is right. If I remain silent and think only of myself, Max's killer might go free."

"But you had nothing to do with Max's murder," Seth said.

"No, I did not," Maryam said. "But there are things I know that might help Jane find out who did." She looked at Jane and nodded her assent.

"Perhaps we can begin with you telling us how you met Max?" Jane said.

"Yes," Maryam said. She took a moment to compose herself. "We met in the museum on Danes Terrace. Max had been to a talk there, about archaeology. After the talk, he browsed in the museum. I was looking at a scale model of a Roman legion when Max approached me. He told me much about Roman Lincoln, and about where I could see Roman remains in the city. We talked for a while. Then Max asked me if I would like to go for a walk with him the next day to look at the Roman sites in the city, and I agreed."

Maryam's eyes misted at the memory. "I thought, why not? It was just one meeting. I did not need to tell Max my secret." Maryam glanced at Darya. "Darya did not approve. How did I know I could trust this stranger? But, somehow, I knew in my heart that I could. Perhaps I was already falling in love."

The women exchanged a smile, and this time, Maryam patted Darya's arm. Maryam continued her story. "I had been in Lincoln for some time by then and I had barely spoken to anyone besides Darya. I did not know who I could trust. Or what to do about my future. Darya and I talked about me seeking asylum, but it seemed that every day on the news there was another story about the government tightening up the law. It did not fill us with confidence."

Darya spoke up. "I came to this country as a refugee in 1979 after the revolution in my country. I did not feel . . . unwelcome, as many do now. I feared that Maryam would be sent home. I was afraid of this boy learning Maryam's secret and betraying her." She shook her head. "But I also knew that Maryam could not hide herself away from the world if she was to have any kind of life here. Otherwise, she would be no freer here than in our country."

Maryam nodded. "When I met Max, I told myself I would meet him only once, but that day, when we met for my tour of Roman Lincoln, everything changed. I agreed to meet him again, and then again. One day, Max told me he had fallen in love with me. He wanted to know more about me, about my family. Until then I had avoided mentioning these things. What was I to do now?"

"You decided to trust him," Jane said.

"Yes. I told him everything. How my mother's family helped me leave my country after I was arrested for taking part in a political protest on women's rights. I was beaten and questioned, then they let me go. I lived in fear of being arrested again.

"A few months later, I travelled to Turkey and then France, and then to the UK, hidden in lorries, all the time fearing that I would be discovered and sent back. It made Max angry to learn what I had to suffer. He understood that I did not want to 'jump the queue', that if there had been any other way for me to escape what I knew would happen to me in Iran, I would not have taken such terrible risks."

Jane swallowed. She couldn't begin to imagine how Maryam had gone through so much at such a tender age. What was she? Twenty? Twenty-one? Younger than Jane's daughter, certainly. And now, another tragedy in her young life with the loss of the man she loved.

Jane coughed to loosen the choking feeling in her throat. Maryam was inspiring. Her heart must be breaking, yet she sat there on Darya's sofa with her head held high, ready to sacrifice her hard-won freedom to help bring Max's murderer to justice. Jane hoped, fervently, that she would not have to betray this young woman's trust. "I'm sorry these things have happened to you, Maryam. I truly am."

A solemn silence permeated the room lasting several moments, before Jane spoke again. "Who else besides Darya, Max and Seth knew your secret?"

"No one," Maryam said.

"You're sure? Max told Seth. Seth told Patrick. How can you be sure no one else got to hear about it?"

Seth intervened. "To be fair, Max only told me because I saw him with Maryam one time." He looked at Maryam. "Maryam and Max were careful to meet discreetly, where they thought they wouldn't be seen by anyone close to Max who might ask intrusive questions.

"But someone was bound to spot them together sooner or later. Of course, once I'd seen them together, I kept pestering Max, teasing him about his secret girlfriend. I wouldn't let it lie. Max knew it was only a matter of time before I mentioned it to my mum, then his parents would get to hear about it, and they would have pestered him even more."

"And Max did seek my permission before he told Seth," Maryam said.

Patrick piped up. "And Seth would never have told me if Max hadn't been murdered."

Jane nodded. She was still sceptical that such a secret could stay hidden, but she didn't press the issue.

"When was the last time you saw Max?"

"Two days before he died," Maryam said. She looked down at her hands, clasped tightly in her lap. "But we spoke on the phone on the day he died. In the morning."

"How did he seem, Maryam? Did you get any sense that something might be wrong?"

"Wrong? No. Not at all. He was the same as always."

Jane asked an awkward question. "How did the two of you see your future together? Did you talk about it?"

"You mean, because I am an illegal alien?" Maryam said.

When she didn't expand, Jane asked a more direct question. "Did Max think you should apply for asylum?"

Maryam's answer was unexpected. "Max was very much against that. He was sure that my application would be turned down because I had entered the country illegally. He said he loved me too much to lose me and could not bear it if I had to return to a country where my life would be in danger."

Jane was about to press her earlier question, when Maryam continued. "Max had plans for our future. He talked of finding some way to raise money to pay for a fake passport for me. We would live together, perhaps have children one day. After many years, who knows, I would have a better chance of being allowed to stay." Maryam shrugged. "I do not know if this is true. We were two young people in love. We believed much was possible."

"You didn't tell me any of this," Darya said.

Maryam smiled at Darya, her eyes full of sadness. "You would have brought us back down to earth. I was, perhaps, not ready for that. I wanted to believe in the dream for longer." She gave another shrug. "It made Max so happy to tell me of his plan. I did not want to hurt him by telling him that it was hard for me to believe it could come true."

"It did not worry you that Max would be breaking the law if he managed to go through with his plan? Was that the real reason you told yourself it was just a dream — because you did not want to face that truth?" A tone of reproach had crept into Darya's voice.

"I don't think so. I was going to let him believe in his dream for a little longer before telling him it was against my wishes for him to take such a risk, and break the law." Maryam looked pleadingly at everyone in turn. "Please believe me when I say that I would rather have been sent back to Iran than see Max sent to prison for trying to help me."

Jane nodded. She wished she could do more for Maryam. She wished above all that she could offer the young woman some kind of hope, but she could make no promises. "Is there anything you can tell me about Max that might help me? Did he mention any enemies, any problems he was having? Anything at all? Did he mention if he had taken any action to try to obtain a forged passport for you?" *Just give me something to go on.*

Maryam gave a pained sigh. The muscles in her face tightened with concentration. She looked almost tearful when she said, "I'm sorry. I cannot think of anything."

Jane stood up. "Let me know if you do."

Darya accompanied Jane, Patrick and Seth to the door. In a hushed voice, she said, "I am very worried about her state of mind. It was so good to see her come alive again after her previous suffering. Now, I don't know what to say, how to offer her hope."

"I'm so sorry," Jane said. "All I can offer is my word that I will do what I can to find the person who murdered Max."

"That is enough," Darya said. She lowered her voice still more. "You will not reveal Maryam's secret to the police? The real police, I mean?"

Jane smiled. For once, it didn't bother her that the role of a special was being downplayed.

Jane wished Darya all the best and walked to where Patrick and Seth were waiting at the car.

"So," Patrick said, "do you understand, after meeting Maryam, why we don't want the police, or anyone else, to know about her secret?"

"Yes," Jane said. "I understand."

"Will you tell DI Warwick about her?" Patrick asked.

"The truth?" Jane said. "I don't know. It's something that she should know about. I mean, you heard what Maryam said about Max's plan to obtain forged documents for her. Who knows what sort of people he might have been associating with if he followed through on that? He could have put himself in danger — maybe that's what led to his death. Did he mention this fake ID thing to either of you?"

"Not to me," Patrick said. "I didn't know about Maryam until after Max was murdered, remember?"

"He mentioned it to me," Seth said. "He was definitely serious about it. He even bought a burner phone, but he didn't have the slightest idea where to start. He talked about the Dark Web and asked me if I knew how to access it. I told him I was an engineer, not a criminal mastermind. I also warned him not to go there."

Seth opened the door to the back seat of the car. Before getting in, he said, "But, look, I don't think we really need to worry about this. Max was besotted with Maryam. I think he was, you know, chasing a dream, like Maryam said. He must have realised his idea wasn't realistic. And, besides, what about money? Max didn't have the means to raise the kind of cash he'd need for something like that."

The burner phone worried Jane. Warwick probably had forensics taking apart Max's other devices by now, but was she aware of the existence of a burner? It should be brought to the DI's attention without delay. But Warwick would want to know why Max had needed a burner and the whole story of Maryam's illegal residency would come tumbling out. Jane shuddered at the thought of being on the receiving end of Warwick's wrath if the DI learned of its existence at some later date and found out that Jane had known about it and kept it from her.

"You okay, Mum?" Patrick asked. She had settled into her seat moments ago, but had not yet put the car in gear.

Jane turned the key to start the engine. "Not really. I feel out of my depth. I promised to do what I could to help find Max's killer, but I'm starting to feel that all I'm actually doing is hampering the official investigation. I said right at the start that there were limits to what I could do. That burner phone could contain vital information. We have no idea whether it's in police possession already, and I can't ask DI Warwick if she knows about it for fear of having to tell her about Maryam. I'm worried, Patrick."

"We just need to prove that Maryam's got nothing to do with Max's murder—"

Jane interrupted her son. "And how do you suggest we do that?"

Patrick was silent. Jane checked the rear-view mirror and saw Seth's anguished expression.

"I'm sorry to cause you all this trouble, Mrs Bell," he said. "Maybe you're right. We should stop right now and leave things to the police."

"No," Jane said, suddenly decisive. "We carry on, but only for a few more days. Then, if we have nothing, I'll have to take all this to Warwick."

CHAPTER FIFTEEN

Steph wasn't sure why a complaint about Jane Bell had landed on her desk. Maybe word had got around that they had a sort of history. The complaint had been made by a Dr Linus Crow, a consultant archaeologist working on a dig in the city.

It appeared that Bell had attended the scene of a burglary at Crow's house on the eleventh of December. The burglar had made off with fifteen pounds in cash. Dr Crow had not reported anything else missing. Bell's report mentioned that a valuable watch had been lying on a bedside table in full view, but she'd stated that the burglar had been disturbed when Crow returned from work unexpectedly. This probably explained why it hadn't been taken.

The complaint from Crow was that Bell had subsequently turned up on his doorstep — not in uniform — giving the impression that she was there on a follow-up visit about the burglary. She'd then asked him a lot of irrelevant questions about the murder of Max Barsby, and also about a local man by the name of John Headley, whom Crow had known at university but hadn't seen in nearly forty years. Most notably, Bell had asked Crow where he'd been on the night of Max Barsby's murder.

"You have to ask why she wasn't in uniform. Particularly as she told Crow the purpose of her visit was to follow up on the burglary," Steph said to Elias. "She must have been aware that Crow would assume she was there in an official capacity." Steph groaned. "Does she really think that not wearing her uniform excuses her from being accused of blatantly abusing her police privileges when she's obviously playing amateur detective?"

"I'm surprised you're taking this so calmly," Elias said.

Steph sighed. "Appearances can deceive. I think I'm too shocked to be annoyed. And I'm bursting with questions. What the hell does Bell know that we don't? It would seem she's made some sort of discovery that's led her to connect this archaeologist to Max Barsby."

Elias raised a tentative hand. "Maybe not such a big leap. Crow's an archaeologist overseeing a dig in Lincoln. Max was studying archaeology. My guess is that he was a volunteer on Crow's dig."

Steph's anger flared. "Then why the hell didn't we figure that out? Why did we know nothing about this Linus Crow, or a dig, until Crow's complaint landed in my lap? Why has no one told us about all this? You'd think Max's parents or one of the people we've interviewed at the university might have mentioned it."

Elias rubbed his chin. "His parents are grieving. It's possible there are a few things they forgot to tell us about. We didn't get much out of them on our initial interview, remember, and the FLO's efforts to form a relationship with them hasn't been well received, by all accounts.

"Not to mention that people don't always make the right connections — a lot of people wouldn't think Max working on the dig might be a relevant piece of information. My guess is that Jane heard about it through her son, Patrick. He's a friend of Max's cousin, Seth Wentworth, remember."

"If that's the case, why on earth wouldn't Bell have relayed that information to us? I can't stop her talking to people, but I specifically asked her to keep us in the loop."

Steph grunted in exasperation. "Bell and her assorted network of friends, casual acquaintances, former colleagues and general busybodies. We should start up a new police database based solely on their gossip."

Elias frowned. "I've got no theories as to where she's got the name John Headley from. No idea who he is or how he fits in. Except that the archaeologist was at university with him. Want me to check him out?"

"Please do. No doubt he'll turn out to be someone Bell knows from her teaching days, or a friend of a friend, or a distant relative, or just someone she chatted to in a queue at the supermarket one day. Someone who, by the merest chance, was able to provide her with crucial information pertaining to Max Barsby's murder. We might as well throw in the towel, Elias, and let the amateurs run the show."

Steph checked the time. "Check out Headley as well as Linus Crow. I've got a meeting with DCI Underwood in five minutes. I should be back in half an hour. Then, I think we'll pay Special Constable Bell a visit."

Steph's meeting — a tedious one about targets and stats — lasted longer than she'd predicted, or at least she thought it had. When she checked the time at the end, it had lasted slightly less than half an hour. She reflected on the subjective nature of time as she made her way to rejoin Elias, who was ready and waiting with the information she'd requested.

"I'll start with Dr Crow. He's sixty-three years old. Born and raised in Lancashire. Went to Nottingham University, where he studied archaeology. Graduated with a first-class degree. He married Hilary Cashmore in 1985, and they had three children. One interesting thing about him is that he wrote a children's book. It was published in 1988 but has been out of print for years. Crow and his wife currently live in Oxfordshire.

"Moving on to John Headley. He also went to Nottingham University to study archaeology. He married Joan Carstairs when they were both in their early twenties. Their first child was born in 1983. Not much else on him. He taught history at schools in Nottingham and, later, Lincoln. His wife, Joan, died in 2017. Neither he nor Crow has as much as a speeding ticket."

"Right. Headley was a teacher. That's probably how Bell got to know him. Have you been in touch with her?"

"She's at home awaiting our visit. She sounded a tad anxious."

"Good," Steph said.

Fifteen minutes later, Jane Bell invited them into her cosy cottage on Danesgate. It must be getting a bit cramped these days with her two kids back living at home, Steph thought. Patrick was standing in the living room, looking ready to make a quick getaway. Sure enough, his next words after greeting them were, "Right, I'll be off upstairs, leave you police folk to talk in peace."

"We might want to have a word with you too, later," Steph said.

Patrick stopped dead and looked straight at his mother with what Steph could swear was an accusatory glint in his eye. Bell shook her head as though to reassure him. Interesting. Steph let it go for now.

When Patrick's heavy footsteps were heard on the stairs, Steph turned to Bell. "You know why we're here?"

"Er . . . I think I can guess. Is it about the complaint Dr Crow made about my visit to his house?"

"Yes. Do you remember what I said about keeping me in the loop if you were set on conducting your own unofficial investigation into Max Barsby's murder?"

"Yes, ma'am."

"It appears that you've been neglecting to do that." Before Bell — whose mouth was already opening — could protest, Steph continued. "You've been harassing Dr Crow, on the pretext of following up on a burglary at his address. You must have been fully aware that Crow would assume you were conducting the visit in your capacity as a police officer — a blatant abuse of your official privilege."

Steph let that sink in before continuing. "What exactly did you think I meant when I asked you to keep me informed of what you were up to? I certainly wasn't giving you a licence to conduct an interview with a potential suspect. If, in the course of your conversations with your 'informants', you managed to uncover any evidence about a possible suspect, you should have come to me first, so that I or a member of my team — with the authority and the requisite training — could conduct an official interview. Again, you have way overstepped the mark. I've said all this many times before. I don't appreciate being made to sound like a parrot, Bell."

"Ma'am . . . if I can just explain—"

"I'm not finished!" Steph's raised voice must have carried upstairs, for she heard the distinctive sound of a chair scraping across a floorboard. Patrick, getting up to come to his mother's rescue? Bell heard it too. Her eyes travelled to the ceiling. But Patrick didn't appear, and Steph took up where she left off, her voice lower but still spitting fire. "I've told you before that your behaving like a loose cannon can undermine the painstaking and thorough, not to mention professional, work carried out by my investigative team. What makes you think you can do a better job?"

Bell was silent. A miracle. Some moments elapsed without a sound — unless Elias clearing his throat counted. Still furious, Steph snapped out an order. "Sit down, Bell. Tell me what you've found out, and how."

"Shall I put the kettle on first?" Bell said meekly.

Steph's throat was dry after all the shouting. She was loath to accept Bell's offer, but Elias gave her a nudge, so she acquiesced. "All right, but make it quick."

While Bell went off to the kitchen, Steph and Elias sat down on the sofa. "That was harsh, boss," Elias whispered.

"Yeah, well, she needed to hear it." Elias didn't disagree.

Bell popped her head around the door and asked if they'd like tea, coffee or maybe a cold drink. She returned moments later with a giant cafetière and three mugs. "Sorry, there's no biscuits. I did have some hobnobs, but Patrick's eaten them all."

"No worries," Elias said. "Coffee's fine." He smiled.

Bell sat, cradling her mug, which, Steph noted with distaste, sported a picture of a gingerbread man. Were these creatures taking over the world?

"So," Bell began, "Patrick and I called at the Barsbys' to pay our respects. While we were there, his parents were talking about Max's love of archaeology, and how he'd been inspired by a book he'd read as a child written by Linus Crow. He was excited to be working on a dig managed by his childhood hero. I take it they told you all about this too?"

No. Steph was damned if she was going to admit that she and Elias had not been party to that information, so she didn't answer.

"Max's mum — or was it his dad? — one of them, anyway, mentioned someone called John Headley too — I'll get to him in a minute. So, back to Linus Crow. As you mentioned, I met Dr Crow when his house was burgled. I thought it was a bit of an odd one that, as the burglar had taken a small amount of cash from the kitchen, but left behind a valuable watch in the bedroom. We assumed it was because he was disturbed. It wasn't until after I'd spoken with John Headley that I thought maybe there might have been something else to it."

Steph was confused. "What does John Headley have to do with the burglary?"

"I think he might have been Dr Crow's burglar."

Steph raised an eyebrow. "Right. Go on, Bell."

"Headley fits the description of the man Crow saw fleeing from his house. But, more than that, Crow and Headley have history—"

"Wait a minute," Steph interrupted. "Crow claims that he hasn't seen John Headley in nearly forty years."

"That might be true, but believe me, ma'am, John Headley's hatred of Crow is still very fresh in his mind. You know that they were undergraduates together at Nottingham University?"

Steph nodded. She listened as Bell recounted how Headley had accused Crow of plagiarism, and how he believed that Crow had ruined his life. When Bell explained how Headley had struck up a friendship with Max — allowing him to work in his home, and even entertaining fantasies of Max marrying his granddaughter — she could understand how galling it must have been for Headley to discover that Max was working with his nemesis, Linus Crow.

"So you see, ma'am, it's possible that when Headley heard that Max had been murdered, he jumped to the conclusion that Crow might have been his killer. It's not really clear why. Probably just because he hates Crow. It's possible that he went to Crow's house looking for evidence to back up his theory."

"Headley told you that?" Steph said.

"No, ma'am. I didn't let on to John Headley that I suspected him of breaking into Crow's house."

"So Headley hasn't been fingerprinted?" Steph asked.

Bell suddenly became very interested in the floor. "Er, no, ma'am. To tell the truth, I felt a bit sorry for him. He's grieving for Max too."

"That's no excuse for not doing your job, Bell."

"No, ma'am. Actually, when I mentioned Headley to Crow, he jumped to his own conclusion and said he wouldn't be surprised if Headley was his burglar. He did put a rather weird spin on it, mind. He came up with the theory that Headley might have broken into his house to plant evidence to frame him for Max's murder. Weirder still, he hinted that Headley might have murdered Max himself just so he could pin the murder on Crow and get revenge for the alleged plagiarism."

"Whoa," Steph said. "He's making some pretty big leaps. So, it's not just John Headley who's got past rivalries fresh in his mind."

Bell agreed, saying, "Makes you wonder what poor Max got himself caught up in, stuck between that pair. Not that I'm suggesting Crow or Headley are guilty of his murder — they'd be more likely to bump off each other — but they're definitely worth investigating, don't you think?"

Steph ignored the question. "So, what else have you got for me, Bell?"

Bell's eyes travelled up to the ceiling again. "Er . . . Nothing, ma'am. That's it."

Steph made a point of looking upwards also. "You're quite sure about that?"

"Yes, ma'am."

"Right." Steph was almost certain Bell was hiding something, and that it had something to do with her son. It was equally obvious that Bell wasn't going to tell her what it was. Reluctantly, she let it go. For now. "I'm going to arrange for fingerprints and DNA to be taken from John Headley," she told Bell. "If we find a match in Crow's rental, he's going to have some explaining to do."

CHAPTER SIXTEEN

Steph was as good as her word. Headley was arrested the next day, following a telephone conversation with Dr Linus Crow. Crow described his intruder in rather more detail than he'd given to Bell and her colleague on the day of the burglary. Then, he'd been unable to form a clear picture of his burglar because he'd been distressed, but since Bell's second visit, he'd experienced a "jolt of recognition". He now claimed that, subconsciously, he must have recognised the fleeing man as John Headley all along.

Crow had mentioned on the day of the burglary that he thought the man he saw running from his house was wearing gloves. No fingerprints matching John Headley's were found in the property, but as it turned out, that didn't matter. Headley confessed to the crime immediately. He also admitted to knowing that it was Linus Crow's house he'd broken into.

"So," Steph said, facing him in the interview room, "we know already that you and Dr Crow have history. You accused Dr Crow of plagiarising your ideas for his PhD thesis." Vigorous nodding from Headley. "So, tell us what you were really doing in Linus Crow's house."

Headley had been sitting with his head bowed — if not in shame, then in dismay at his current predicament. Now, he looked up and sighed. "I . . . It was something that Max told me the day he was murdered."

Steph looked at Elias and saw her own surprise mirrored on his face. "You saw Max on the day he was murdered? Where, and when?"

Headley muttered something that sounded like, "He turned up in the evening."

Steph wondered if she'd heard correctly. If true, Headley had seen Max just hours before his death. This would place Headley right at the centre of the investigation. "What time in the evening?"

"Max came to me at seven thirty. He left around eight."

"Why didn't you come to us with this information before now, Mr Headley? You must have known we would be interested in tracking Max's movements on the night he was murdered. I have to say that your failure to approach us makes things look bad for you."

Headley gasped. "That's one of the reasons I didn't tell you about it. I knew I'd automatically become a suspect."

"Tell us now," Steph said dryly. "What was the reason for Max's visit?"

"He came to me to ask my advice," Headley said. "He'd found something he wanted to show me. An artefact from the dig. He was excited. He thought he knew what it was and wanted a second opinion from an expert."

Interesting that Headley regarded himself as an expert in archaeological matters. Steph was aware that Headley's studies had ended with his graduate degree, but she also knew that he was a keen amateur historian and archaeologist. She didn't doubt he believed himself every bit as qualified as Dr Linus Crow. "Why did Max take this artefact to you and not Dr Crow? Did he even have Dr Crow's permission to remove it from the dig?"

Headley shook his head. "No. He shouldn't have done that. I think Max chose to bring it to me because we were friends, and he respected my judgement."

"But he would also have respected Dr Crow's judgement, wouldn't he? After all, Linus Crow was his childhood hero. The man whose book sparked his interest in archaeology and inspired him to study the subject."

Steph could see how her remark rankled. The way Headley flinched, the sharp intake of breath, as if in pain, the sneer that came after. Bell was right. It must have been torture for this man to see Max volunteer on Crow's dig.

"I don't know. I assume Max trusted my opinion more."

"I see," Steph said, her tone making it clear that she thought Headley was suffering from a severe case of sour grapes. "So, in your expert opinion, this artefact that Max found, what was it exactly? Was it valuable?"

Headley took his time to consider the question. Once or twice, he looked to be about to speak, then seemed to retreat back into his thoughts. The sound of Steph's fingers rapping against the table top startled him into answering.

"It is my belief that it was, indeed, a most significant find, DI Warwick. I can scarcely believe I'm saying this, but it appeared to be a gold aureus depicting the head of the Roman emperor Caligula. A most rare and precious find. Coins of this era are especially valuable because they were produced before the mass minting of the third century onward. Not to mention that the emperors of the Julio-Claudian dynasty — of which Caligula was one — were among the most important, historically speaking."

Elias piped up. "It makes no sense that Max would remove such a find from the dig without permission. Everyone we've spoken with has emphasised his passion for archaeology, and his honesty."

Headley only repeated his earlier assertion. "It was wrong of him to do so."

"When Max brought the coin to you, what advice did you give him?" Steph asked.

Headley's excitement vanished. His expression took on a dark set. "I advised him to show it to Linus Crow. I had no other choice. Max came to me for advice. I had to make sure he understood the seriousness of what he had done in removing the coin from the site. If it came to light that he had done so, the integrity of the find could have been compromised."

"Really?" Steph said. "Why?"

"Removing the coin from the site might have resulted in accusations that Max had obtained it elsewhere, or even stolen it. Even the most insignificant finds must be recorded."

"I see," Steph said.

"I couldn't advise Max to do something that would compromise the find. I'm an honest man, DI Warwick. Despite what you might think, my passion for archaeology outweighs any enmity I may bear towards Linus Crow. This find was of immense interest and importance. It outweighed any personal concerns."

Elias jumped in again. "Wouldn't Max have been well aware of his responsibilities towards any artefact he found on the site?"

Headley gave a weary nod. "Yes. I was puzzled that he'd removed it, but I didn't press him on it."

Suspecting she now knew why Headley had broken into Crow's house, Steph asked, "You say you are an honest man, but you broke into Linus Crow's house. Why did you do that, Mr Headley?"

Headley looked from Steph to Elias. "Because Max agreed to take the aureus straight to Crow. As for why I broke into Crow's house, it should be obvious from what I've just said. Crow hasn't said a word about the coin, has he? Not in public, anyway. I'm assuming you had no idea Max went to him with it that night.

"I went to Crow's house because I suspected Crow had taken the aureus from Max, and then killed poor Max to stop him mentioning it to anyone else. I hoped to find the coin hidden somewhere on his property. I only stole the money to make it look like a real burglary."

"How much would one of these coins be worth?" Steph asked.

Headley shrugged. "Whatever a collector is willing to pay, but certainly many thousands of pounds. To me, the monetary value of such a coin would be of no concern."

"Why do you think Dr Crow would want the discovery of such an important artefact to be concealed?" Steph asked.

Headley threw his arms in the air. "Well, that's your job to uncover, isn't it? I'm an archaeologist, not a detective, but I can give you a couple of reasons just off the top of my head."

"Please do," Steph said.

"Something to do with delays to the building works, possibly? Maybe Crow was taking backhanders from the owner of the construction company to keep delays to the project to a minimum. Or maybe Crow just wanted to have the coin for himself, knowing he could get a good price for it." Headley was on a roll. "Maybe the aureus wasn't all that Max found. There could have been other valuable artefacts for Crow to get his thieving hands on as long as he got poor Max out of the way."

Steph sat back in her chair with her arms crossed, wondering if there was any limit to the crimes Headley believed Crow capable of committing. Headley was, undeniably, a pompous eccentric, if not outright bonkers, but he had just come up with a number of potential motives that weren't all that outlandish.

"Right. And did you find anything at Dr Crow's house?"

"No. But I ran out of time. Crow came back unexpectedly. I had to make a run for it." He looked from Steph to Elias pleadingly. "You need to search his place carefully — and his office at the dig. It's probably already too late — he'll have moved the evidence by now, but you must do it, nevertheless." With a moment's afterthought, he added, "You owe it to Max."

"Yes, thank you, Mr Headley. We know how to do our job. Just so you know, we'll also be searching your house," Steph said.

Headley was unperturbed. "Feel free. Unlike Crow, I have nothing to hide." He sighed. "So, I suppose I'm going to be up on a burglary charge?"

"Actually, no," Steph told him. "We've spoken with Dr Crow, and he's generously decided not to press charges." Out of sheer mischief, she added, "You owe him one."

Predictably, Headley exploded, "I will not be in debt to that . . . that . . . charlatan!"

"Go home, Mr Headley. Think yourself lucky you're not being charged with breaking and entering. On the other hand, you are now a credible suspect in a murder investigation."

"I didn't kill Max. He was like a son to me."

Steph warned Headley not to breathe a word about the story he'd just told them. She then got up, leaving Elias to see Headley off the premises. When he returned, she asked what he'd made of Headley.

"Bit sad, isn't he?" Elias said. "Bitter about his lack of success in the area he'd hoped to excel in. Blames Crow for that, although it seems to have been for financial reasons that he was obliged to give up his studies. As to whether he's capable of murder, yes, in the right circumstances, just like most of us."

"Sad — and disappointed," Steph said. She dragged her fingers through her hair — it felt greasy, in need of a wash. "He's one to watch. Max was with him the evening he was murdered. If Max did take this aureus to Crow, then he's one to watch too.

"Let's speak with Crow next. Find out if Max took Headley's advice. If so, why the hell hasn't Crow told us about Max coming to him with the coin? It's ridiculous how much time we've wasted on this investigation through people not giving us the right information. It's a week since Max was murdered. We've been focussing on Harry Scott, not knowing the existence of any of these potential suspects."

Elias made a stab at cheering her up. "Look on the bright side. You're one up on Jane Bell now. She didn't know about Max finding a valuable coin."

Steph gave him a glare. "You mean she didn't mention that she knew of it. Who knows what that woman knows that she's not telling us?"

Best not to ponder on that. Steph moved on. "Headley's not an expert. How credible is his claim that this coin was genuine? Or even made of gold?"

"I think it's quite credible. He's very passionate about archaeology," Elias said. "But there is one thing bothering me."

Steph laughed. "Only one?"

"We don't really know why Max removed the coin from the site and took it to Headley. Everyone we've spoken with has mentioned Max's passion for archaeology. I just find it hard to believe that he'd, as Headley pointed out, risk ruining the integrity of the find. I can only think of one reason why he'd do it."

"Are you thinking that Max might have been in some sort of trouble? That he might have been desperate enough to consider selling the coin to get him out of it?"

Elias nodded. Steph stroked her chin. "It's certainly a possibility. And you're right in saying it doesn't ring true that Max was merely seeking Headley's opinion on the coin. Max was clued up. He would probably have known it was a rare find — although I accept that, perhaps, he couldn't quite believe it, and was seeking confirmation." She sighed. "Still, I don't buy that he showed it to Headley rather than Crow, or someone else at the dig, simply because he trusted Headley's judgement more."

"Maybe it was because he had reason not to trust Crow, or the people at the dig," Elias said.

"Hmm. That's an intriguing thought, isn't it? If that was the case, Max didn't mention it to Headley. Not that Headley's told us, anyway, and I tend to think he wouldn't hold back if he had something on his arch enemy. Let's speak with Crow first thing tomorrow."

CHAPTER SEVENTEEN

Patrick was looking forward to his second day at the dig. All in all, he considered that his first day had gone pretty well. Even if he'd made no big breakthroughs in the case, he had at least got to know the team.

It was a bright morning. Patrick decided to walk to the site instead of borrowing his mother's car, or pestering her for a lift. It was a few miles' distant, but the exercise would do him good, and he'd have time to think. When he drew near the dig and caught sight of the portacabin, the conversation he'd overheard between Roadknight and Linus Crow came to mind. A case of the two men simply airing understandable concerns about a delay to the schedule? Or something more sinister? Perhaps today would help him make up his mind.

Patrick was greeted warmly by the others in the team, which made him feel even more guilty about deceiving them. Jacob and Grace were particularly friendly. They told him how much they were enjoying their archaeology course, and shared useful information about their lecturers and the course content.

"Most of the staff are really nice," Grace said. "It's a small department so you get to know them quite well, especially when you go on field trips."

"Dr Carr is nice," Jacob said, colouring slightly.

Grace must have noticed. "You're not the only one who fancies her. Her lectures are always full. But yeah, she's great. Really takes an interest in her students." Grace seemed to reflect for a moment. "She was Max Barsby's personal tutor."

"How do you know that?" Jacob asked.

"Because she's my personal tutor too. I was waiting outside her office for an appointment one day. Max came out of the room, and when I went in, Dr Carr — Bianca — commented that she'd had a busy morning catching up with the students she 'looked after', as she put it."

Patrick's ears were open full flap. He hadn't even mentioned Max, and here he was the topic of conversation.

"Also, Bianca invited all her students for coffee at the refectory café one afternoon. Max was there. He was very serious, gave the impression of being very clever and studious. Bianca sang his praises. She said he was one of the most gifted archaeology students she'd ever had the pleasure to teach and she suggested we go to him if we ever needed guidance on work-related stuff."

"How did Max react to a comment like that?" Patrick said.

"He was embarrassed, I think. Didn't like attention being drawn to him, but he mumbled something like, of course, he'd be happy to give advice to anyone who asked him, if he could. I never took him up on it, though."

"Did you hear about the fight Max had with Harry Scott on a field trip to Vindolanda?" Jacob said.

Grace frowned. "Harry Scott?"

"Second-year archaeology student. Or was. He quit his course. You might know his ex-girlfriend, Sophie Egan? She works some evenings in the student bar."

"I know Sophie," Grace said. "By sight at any rate. I don't *know her* know her, if you see what I mean. And I can place Harry Scott now too. He's hench. So, Sophie was dating Harry, and he and Max Barsby were involved in an actual fight? What, over Sophie?"

Patrick couldn't believe his luck. He was picking up whole nuggets of information without uttering a word. He carried on working, listening intently.

Jacob lowered his voice, although Sue and Iain were engaged in a conversation of their own and were unlikely to be listening. "Yes. The rumour was that the fight was over Sophie Egan. Harry ended up having to leave his course because of it. Or so I heard."

"No! Get out!" Grace said. "Sophie was cheating on Harry with Max? Actually, I can sort of see it. Max wasn't that good-looking, but I can see why some women would fancy him. He was intense."

"That's the goss, anyway," Jacob said.

Patrick wondered why Seth had never mentioned Harry Scott. He decided to weigh in. "The fight must have been pretty serious if Harry had to leave over it."

"It was," Jacob confirmed. "Harry pushed Max onto a campfire. Max could have been burned alive. It was only down to some speedy rescue action by a couple of members of staff and students that he wasn't."

Patrick suspected that Jacob had a flair for the melodramatic. In his experience, campfires tended to be damp squib affairs. Still, like Jacob said, pushing someone onto a fire was a serious affair. "Wow. That's heavy."

"Poor Max," Grace said. "He survived an ordeal by fire only to die in the water." They were all silent for a moment or two.

"We don't actually know that he drowned," Patrick said, hoping to repair the conversation.

"His body was pulled from the Witham," Grace pointed out.

"I read that he was murdered first — bludgeoned with a heavy object — and then thrown in the river," Jacob said.

Grace shuddered. "This conversation is getting morbid. Can we maybe talk about something else?"

Nooo. Things were going so well. Patrick didn't dare voice his objection, but, once more, luck was on his side. Jacob wasn't ready to drop the subject.

"Sorry, Grace. But it's a big thing, isn't it? A student getting murdered. An archaeology student at that. Maybe we all need to be extra vigilant."

"I wonder who the police are looking at?" Patrick said.

"Well, Harry Scott for starters, I would guess," Jacob said. "No doubt they'll be talking to Sophie Egan too, and maybe some members of staff." He looked at Grace. "They'll probably have spoken with Dr Carr and Professor Hogue, at least."

"Who's Professor Hogue?" Patrick asked.

"Emilia Hogue. She's the head of archaeology," Grace said.

"I suppose it's only a matter of time before the police visit the dig and talk to all of us," Grace said. "Max was working here the day he was murdered." She looked thoughtful for a moment. "He certainly didn't behave like he knew what was coming. I remember he seemed quite excited that day."

Jacob shrugged. "I didn't notice."

Patrick looked around, feeling suddenly uneasy about the prospect of the police — DI Warwick in particular — showing up at the dig and recognising the latest volunteer.

"Maybe it was the thing he was excited about that got him killed," Jacob suggested.

Really, Jacob was doing Patrick's work for him. He asked, "Any clues what it might have been?"

Grace gave a shrug. "Nope. Unless . . ." She gazed at her dirt-encrusted trowel, a thoughtful expression on her face. "Maybe he had a date. Oh my God. I swear, I've literally just remembered that I saw Max later on that day, in the evening, at a bar on the Brayford. He was with someone, a woman." Her eyes widened. "Oh no! Do you think she could have murdered him? Maybe I actually saw Max with his murderer. I should tell the police."

"It was probably just his date — Sophie Egan maybe, if Harry was out of the picture?" Jacob said.

Patrick felt a surge of excitement. He was bursting with questions. When Jacob didn't say anything, he asked Grace what time she'd seen Max with the woman.

"It must have been around nine. I was meeting a friend for drinks in another bar on the Brayford and I walked into the wrong bar. As soon as I realised I was in the wrong place, I walked straight back out again. I would have said 'hi' to Max, but I was already late for my friend."

Patrick nodded. "You didn't recognise the person he was with?"

"No. I really only got a fleeting glimpse. I wish I'd taken more notice now."

"You weren't to know it might be important," Jacob said. "It probably wasn't, to be honest." Grace gave him an appreciative smile.

Patrick understood the significance of Grace having seen Max in the bar so late on the evening that he was murdered. As Grace feared, the woman might have been involved in Max's murder. And even if the mystery woman had nothing to do with his death, she might have vital information about his last movements on that night. Was DI Warwick aware of the woman?

There had been an appeal for witnesses to come forward — anyone who'd seen Max in the last hours of his life. If the woman had nothing to hide, surely she'd have come forward already. If, on the other hand, she was somehow implicated in Max's murder . . . Either way, DI Warwick could well be completely unaware of her existence. She should be told.

But . . . A sudden, unsavoury thought occurred to Patrick. Could the woman have been Maryam? Maryam said she hadn't seen Max on the day he died, and Patrick had believed her. But what if she'd lied? If Patrick informed Warwick about the mystery woman, Warwick would check CCTV of the bar, and Maryam might be identified. Her secret would be discovered.

Patrick also feared that, even if he didn't mention the meeting in the bar to Warwick, Grace might bring it up when she was interviewed. Now that Warwick was aware Max worked as a volunteer at the dig, she was sure to follow it up. What a mess.

In an attempt to downplay the woman's importance, Patrick said, "Jacob's right, Grace. The woman was probably just someone Max got talking to in the bar. I wouldn't stress about not telling the police about her."

Grace nodded, but she didn't look wholly convinced.

The next hour was spent on the job at hand — scraping, brushing and sifting, mostly. Although he was becoming a dab hand at all this, Patrick was more convinced than ever that he'd made the right career choice. He wasn't really in his element hunched over in a trench with a bitter wind blowing across the field from the north-east and nothing more exciting to look forward to than an afternoon of washing the fragments of pottery he'd bagged up in the morning. A computer and a spreadsheet were more his vibe. So, he was glad when, around eleven, Sue announced it was time for a break, and they all trooped over to the portacabin for a hot drink and some much-needed warmth.

That evening, Patrick told his mother about Max's fight with Harry Scott. "I wonder if Seth knew about it? He's never mentioned it. Maybe he didn't think it was relevant. I'll have to ask him."

He also told Jane about Grace seeing Max in a bar with a woman on the night he was murdered.

"We have to tell DI Warwick about this," Jane said. When Patrick didn't answer, she added, "You're worried in case she was Maryam, and that Warwick will be able to spot her on the bar's CCTV, aren't you?"

Patrick frowned. "Maryam said she didn't see Max that day. I want to believe she was telling the truth, or that there was a good reason why she had to lie about it." He sighed. "Anyway, Warwick is bound to get round to questioning the people on the dig soon enough, and she'll hear about the mystery woman from Grace."

Patrick noted the worried look on his mother's face. After a few moments, she said, "Sorry, Patrick. I do have to admit to hoping Warwick interviews Grace soon. Identifying that woman could lead to a big break in the investigation. And—"

Knowing what was coming, Patrick interrupted. "I know. If Warwick doesn't learn about the mystery woman from Grace, you'll tell her yourself."

CHAPTER EIGHTEEN

Steph and Elias pulled up outside Linus Crow's rented house, first thing in the morning after their interview with John Headley. They were hoping to catch Crow before he left for the dig.

Crow answered the door wearing a pair of striped pyjamas and a fleecy dressing gown, an expression of puzzlement on his face, which turned to exasperation when he learned they were police detectives.

"This is to do with John Headley, isn't it? Damn the man."

"Mind if we come in?" Steph said. It wasn't really a question.

"Fine," Crow said, impatience and annoyance in his tone. "I'm not sure why you have to disturb me at this hour of the morning, but come in."

"Sorry if we got you out of bed," Steph said.

"I was already up." Crow led them into the kitchen, where the aroma of freshly brewed coffee confirmed that he was telling the truth. "Can I offer you some coffee?" The offer sounded begrudging.

"Thank you," Steph and Elias replied in unison.

All the while he was fiddling with the coffee machine, Crow complained bitterly about his visit from Jane Bell.

"You heard she asked me what I was doing the night Max Barsby died? The cheek! As if I had something to do with it. Outrageous."

"Special Constable Bell's behaviour was out of line and unacceptable. I reprimanded her personally. She won't trouble you again," Steph said.

Crow handed out the drinks. "Good. So, why are you here?"

Steph explained that they were investigating the murder of Max Barsby. "We have been advised that Max was intending to call on you on the night he was murdered. Can you confirm whether Max was here that night?"

Crow's nostrils flared. "I'll wager I know who your adviser was. John Headley. Am I right?" He launched into another angry diatribe against his former acquaintance.

"Headley bears an ancient grudge against me because I succeeded academically where he failed miserably. If you've spoken with him, you'll have heard all the details, so I won't go into all that. I'll simply answer your question: No, Max Barsby did not come to this house the night he was murdered. I did not see him that night. I was here, alone, all evening, working. So, you can inform your 'adviser' that I don't have an alibi for the time of poor Max's murder." He frowned. "Although I did see the woman who lives next door at around nine that evening. She knocked on my door to ask me if I'd like to subscribe to a neighbourhood newsletter she helps produce."

"Right," Steph said. "We have heard about the dispute between you and Mr Headley—"

"All of his making. I've tried to forget about him since we parted ways, but it appears his hatred of me has been festering all these years." He frowned, a look of curiosity in his eyes. "You said Headley told you Max was intending to visit me that evening. Did he say why?"

"He said Max had made what might have been a very significant find on the dig. Max removed it from the dig and showed it to Headley," Steph said. "Headley's advice to

Max was to show it to you immediately. That was after he'd reprimanded Max for removing it from the dig without your permission."

Crow looked astonished. "He said that? Did he say what it was that Max allegedly found?"

Elias explained. "A gold aureus of the Julio-Claudian era depicting the head of the emperor Caligula."

Crow rolled his eyes and roared with laughter. "Preposterous! That man wouldn't be able to tell the difference between a genuine Roman aureus and a thrupenny bit."

"Would I be correct in saying that a find like that might lead to delays — expensive delays in the case of Roadknight Construction?" Steph asked.

"A find like that would far outweigh any concerns about the building works," Crow said. "For an archaeologist, at any rate. And I'm not talking about its monetary value. But . . . the likelihood of a coin like that turning up . . . especially in Britain. I'm not saying it's impossible, mind. But the chances are . . ."

Crow suddenly grasped the significance of Steph's question. "Are you — or is Headley — actually suggesting that I murdered Max Barsby to prevent him telling anyone else about his discovery? Because I didn't want it to interfere with Roadknight's project? I can assure you that is absolute nonsense. Besides, as I said, I didn't see Max that evening. As for the veracity of what Max allegedly found, all I can say is that I would have to see the coin to comment on it. Are you sure Headley isn't making the whole thing up?"

"As I said, Headley claims that Max agreed to show the coin to you. He left Headley's house around eight. We don't know his movements after that."

"Doubtless Headley claims Max came here and I bumped him off. I take it that's why Headley 'burgled' my house. He was looking for evidence." Crow shook his head. "Well, he didn't find anything because Max didn't come here. As I told that interfering wannabe detective woman, I wouldn't be surprised if Headley came here to plant something to implicate me in the murder. I thought I was being a bit paranoid at the time. Now I'm not so sure."

"Dr Crow, do you give your consent to a search of your house?" Steph asked.

Crow threw his arms in the air. "Be my guest. Can you start with the bathroom? I'd like to take a shower as soon as I can."

Steph signalled to Elias, who got up and headed out of the room and off upstairs. Steph got up too and began searching the kitchen. While she looked around, Crow sat at the kitchen table eating a bowl of cornflakes and checking his phone messages.

Elias joined them after a few minutes. "All done," he said. "I'll check the bedrooms while you take your shower, Dr Crow." Both men went off together. Steph carried on searching downstairs. Not that she expected to find anything. If Max had given the coin to Crow, Crow would have had plenty of time to move it elsewhere by now.

By the time they had finished searching the house, Crow was showered and dressed, and impatient to leave for the dig. "Satisfied?" he asked after Steph confirmed that nothing had been found.

"I won't be satisfied until I learn who was responsible for taking that young man's life, Dr Crow. One last question: How easy would it have been for Max to hide what he'd dug up from his colleagues at the dig?"

"Max was working under the supervision of two members of my team, Dr Sue Sellars and Dr Iain MacDonald. Something as small as a coin would be fairly easy to slip in his pocket, I'd say."

Crow then echoed what Elias had said earlier. "I just can't see Max doing something like that. He struck me as an honest young man who was passionate about archaeology."

"We need to speak with Sellars and MacDonald. And everyone else on the dig. And take a look at the area where Max was working," Steph said.

Crow checked the time. "I've got meetings most of today."

"Fine. Tomorrow morning, then, but in the meantime, one of my officers, PC Fairbairn, will search your office today. You can tell your staff the search is related to the investigation into the murder of Max Barsby, but on no account should you mention anything that we have discussed with you this morning. I do not want Headley's story about Max and the aureus becoming common knowledge. Do you understand?"

"Perfectly," Crow said. "You certainly don't need to worry about anyone hearing that story from me. As far as I'm concerned, it's a load of old codswallop, like everything else that comes out of John Headley's big, angry mouth."

Steph was inclined to agree, but she didn't say so. She watched Crow drive off with a feeling of frustration, then turned to Elias. "Well, we didn't expect to find anything, but I got the feeling Crow was telling the truth. Not that I trust feelings, as you know. I also got the impression he was excited about the possibility of Max finding this aureus. Even though he's sceptical about it."

Elias frowned. "Who on earth is telling the truth here? Did Max really find something and show it to Headley? Or is Headley just making the whole thing up — as some kind of petty revenge for what he sees as Crow's treachery? Or to cast suspicion away from himself?" He shook his head. "If Headley was lying, we could end up wasting a lot of time over this coin."

"As you suggested yesterday, Max might have been in some kind of trouble and needed money quickly. Money he hoped to obtain by selling the aureus," Steph said. "If Headley and Crow are both telling the truth, what did Max do — and who did he meet — between leaving Headley's house and ending up in the river?"

Elias threw something else into the mix. "And what about Harry Scott? Don't we need to keep him and any other potential suspects in mind?"

"You're right," Steph agreed. "We mustn't let ourselves become overly sidetracked by this coin. In the absence of any evidence, we need to take the wide view." She gave a grim smile. "Let's hope we can unearth something of value at the dig tomorrow."

CHAPTER NINETEEN

When Steph and Elias arrived at the site of the dig the following morning, Crow was waiting for them on the steps of a portacabin, which he explained served as his office, as well as the crew room and work room. Inside, they were introduced to Crow's colleagues and two students from the university who were drinking coffee at a long table. Crow looked around. "Where's the new lad?"

"He's not here today," Sue Sellars said. "He only volunteers twice a week, remember?"

"Ah, yes. I'd forgotten," Linus said. For Steph and Elias's benefit, he explained. "We have a new volunteer. A young man who is thinking of applying to study archaeology. He only started here this week so I doubt there'd be any point in your speaking with him."

Linus addressed his team. "DI Warwick and DS Harper would like to speak with you all individually about Max Barsby. I appreciate that this might be upsetting, but it is necessary, and I know you will all cooperate with the detectives."

The interviews were fairly brief. No one had known Max for very long. Iain MacDonald praised his intelligence and his commitment to the dig. He had found Max to be a polite, respectful young man, although he did add a caveat.

"I'm not necessarily the best judge of people. I tend to just keep my head down and get on with the job. Sue's the one you want to be talking to for all the personal, feely stuff."

He wasn't kidding. As soon as she sat down in front of them, Sue teared up. She had been fond of Max, she said. "He was a quietly confident person. He mainly talked about archaeology. So excited to be working alongside Linus, whom he'd idolised from boyhood, after reading a children's book Linus wrote years ago."

When Steph nodded, Sue continued. "Max wasn't one to talk much about his personal life, but I kept chipping away at his reserve, and eventually he began to open up to me. I know he was close to his cousin, Seth. He didn't mention a partner — but I got the impression there was someone. I couldn't resist asking him if there was someone special in his life. Eventually, he admitted he had a girlfriend. His face positively lit up when he said it." Sue sighed. "I know love when I see it, and believe me, Max was in love. Even so, he was reluctant to talk about her."

"What was her name?" Steph asked, impatiently.

"Mary-Ann — bit old-fashioned, isn't it?" Sue said. "But don't ask me for any more information about her because I don't know anything more. When I asked what Mary-Ann did, he was a bit evasive — cagey even, come to think of it, as though it was a big secret. I asked a few more questions about her, but he just clammed up, or changed the subject. At the time, I just thought he thought I was being too nosey. Now, of course, I'm wondering."

A bit nosey. Sue didn't specify what she was wondering about, but it was obvious. Steph humoured her. "What are you wondering about?"

"Well, did this girl have something to do with why he was murdered? Maybe Max didn't want to talk about her because there was some mystery surrounding her. Was she married, perhaps?"

"We'll check her out," Steph said. "Max was at the dig on the day he was murdered. How did he seem that day?"

"Now you mention it, he did seem a bit — what's the word? Agitated. As if he had something on his mind. Do you think he might have been in some kind of trouble that led to his death?"

Steph shrugged. She was keen to move on, and Sellars struck her as someone who talked a lot without saying much. After a few more routine questions, she allowed her to return to the dig. "Can you ask Jacob to come in next, please?"

As soon as Sue left the portacabin, Elias said, "I was expecting her to say Sophie when you asked the girlfriend's name."

"So was I," Steph said. "Shame she didn't get a surname, but as Sue said, Mary-Ann is a bit of an unusual name these days. Might make it easier to track her down. Of course, Max might have given a false name — or even just invented a girlfriend to shut Sue up."

"What did you think of Sellars' theory that there was some mystery surrounding Mary-Ann?"

Steph shrugged. "Not a lot. I'm sure she'd like there to be."

At that moment, Jacob knocked on the door. Steph called him in. He sat down in the chair vacated by Sue, his head bowed. He looked very young — like a school student rather than an undergraduate. Or was that just Steph's age catching up with her? Steph asked how long he'd known Max.

"Only since I'd been on the dig, although I'd seen him around the campus." He looked at them through his round glasses with large, doleful eyes. "You just don't expect something like this to happen, man."

Steph hadn't been much older than Jacob when her best friend was murdered by Steph's ex-boyfriend, whom she'd subsequently witnessed taking his own life. "No. You don't," she said. For a moment she experienced a sudden, overwhelming crush of emotion. She felt Elias's eyes on her. She cleared her throat and continued.

Jacob hadn't asked Max if he was in a relationship. He had no insights to offer as to Max's state of mind on his last day at the dig, saying in answer to both questions, "We mainly talked about football."

The interview was over quite quickly, and Grace Toyne replaced Jacob in the chair. Of the four, Grace was easily the most upset. Her eyes shone, ready to shed tears the second Steph mentioned Max Barsby. She opened her eyes wide and waved her fingers in front of her face as though fanning herself.

"Sorry, sorry," she said repeatedly.

"Take your time," Elias said. "We know this is difficult."

Steph waited patiently until Grace was calmer. She tried not to look at her watch.

"I didn't know Max very well, but he seemed nice," Grace said at last. "He didn't deserve what happened to him. Do you have any idea who did it, or . . . why? That's what I don't get. Why would anyone want to hurt Max? He was so . . ." Grace's voice tailed off, as though she couldn't think of another word to describe him. Eventually, she said, "Clever."

Steph put the same questions to her that she'd put to the others. When she asked if Max had ever mentioned a girlfriend, Grace seemed suddenly nervous. "He never mentioned it, but on his last day at the dig, he was kind of . . . edgy? Like, distracted? Almost like he was agitated, but not in a bad way, more sort of . . . excited? I joked with him, saying something like, 'You're very full of it today. Got a hot date tonight?' He got all embarrassed and didn't say anything."

Grace then started mumbling something about how she and the other volunteers had been talking about Max just the previous day, and how something someone had said had prompted her to remember that she'd seen Max at a bar overlooking the Brayford Pool at around nine o'clock on the night he was murdered. He had been with a woman. Maybe she was his girlfriend. Unfortunately, Grace was unable to give them a description, other than that the woman had been wearing a dark coat, and that, "Her hair must have been dark too, because if it had been fair, it might have stood out against her coat more."

With or without a description, this was still the best lead they'd had for a while, particularly as regards the timing. It confirmed that Max had spoken with someone other than John Headley and, possibly, Linus Crow on the night of his murder.

When the interviews were over, Crow rejoined them and all three made their way across the field to where the team was at work. It was a relief to leave the slightly claustrophobic atmosphere of the portacabin and step out into the fresh air. Sue Sellars gave them a wave. "Come to see where it's all happening?" she said in a cheery voice.

"Or not happening," Iain MacDonald said. "Nothing exciting turning up today."

Jacob looked up. "I found a dead rat." Everyone laughed.

"The reality of working on a dig is less glamorous than people think," Crow said. "This is where Max was working." He indicated an area of ground that had been marked out with stakes. "Under Sue's supervision."

Steph listened while Sue explained the work that Max had been doing. "Very much what Grace and Jacob are occupied with right now," Sue said, pointing over to where the two students were scraping away at the sides of a muddy trench, using the straight edge of their trowels, a look of intense concentration on their faces.

"What about security?" Steph asked, trying to sound casual.

"What do you mean?" Sue asked.

"How do you ensure that nobody pockets a valuable artefact, for example?"

Sue looked taken aback by the suggestion, and Iain MacDonald, who had for the most part been ignoring Steph and Elias, looked up from his task with a scowl.

Sue explained. "Most of what we find is of little value in monetary terms. You're probably being misled by stories about amateurs stumbling upon hidden hoards with their metal detectors. That's not what we're expecting to find here." She sniffed. "And besides, I consider our students to be completely trustworthy. They've all had experience of working on other digs, and arrived here with letters of recommendation."

"Right," Steph said. "Just thought I'd ask. Probably the police officer in me."

Sue gave them a quick tour of the site. Steph was struck by the lack of high tech in evidence. Most of the work seemed to be carried out using what looked like common gardening tools, or the kind of simple probes used by dentists to poke around in your mouth. Finds were washed in plastic washing-up bowls and dried in plastic seed trays lined with newspaper. The most sophisticated piece of equipment on show was a wheelbarrow. Crow wasn't kidding when he'd said there was nothing glamorous about the work.

Of course, Elias seemed to be getting a lot out of the tour. He kept asking how this or that was done, and spent far too long examining tiny fragments of pottery that Sue referred to as 'sherds'. What was a sherd, anyway? Wasn't the proper word 'shard'?

At last, the tour was over. Steph had a final request. "One last thing — I'd like to question your new recruit."

"He only started this week," Sue said.

"Dotting the i's and all that," Steph said.

"His name is Patrick King," Crow said. "If you accompany me back to my office, I can give you his contact details."

Steph and Elias exchanged a look. "Probably no need," Steph said. "I think we know where to find him, but please show us just in case."

The information Crow supplied on his new recruit confirmed what Steph suspected. Patrick King and Patrick Bell were one and the same.

After thanking the members of the team for their time, Steph and Elias left them to carry on with their work. As they made their way back to the car, Steph seethed. "What the hell is Patrick Bell doing volunteering on that dig?"

"Could be a case of 'like mother, like son'. He feels invested in the investigation because he knew the victim," Elias said.

"Not helpful, Elias. I'll be having words with those two."

Elias kept chuntering on about how exciting it must be to work on a dig.

After a while, Steph, still smouldering over Patrick Bell, had had enough. "Seriously, Sergeant? It looks like pretty tedious work to me, scraping away all day in a hole in the ground, although you seemed to be enjoying yourself. Maybe you should be volunteering alongside Bell's irritating son."

"It's the possibility of finding something of interest, and the connection with the past, with the people who have gone before," Elias enthused.

Steph grunted. "It's the present that interests me. Facts and evidence. Particularly finding out who killed Max Barsby. I want to know whether this coin was what Max and Headley thought it was, or whether Headley was just making the whole thing up to drop Crow in it."

Elias nodded. "At least we've got some new leads to follow now — the woman sighted in the bar with Max, and this Mary-Ann Sue mentioned, who might or might not have been the woman Grace saw with Max."

"Plus, although we don't know whether Max really did go to Crow's house on the night of his death, it's possible that he spoke to at least one other person the night he died."

Steph wasn't impressed. "What we have on this investigation are too many unknowns. Too many facts that might not be facts."

"Including an ancient 'arte-*fact*'," Elias said.

Steph cringed at the pun. "I'll get Joey Fairbairn and Olena Melnyk to show Max's picture around in that bar to see if any of the staff remember seeing him there with his unidentified female companion. They might also be able to provide a list of punters who were there that night too. And we can appeal for people who were there to come forward if they remember anything. One way or another we are going to find out how and why Max got himself killed that night."

CHAPTER TWENTY

It was Thursday 17 December, just over a week before Christmas. Jane and Patrick were getting ready to go to a vigil for Max Barsby that was being held at the university campus. Seth had contacted Patrick and asked if they'd like to attend. Was it terrible to consider the occasion as the perfect opportunity to observe the people who had known Max, perhaps even ask them some questions? Jane couldn't decide.

Patrick came downstairs dressed in his full-length black woollen coat. He looked very handsome. "Thought I'd make the effort," he said, seeing Jane appraise him. "It's a solemn occasion, isn't it? A bit like a funeral."

"Yes," Jane said. Sadly, the Barsbys would have to wait a while to bury their son. His body was still being retained by police and would not be released until authorised by the coroner. Jane had intended to wear her warm, khaki-coloured parka, but seeing Patrick's choice of dress made her change her mind and she went upstairs to get her own navy woollen coat from her wardrobe.

Thus attired, they walked down to the university. They arrived to find a small group of people already assembled on the square near the Grand Central Warehouse, a former railway building that had been repurposed as the university's library.

"There's Seth," Patrick said. They walked over to join him.

With Seth was his mother, another man who looked so like Seth that he had to be his father, and Seth's two older sisters, who were supporting Max's parents. Jane felt that she had let them all down. Even though she had promised little, it seemed to her that she had delivered even less.

She longed to tell them that she had made a significant discovery and, of course, she had, but now she feared that concealing Max's secret from DI Warwick might have stymied the official investigation.

Within only a few minutes, a sizeable crowd of people had assembled. Most were holding candles. Jane scrutinised their faces, wondering how many of them had known Max well. The majority were young students who had turned out for one of their own.

One face jumped out at Jane, causing her to start and almost drop her candle. A hooded Maryam, standing just on the periphery of the gathering, which had somehow begun to form a loose, protective circle around Max's family. For a moment Jane and Maryam locked eyes. Then, Jane gave Maryam a slight nod. Jane looked at Patrick and saw that he, too, had spotted Maryam.

Patrick told Jane that some of his colleagues from the dig were present. He pointed them out discreetly. "Linus isn't here. He's gone home for the weekend to attend a big family get-together tomorrow."

Emma Wentworth cleared her throat. She gave a brief speech.

"Thank you all for coming here this evening to remember Max. Some of us are family, others friends or colleagues. We're all here because we cared about Max. Max was a bright, lovely young man who had a promising future ahead of him in his chosen field of archaeology, which, as anyone who knew Max even a little will know, was his absolute passion. He didn't deserve to have his life taken away from him so cruelly."

Emma continued for a few moments more, speaking on behalf of Max's parents, neither of whom were in any shape to address the gathering.

When she had finished, a dark-haired woman came forward to speak. She introduced herself as Dr Bianca Carr, one of Max's tutors. She, too, praised Max's intelligence, his integrity and his passion for his subject. Her voice breaking, she ended by saying that it had been a pleasure to have known him, however briefly. When she stepped back into the circle, she had tears in her eyes.

Next, a young woman stepped into the centre. Seth nudged Patrick and whispered a name, which Jane also caught. Sophie Egan.

Sophie referred to Max as her 'dear friend', whom she would miss terribly. She more or less repeated what Emma Wentworth and Bianca Carr had said before dabbing at her eyes and saying 'sorry' repeatedly, and shuffling back into the circle.

A couple of Max's friends spoke next, including Seth. Then, an awkward couple of minutes passed when everyone had said their piece, and no one seemed to know what to do next. Finally, Emma Wentworth asked everyone to join Max's family in singing one of Max's favourite songs by a well-known indie group. Seth and his mates started them off and everyone who knew the words joined in.

Jane sneaked a peek at Maryam and saw that her face was wet with tears. She longed to go across and offer the bereaved young woman some comfort, but dared not, for fear of exposing Maryam to unwanted attention. After a moment or two, Maryam pulled her hood closer around her face, turned her back on those gathered and walked slowly away.

When the last verse had been sung, people began to disperse. Jane tapped Patrick's arm, nodding after Dr Carr and Sophie Egan, who were walking off together. "We should speak with them."

"DI Warwick has already interviewed them, hasn't she?" Patrick's tone was less than enthusiastic.

"Yes, but perhaps we can find out something Warwick hasn't," Jane said. "And if we do, we pass it on to her immediately this time."

"Trying to get back in her good books?" Patrick said.

"Am I that transparent?"

"Totally."

They fell into step behind the two women and followed them to a pub near the campus.

At the bar, Jane struck up a conversation with Carr as casually as she could. "Excuse me, Dr Carr. My name is Jane Bell. I've just come from the vigil for Max Barsby. Your speech was very moving. I'm sure it was a great comfort to Max's family to hear you speak so highly of him."

Dr Carr frowned, as if about to ask Jane if she knew her. Then she smiled. "Thank you. Did you know Max?"

"My son, Patrick, went to school with Max's cousin, Seth."

"Max was very close to Seth," Dr Carr said.

"Yes." Jane hoped that Dr Carr would assume Patrick had known Max well too.

Dr Carr's order arrived. Two glasses of red wine — one presumably for Sophie Egan. "Look, I'm here with one of my students — she was in Max's year and knew him quite well. Her name's Sophie. She said a few words at the vigil." She nodded towards an alcove where Sophie was sitting, scrolling through her phone. "We're just over there. Come and join us when you get your drinks if you like."

"Thank you. I'm with my son. We'll join you in a few moments."

Jane signalled to Patrick, who had been sitting at a table nearby. He got up and headed to the bar.

"We're joining them," Jane whispered.

They collected their drinks and made their way across to the two women. Jane introduced Patrick. Dr Carr introduced Sophie and invited them to call her Bianca.

"It's nice to meet you both," Jane said. "I'm just sorry the circumstances are so sad."

"It was a nice vigil," Sophie said. "I wanted to say more, but my throat closed up."

Bianca patted her arm. "We were all overcome by emotion." She looked at Patrick. "You must miss your friend, Patrick."

"I'm a friend of Max's cousin, Seth, actually, but I did know Max a little. I came along to support Seth and pay my respects. I was shocked to hear what happened to Max."

"We all were," Sophie said.

Patrick took a sip of his wine. "I hope the police find out who did it quickly."

"They've been to the university to speak with members of the archaeology department," Bianca said. "Including me. It was quite disturbing. Not that I think they regarded me as a suspect, but it was still . . . upsetting."

"They spoke to me too," Sophie said. She looked at Bianca. "Because of the thing with Harry Scott."

"Seth told me about that," Patrick said. "Did you know Harry Scott well?"

"Harry was my boyfriend at the time," Sophie said. "He thought I was cheating on him with Max. I wasn't, although I did flirt with Max a bit. I shouldn't have done that. I feel terrible about it now, given all that's happened."

"If they've questioned both of you, they must have given Harry the third degree," Patrick said. "They'd surely have considered he had motive."

"Harry was a jealous, hot-headed idiot," Sophie said. "I wouldn't be surprised if he killed Max. The sooner they lock him up the better."

"Well, we don't actually know that he is a murderer," Jane said, even though she wasn't convinced of Harry Scott's innocence either. Harry had been enraged enough by jealousy to push Max onto a fire. Unless he had a cast-iron alibi for the night of Max's murder, he must surely still be on Warwick's radar.

Sophie downed the last of her drink and announced that she had to go. "My dad drove me here from Hull for the vigil. He's been waiting to take me home. I'd better not keep him any longer."

After Sophie's departure, Jane felt a sense of urgency. What if Bianca also decided it was time to go? They hadn't learned much so far. She decided to ask some direct questions.

"Relationships can be so complicated, so fraught with difficulty. I suppose, as a personal tutor, you have students coming to you for advice on relationships all the time. Or with other kinds of problems. Did the police ask if Max confided in you about any trouble he was in — romantic or otherwise?"

Bianca smiled. "Yes. Of course. Students often come to me about all sorts of problems, even though I'm really only supposed to advise them on issues affecting their work. Often, it's a case of referring them on to student support or welfare services.

"Regarding Max, yes, the police asked whether Max mentioned having any problems. It's what you'd expect when they're investigating a murder. They also wanted to know what kind of mood he was in in the days leading up to it, and if I knew of anyone who might want to harm Max. I couldn't think of anyone, except Harry Scott. I did ask Max how he was after the incident at Vindolanda, but he didn't seem to want to talk about it."

"Sorry for asking," Jane said. "It's just, Max's cousin, Seth, asked if I could help the family in any way. Sadly, I feel I haven't been much help."

Bianca listened, nodding. "I wasn't of much help to the police. There was nothing I could tell the detectives who interviewed me."

Bianca finished her drink and then she too told them that she had to leave. Jane and Patrick were in no hurry. They had another drink.

"That wasn't very informative," Patrick said, lifting his pint. He had switched to beer, despite Jane's warning about mixing the grape and the grain.

"I suppose we now have confirmation from Sophie that Harry Scott was jealous of her friendship with Max. As you said to Sophie, Warwick must have given him the third degree. It's looking like Harry is the main contender for Max's murder. Well, I doubt there's anything we can uncover about Harry that Warwick and her team haven't unearthed already. Still, the fact that she hasn't arrested him suggests she doesn't have enough evidence. Not yet, anyway. Killing someone is a big step up from giving them a push."

Patrick looked thoughtful. "Harry told Sophie that Max was in a relationship. What if Harry thought Max was — I don't know — pranking him or something? Pretending he was with someone, while seeing Sophie behind Harry's back. Maybe he thought Max and Sophie were having a joke at his expense."

"Where are you going with this, Patrick?"

"So, what if Harry decides he needs proof that Max isn't a threat to his relationship with Sophie? Maybe he wants to find out who Harry's girlfriend is, to prove to himself that she's not Sophie. He follows Max, sees him with Maryam, and somehow manages to work out that Maryam is an illegal immigrant. Then, he confronts Max. He threatens to out Maryam to the authorities. They fight and Harry kills Max. Possibly by accident."

Jane sat back, intrigued by the possibilities thrown up by Patrick's scenario. She took her time to answer. "You won't like me saying this, Patrick, but I think it's time to tell DI Warwick about Maryam. She has so many potential connections to this case that we simply can't keep Warwick out of the loop any longer. Warwick's team will be able to check CCTV, and use other means not available to us to find out whether Harry went anywhere near Maryam's house. If he did, she'll be able to arrest him and haul him into the station, fingerprint him and take DNA samples. If Harry killed Max, then he's bound to have left some trace."

Before Patrick could comment, Jane continued. "Maryam is central to our other scenario too. Warwick needs to know that Max was considering obtaining forged documents for Maryam. He might have put himself at risk to do so. It needs to be investigated properly. Either of these two scenarios could provide the reason for Max's murder. You do see it's time to tell Warwick what we know, don't you, love? We can also tell her what Grace said about spotting Max with a woman the night he was murdered, in case she hasn't discovered this already."

Patrick gave a sigh of defeat. "I guess you're right, Mum. I hope you've got a hard hat because you're going to need it when she hears what you've got to say."

Jane stroked her head, already feeling the blows, but it was DI Warwick's tongue she feared most, plus the worry that, maybe, this time she might just have gone too far to hang on to her job.

CHAPTER TWENTY-ONE

Steph was surprised to find a text from Jane Bell when she checked her messages first thing on Friday morning.

Need to speak to you regarding an urgent matter relating to the Max Barsby investigation. Do you have time to pop round this morning?

She showed the text to Elias when she arrived at work. "*Pop round.* Does Bell think I'm at her beck and call now?"

"She does say it's urgent," Elias said. "Do you think her son has made some sort of discovery at the dig?"

"We'd be the last to know. I haven't had words with the pair of them about that yet. Let's go round there now." Steph stabbed out a text to Jane Bell, telling her to expect a visit in the next ten minutes.

As soon as Bell answered their knock, Steph could tell from her drooping shoulders and evasive eye contact that she was feeling guilty about something. Time to find out what she had been keeping from them. Steph sensed that it was more than Patrick's presence at the dig.

Steph declined the offer of tea or coffee, warning Elias with a look not to accept. No way was Bell getting to control the agenda.

Bell invited them to sit down, and then hovered, nervously, before taking a seat in the armchair furthest from where Steph had chosen to sit. Elias occupied the sofa between the two.

"So, you didn't think to mention when we were here on Tuesday that your son is volunteering at Linus Crow's dig?" Steph said, getting stuck right in.

Bell flinched. "Er. Yes. I must have forgotten to mention that. He only started on Monday this week."

"I don't remember you mentioning Patrick's interest in archaeology before. What a coincidence that he's volunteering at the very same dig Max Barsby volunteered at."

Steph thought back to their previous visit. The look that had passed between mother and son. The way Bell had cast her eyes up at the ceiling guiltily when Patrick had gone upstairs. Well, if Bell had been holding back on something important out of loyalty to Patrick, Steph wasn't going to let her off lightly. "Well, SC Bell. Care to comment?" Steph's voice had risen, almost to a shout.

Bell opened her mouth to speak, but at that moment there came a thunderous sound from the stairs and, seconds later, Patrick burst into the room. "DI Warwick. Mum's not to blame. If you want someone to shout at, shout at me. I'm the one who's put her in an awkward situation." He turned to his mother. "Go on, Mum. You'd better tell her about Maryam, and all the rest of it, like we agreed last night."

Bell's sigh of relief was deafening. Steph's eyebrows rose. *Trouble. Definitely trouble.* Whatever Bell was about to reveal, it had obviously been weighing on her mind, a source of great conflict for her. And who the heck was Maryam?

"What now, Bell?"

"The thing is," Bell said, taking a breath, "leaving aside Patrick being at the dig, there's something else. Something I learned about Max that I don't think you'll have found out from anyone else, it being a bit of a secret. I found out from Patrick, who found out from Max's cousin, Seth Wentworth.

"Actually, it's something that I should probably have told you about before now, but Patrick asked me to give him some time to check it out himself first, because he thought maybe if you knew about it you would jump to the wrong conclusions, so I agreed to give him some time to find out what he could, but . . . ahem . . . he hasn't really had much success and—"

Steph held up a hand to signal that she was running out of patience. "Just get to the bloody point, Bell."

"Okay, ma'am. Max was in a relationship with a woman who entered the country illegally."

Steph took a moment to process what Bell had just said. "How long have you known about this?"

Bell squirmed in her seat. "Er . . . Let me think. Er . . . Since last . . . ahem . . . Saturday it must have been. Yes. Saturday . . . ma'am."

"For pity's sake, Bell. That was six days ago. Six days! We sat in this very room on Tuesday morning and you didn't mention a word about this? You must have known that we were scrabbling about looking for potential suspects among the people Max spent time with, and yet you *wilfully* kept this from us?"

Bell stared at the carpet. "I . . . I'm sorry, ma'am. I wanted to mention it, but I'd promised Patrick and—"

"I don't care if you promised the head of MI5, Bell. You are a police officer. There's no room for divided loyalties in this job. You do your duty. At all times."

"I'm sorry, ma'am."

Patrick chimed in. "I thought I could check out Max's girlfriend and eliminate her from suspicion so there'd be no need for the police to know about her. If I'd discovered anything significant, I would have told Mum immediately, and she would have contacted you."

Steph stared at him, open-mouthed. "You thought you could check her out? So, you're a police officer now, as well as an accountant and an archaeologist, are you, Patrick? You have the authority and the training to interview potential suspects and eliminate them from my investigation? Jeez! Talk about like mother, like son."

Turning back to Bell, Steph continued. "First I find out about John Headley and Linus Crow through a complaint lodged against you, and now this? Are you ever going to learn, Bell?"

At least Bell refrained from apologising again. She sat there, looking meek and miserable, making no attempt at retaliation. It occurred to Steph that, on this occasion, at least, Bell was fully aware she was in the wrong.

Steph addressed them both. "Your actions might have cost us six days in the progress of this investigation. Six days—"

Patrick interrupted. "Excuse me, DI Warwick, but you've just admitted that you knew nothing about John Headley and Linus Crow until after my mother brought them to your attention. You failed to find out about Max's relationship with Maryam. Exactly what has your investigation uncovered so far? Because it seems to me that, without our input, you'd have no leads at all. Which, incidentally, is why Max's family asked for my mum's help in the first place."

You could have heard a pin drop. Bell looked at her son in apparent horror. Steph eyeballed Patrick and he glared back at her unflinchingly. It was left to Elias to cut through the tension.

"Please sit down, Patrick. You're not helping."

Patrick's bulky six-foot-four frame, together with his angry demeanour, did come across as intimidating. Not that Steph felt intimidated, but she was relieved to see Patrick take a seat. She gave Elias a nod and turned back to Bell. "I should suspend you."

Bell mumbled something that sounded like, "Wouldn't be the first time." Steph pretended not to have heard. She had, once before, suspended Bell for interfering in a murder investigation. The memory gave her pause for thought as she recalled that, before that investigation was over, Bell had saved her life twice over, and along with Elias Harper, rescued her career. So, instead of exploding again, she took a couple of calming breaths.

155

In a more measured tone, she said. "The damage is done. Who knows to what extent it has jeopardised this case, but we need to move on." She looked at Patrick. "Tell us about this Maryam."

Steph listened while Patrick described Maryam's perilous journey to England, and how she had first met Max in the museum. So far, so romantic.

"Max loved her. He just wanted to help her."

"There is only one way he could have helped her. By encouraging her to seek asylum in this country," Steph said.

"They were afraid she'd be sent back to Iran."

"I appreciate that, but what was the alternative? Spending the rest of her life in the shadows?"

Patrick and his mother exchanged a look. *Now what?* Steph shot Bell a questioning look.

"Maryam told us that Max had a plan," Bell said.

"Go on."

Bell blurted it out. "He had it in his head that he could obtain fake ID for Maryam."

"Ah," Steph said, surprised. "And how did he think he could raise the funds and the contacts to do that?"

"We don't know," Patrick said. "But Seth says Max asked him how to access the Dark Web, and that he'd bought a burner phone. Seth advised him against going down this route and, in any case, he had no idea how to access the Dark Web himself. Although, being a techie, he could probably work it out. But even if he could, he wouldn't have gone near it."

"Glad to hear it," Steph said. "Our digital forensics team have Max's devices, but there was no burner phone. Do you or your cousin have any idea of its whereabouts?" Patrick shook his head. "What about Maryam? Would she have it, or know where Max kept it hidden? I need to speak to her without delay."

Patrick groaned as if in pain. "Do you really have to speak to Maryam?"

"Yes, Patrick. We really do." Steph looked at Jane and Patrick in turn. "What else do you know that you haven't told us about?"

"Nothing. That's it," Bell said.

"Patrick? Have you uncovered anything from talking to people at the dig?"

"Not much. There was some sort of fight involving Max and another student called Harry Scott. It was rumoured to be because Harry thought his girlfriend at the time, Sophie Egan, was cheating on him with Max."

"Yes, we know about that."

"Oh, and Grace at the dig told me she saw Max with an unknown woman the night he was murdered, but I expect you know about that too?"

"Yes, thank you, Patrick," Steph said, with only slight sarcasm. "Anything else, or is that really it?"

"That's it." Patrick's tone was chilly and disrespectful.

Bell put her hand up like a child in a classroom. "Er . . . Patrick has a theory."

Steph gave a great sigh. "Let's hear it, then." She listened as Bell described how she and Patrick had attended a vigil for Max Barsby the previous evening, and how afterwards, she and Patrick had spoken with Dr Carr and Sophie Egan."

When Bell had finished, Steph summed up. "So, in brief, your theory is that Harry needed to satisfy himself that Max was seeing someone and wasn't interested in Sophie, so he followed Max, and found out about Maryam. He then worked out that Maryam was an illegal immigrant and confronted Max, threatening to report Maryam to the authorities. They fought, and Harry ended up killing Max."

"Yes," Bell said.

"Right." Steph didn't comment further. Instead, she gestured to Elias that it was time to go, but Patrick piped up. "There's another idea we had that doesn't involve Maryam or Harry Scott. I overheard Roadknight talking to Linus Crow about the investigation into Max's murder, and how it was likely to lead to delays. Crow was quick to reassure him."

Steph listened as Patrick outlined his other theory that Max had been murdered to keep him quiet about something that would have meant more delays to the construction project. Steph immediately thought of the gold aureus. She assumed that Bell and Patrick did not know about that. Well, she was in no rush to enlighten them.

"Right," she said again, when Patrick had finished. "You have been busy. Any more theories?" Silence.

Steph signalled to Elias again, saying, "Let's go." Bell jumped up and showed them to the door, while Patrick remained seated.

"I hope you make good progress on the investigation," Bell called after them as they ascended the steps from her door to street level.

"Well, if we do, it will be no thanks to you or your meddlesome son, will it, Bell?" By the time Steph reached the street and turned to look back for Bell's reaction, the door had been closed. "I really thought she was beginning to change," she complained to Elias. "Then she goes and pulls something like this. But at least we now have a potential explanation for why Max removed the aureus from the dig. It's possible he hoped to sell it to pay for forged documents for Maryam. Who knows what dangerous company he might have fallen into in his efforts to do so. He was passionate about archaeology, but more passionate about helping the woman he loved, it would appear."

"Yes," Elias said. "And, at the risk of sounding like I'm defending the Bells, it was sort of true what Patrick said. They have provided us with information we couldn't have obtained easily by ourselves. Think about the scenario they've come up with involving Harry Scott. We've struggled with finding a credible motive for him killing Max. It is sort of credible that he found out about Max's secret girlfriend and threatened to report her. Just to get back at him for Vindolanda."

With reluctance, Steph conceded the point. "Maybe, but you know what pisses me off? Apart from the pair of them withholding valuable information? It's that they both thought my first instinct would be to report Maryam to immigration. I mean, we might eventually have to, but I'd take no pleasure in doing so."

Steph sighed. "I have to admit, the theory about Harry does have legs." More sourly, she added, "Perhaps we'd have got there too, if we'd been party to Max's big secret." She shook her head. "It was bad enough when it was just Bell's interference we had to contend with. Now it's Bell and Son. Interferers, Inc."

"Has a ring to it, doesn't it?" Elias said.

Steph's glare warned of incoming flak. Elias ducked to avoid the fallout.

CHAPTER TWENTY-TWO

The woman who answered Elias's knock took one look at their faces and uttered a single word. "Police."

Steph stepped forward. "Yes. I'm Detective Inspector Steph Warwick, and this is my colleague Detective Sergeant Elias Harper. And you must be Darya Shirvani. You have a young woman living with you. Her name is Maryam Bandari. We'd like to speak with you both in connection with the death of Max Barsby."

Darya hovered in the doorway. She cast a nervous glance over her shoulder. There was the sound of a door slamming.

"She's bolted. Quick, Elias!" Steph signalled to Elias to go around to the back of the house. He took off at a run. Steph barged past Darya and sped through the house to find the back door. She opened it, spied the open gate leading from the back garden and hoped that Elias would be in time to intercept Maryam. By the time she'd run the length of the garden to the gate, Elias was there with the young woman in tow.

"Maryam," Steph said. "I'm sorry if our presence alarmed you. We're not immigration officers. We just want to talk to you about Max."

"You will report me," Maryam said, her voice angry and afraid.

"I don't know," Steph said truthfully. The guidance on whether police were required to report illegal immigrants had shifted backwards and forwards over time. Steph was aware that illegal immigrants were often victims of crime and, as such, were entitled to police protection. Fear of deportation meant that they were afraid to approach the police for help. Maryam wasn't a victim, and Steph could make her no promises. "Look, let's just go inside and talk."

Elias, who had a loose grip on Maryam's arm, let her go. They made their way back inside. Darya hugged Maryam, then all four sat down at the kitchen table.

"Was it Patrick and his mother?" Maryam asked.

"Yes, but not willingly," Steph said. "What you need to understand is that Max was murdered, and that the person who killed him is still at liberty. Is that what you want? For Max's murderer to go free?"

Maryam's eyes flashed with anger. "Of course not."

"Then help us."

"How can I help you when I do not know anything? I told the other police officer—"

"Jane Bell is not a detective," Steph said. "Talk to me."

Maryam looked to Darya. The older woman's eyes were full of compassion. "I think you must, Maryam."

Without breaking eye contact with Darya, Maryam spoke in a quiet voice, "What do you want to know?"

"I won't ask you to repeat yourself. SC Bell has already told us how you and Max met and fell in love. You kept your relationship a secret from all but Darya, and Max's cousin, Seth Wentworth. Then, after Max died, Seth told Patrick and asked for Jane Bell's help. Are you quite certain that no one else knew?"

"I told no one else. Max would not have told anyone else without first speaking with me. Of this, I am certain."

"Right. You and Max went out and about together. I know that you avoided places where Max might be recognised by the people close to him, to avoid awkward questions, but it's quite possible the two of you were seen together, that someone else guessed your secret."

Maryam shrugged. "It is possible, but we were careful. Mostly, Max came here, to Darya's house. Max said we would go to London one day, after he graduated. He talked about doing a master's degree in London, then a doctorate. He could rent a flat, I could get some kind of job. In my country, I was a student of medicine for one year. It is still my dream to become a doctor, but I told Max I would do any job, however menial. We hoped that, in time, I could apply to stay and study in this country."

"When did you last see Max, Maryam? Was it the day he died?"

Maryam shook her head. "No. Two days before that. Max was here for a few hours in the evening. The last time I spoke with him was on the day he was murdered. He called me in the morning to tell me he would not see me that evening because he had to finish an essay."

Steph nodded. She pressed on. "SC Bell told me you left Iran because of gender inequalities, and because your political activity was attracting the attention of the authorities. Is that right?"

"Yes. So many restrictions on women. I have a big mouth, as you say here. It got me arrested and beaten once, and was surely going to get me into trouble again."

"I'm sorry," Steph said. She had a lot of sympathy for Maryam's plight and had to remind herself of the focus of the interview. She directed her next question at Darya. "What did you say to your friends and neighbours to explain Maryam's presence here?"

"I told them that Maryam is my niece, that she lived in Iran until she was twelve years old and then moved to London with her parents when the family emigrated to this country. Recently, Maryam decided she'd like to come and stay with her favourite aunt for a while. People accepted what I said. When they asked what Maryam did, I told them that she was working from home as a translator. That she was a quiet girl who kept to herself. No one seemed suspicious."

Steph thanked Darya and moved on. "Maryam, Seth told Patrick that Max had come up with the idea of obtaining forged documents for you. That he even bought a burner phone and talked about accessing the Dark Web. What do you know about this?"

Darya shot Maryam a look full of concern. "Is this true? You never mentioned that he was taking his idea to such dangerous lengths. And you said that you were going to discourage him from even trying."

"I was intending to tell Max it was completely against my wishes for him to break the law or put himself in danger, but I never got the chance," Maryam said. "I just wanted him to believe in the dream of our happy future for a little while before I told him I could not let him take such terrible risks for me. I did know about the phone. He gave it to me for safe keeping. I have it upstairs. He did not use it."

"You checked it?"

"Yes."

"I'd like you to give the phone to my sergeant before we leave, Maryam," Steph said.

"Yes."

"Do you think there's a chance Max might have pursued his idea of obtaining forged documents before you were able to dissuade him?"

Maryam bowed her head. Looking utterly miserable, she said, "This, I cannot know for sure. If only I had spoken with him sooner."

It was an important angle for the police to pursue. If Max had dabbled in something illegal, it could have cost him his life.

"Just one more thing, Maryam. Did Max ever mention to you that he had found something valuable at the dig he was volunteering on?"

Maryam answered without hesitation. "No. Sadly. It would have made him so happy to find something important."

Steph nodded. "Thank you, both. That's all for now."

Before they left, Maryam brought down the burner and gave it to Elias, who slipped it inside an evidence bag. As they prepared to leave, a question hung in the air. Steph addressed it. "As I said, we're not immigration officials. It's not my job to enforce immigration law. It's my job to investigate murder, and that remains my focus. That being said, I can't give you any assurances. If Max was murdered because of some action he took concerning your status as an illegal immigrant, it might not be possible to shield you." She felt obliged to add, "Applying for asylum is your best way forward. If you decide to make a claim, I will make it known that you cooperated with my investigation."

When they left Darya's house, Steph instructed Elias to drive back to the station. On the way there, she checked the burner. Predictably, it was out of power. Not that she expected to find anything on it. She was certain Maryam wouldn't have lied about finding nothing, knowing that it would be easy for them to check. And, as she pointed out to Elias, Max could easily have bought another phone and concealed it from Maryam.

Steph sighed. "Right now, I'm leaning towards Max having got mixed up in something illegal that led to him getting himself killed. The mystery woman he met on the Brayford might have been a contact, or an accomplice he'd made in his bid to obtain false documentation for Maryam by selling the aureus."

Elias whistled. "You think he might have found a buyer for it?"

"Why not? He showed it to Headley, just to check if it was the real deal, say. He could always tell Headley later on that they'd been mistaken. Crow maintains he never saw the coin. If he's telling the truth, then we could speculate that, after showing the coin to Headley, Max went on to meet the mystery woman. If she was someone he'd contacted about the fake documents, he'd be confident that he'd be able to cover the cost."

"But why show it to Headley in the first place?" Elias said.

"I don't know. For a second opinion, like I just said. Maybe he didn't even realise its worth until Headley got excited about it being an aureus. He couldn't show it to Crow, could he?"

"Okay." Elias swung left into the station car park. "If the coin was worth as much as Crow suggested, selling it would certainly bring in enough money for Max to obtain what he was after."

"Absolutely." Steph thought for a moment. "Going back to the reason for Max showing the coin to Headley, what if he did it as some sort of insurance that, if he got himself into trouble, Headley would contact the police?"

"That sounds plausible," Elias said.

Elias parked the car and they both got out. Steph spoke across the roof of the vehicle. "And, just so we don't lose sight of the Harry Scott angle, I'll get PCs Fairbairn and Melnyk to test Patrick Bell's theory about Harry following Max and finding out about Maryam. They can trawl through any available CCTV footage of the streets around Darya Shirvani's house in the months leading up to Max's death. If Harry's spotted trailing Max, or even caught in the vicinity, he'll have some questions to answer."

CHAPTER TWENTY-THREE

Steph intended to spend Saturday morning catching up on reports and admin activities, but at nine thirty, Elias interrupted her with news of an unexpected phone call from the help desk. He filled Steph in.

"Linus Crow was attacked at the dig last night. He was left unconscious. When he came round, an ambulance was already on its way. Someone else had called it."

"Who?" Steph said.

"Unknown."

"Is he okay? And why am I only hearing about this now?"

"The report of the officer who attended the incident stated that Crow had a slight concussion and was being kept in hospital for observation last night. He recorded it as burglary and assault. It wasn't picked up as relevant to our investigation until the duty desk sergeant came across it this morning." Elias gave a mighty sigh. "Just our luck. A complication in the case with only six more days to go until Christmas."

"Oh, I'm sorry. Did you have plans? Had you been hoping the case would be solved and tied up in a nice big bow before the twenty-fifth?" Steph's tone was dripping with sarcasm.

Elias shrugged. "Well . . . you know."

"Christmas is cancelled," Steph said. "Bar a miracle."

Before leaving for the hospital, Steph tasked one of her team with obtaining the 999 call from the ambulance control room. It might be possible to identify the caller.

Linus Crow already had a visitor when they arrived at the hospital. His wife was by his bedside, having travelled up from Oxfordshire the previous night. Crow looked cheerful enough, sitting up in bed dressed in a blue-and-white gown, and holding his wife's hand.

"I'm Jill Crow," his wife said, as Steph and Elias approached. "We were advised you'd be coming. Linus has already told me your names."

Steph nodded. "Nice to meet you, Mrs Crow, although I'm sure the circumstances could be better." She turned to Crow. "How are you feeling, Dr Crow?"

Crow's hand moved to the back of his head. He winced. "Glad to be alive. I've been assured my injury isn't serious, and that I should be able to leave within twenty-four hours of when the blow was administered."

Steph nodded. "You were attacked outside the portacabin at around six forty-five last night. Can you confirm that for me?"

"Yes. That's about right. I'd gone to the site to pick up my wallet, which I'd left in my desk. I was supposed to be travelling back to my home in Oxfordshire for the weekend. I'd been looking forward to spending some time with my family. Jill was organising a big family gathering for today, since not everyone could make it for Christmas. All four of our children, plus partners and assorted grandchildren, were coming round for a big pre-Christmas celebration this afternoon." Crow looked at his wife, his expression apologetic.

"Don't worry about all that, Linus," Jill said. She squeezed her husband's hand. "We'll rearrange the get-together early in the New Year. The important thing is that you're all right."

Linus sighed. "To tell the truth, I wasn't just looking forward to spending time with my family. I was also looking forward to escaping Lincoln and work for a few days. The murder of Max Barsby shook me up more than I'd realised."

"That poor boy," Jill said. "Linus told me how Max had hero-worshipped him from boyhood. But that wasn't the only reason you took to him, was it, Linus?" Jill looked at Steph and Elias. "Linus was impressed by Max's passion and his enthusiasm for archaeology, as well as his breadth of knowledge for one so young. He was sure the lad had a bright future in front of him."

Linus nodded. "So, all in all, it was a relief to pack my bags after work yesterday. As it would be quite late by the time I arrived in Abingdon, I'd decided to have a bite to eat somewhere in the Bailgate area before setting off for the station. But, the best laid plans, as they say. Just as I was locking up to go out, I slipped my hand in the pocket of my jacket and discovered that my wallet wasn't there. I remembered putting it in the drawer of my desk at work, but I couldn't recall retrieving it when I left.

"It was an inconvenience, but I knew I could still make my train if I skipped going out to eat and picked up a takeaway on my way back from the office instead."

Steph listened, impatient for Crow to get to the important details. Still, she understood his need to talk about the events of the previous evening.

Crow continued. "When I got to the dig, I noticed a light was on in the portacabin. No one should have been there at that time. I assumed that someone else must have forgotten something. Nevertheless, I must admit, I felt a bit uneasy."

Crow paused. He seemed a little less sure of himself now, as he relived the moments leading up to the assault.

"I walked up the steps leading to the door and turned the handle. I think I called out, 'Who's there?' Just then, the light went out. I was about to back away down the steps when someone pushed the door open, knocking me off my feet. I fell backwards down the steps. Before I could get up, the fellow was on me. He must have got behind me and bashed me over the head with something — I don't remember that part — no explosion of pain or anything, and certainly no seeing stars. I went out like a light. The next thing

I remember is coming to and calling 999. Then, all I could think about was Jill and my family, and how there'd be an empty chair at the dinner table the following day if I didn't make my train home."

Jill Crow made a tutting sound. "Oh, Linus. You foolish man." They embraced.

Steph looked away. She gave them a few moments and was about to ask a question when Linus said, "The strange thing is, someone had already called an ambulance. Did you hear about that?"

"Yes," Steph said. "The call went in at six fifty, so only about five minutes after you arrived at the site, and probably moments after you were attacked, suggesting that your attacker might have been the one who made the anonymous call."

"What sort of weirdo knocks you unconscious, then immediately calls for help for you?" Jill Crow said.

Steph shrugged. "Someone who didn't really want to hurt you? Perhaps you interrupted a burglary."

"Another one? Is this Headley again? That man is unhinged," Linus Crow said.

Steph was quick to correct him. "We don't know who it was, Dr Crow. Best not to jump to conclusions."

"John Headley?" Jill said. Her tone suggested a familiarity — and contempt — with the name. Linus Crow must have told her of his recent doings with Headley, but her reaction seemed to go beyond that. The couple exchanged a look.

Crow frowned at his wife. "No need to go into any of that, darling."

"Any of what?" Steph asked sharply. "You need to tell us everything you know."

Crow sighed. "I've published articles in various journals over the years, which have been mostly well received, but one anonymous reviewer — I'm sure it's the same person every time — has criticised everything I've written. The reviews and comments became more frequent — and more vitriolic with the arrival of social media."

169

"You believe John Headley is your anonymous critic? Why didn't you mention this before?"

"Because I never felt threatened in any way. And I had no proof it was Headley, other than that I believed it would fit his style. It seemed like the work of someone petty-minded and grudge-bearing. And his comments were of no consequence. They counted for nothing in academic circles. Most of my colleagues regarded them as pathetic and sad — not to mention ill-informed."

Jill Crow expressed her opinion of the reviews. "I could see that's what they were, but it was still disquieting to think that there was someone out there putting so much effort, not to mention malice, into attacking my husband and his work."

"We will investigate the assault, and see what can be done about identifying your troll," Steph assured them both. "Did you get a look at your attacker?"

Crow shook his head. "It was dark, and I was in a bit of a state after falling down the stairs." He looked suddenly tired. "Are my colleagues at any risk, Inspector?"

Steph considered the question. It was a pertinent one. There was now a murder and an assault connected with the dig. Was that mere coincidence?

"I'm pretty sure your assailant wasn't the same person who murdered Max Barsby. The blow to your head wasn't meant to kill, and the person who inflicted it acted quickly to ensure you received medical attention. That being said, I can't say with absolute certainty that there is no risk. I'll speak with your team first thing on Monday morning and advise them of the need to be vigilant."

* * *

When Steph and Elias arrived at the dig early on Monday morning, a grim-faced Sue Sellars opened the portacabin door to greet them. She and Iain MacDonald had been assisting the police over the weekend, letting officers in to dust for fingerprints, and providing information on what might have been missing or disturbed.

Now, Sue led them into the warm interior of the porta-cabin, asked if they'd like coffee and went off to make it for them, while Steph and Elias joined the others around the table. Steph raised an eyebrow when she saw Patrick Bell sitting next to Iain MacDonald. She'd forgotten that he was volunteering at the dig. Also present were the students, Grace Toyne and Jacob Abbot. The onslaught of questions began immediately.

"Did someone try to kill Dr Crow?" Grace.

"Do you know who attacked him yet?" Patrick.

"When is he coming back?" Jacob.

"Are we in any danger?" Grace again.

Steph held up a hand to staunch the flow of questions. Sellars broke the tension when she walked across the room carrying two steaming mugs of coffee. "Here you go, officers."

Steph wrapped her fingers around the mug, glad of the warmth. "I know you must have a lot of questions, but, at this moment in time, I have very few answers for you. Our working theory is that Dr Crow disturbed a burglar—"

Patrick Bell snorted. "What? Again?"

Steph gave him a filthy look. "As I was saying, the suspected burglar attacked Dr Crow but didn't hit him with sufficient force to cause serious injury. He, or she, also called an ambulance within seconds of inflicting the blow. So, we do not think they set out to harm Dr Crow. It's possible he just happened to be in the wrong place at the wrong time." Steph looked at Grace. "So, to answer your question, no, I don't think anyone is in any danger."

Grace looked unconvinced. "First poor Max, now Dr Crow. I'm not sure I want to carry on working here after everything that's happened."

Jacob gave her a sympathetic look.

Patrick Bell waded in. "I'm sure DI Warwick is right. We're probably not in any danger, but we should all be more security conscious going forward. Make sure we leave our cars and the portacabins locked when we're not in them, maybe avoid being alone on the site, especially after dark, that kind of thing."

Patrick smiled at Steph, as if expecting brownie points for wading in to support her efforts to preserve calm. *Sorry, Patrick.*

Iain MacDonald, who had been silent so far, asked the question Steph had most anticipated. "So, do you think the assault on Dr Crow has anything to do with the murder of Max Barsby?"

Steph was honest. "As I've said, we're working on the theory that the assailant was a burglar who was disturbed. There's nothing so far to suggest the two are connected."

There was a burst of conversation around the table, mostly about whether people agreed with her or not. Steph waited, impatiently, for their chatter to die down. Then, against her better judgement, she asked a question. "Going back to Max Barsby. Did Max mention to any of you that he had found something valuable on the dig? I don't mean something valuable solely in terms of its historical interest. I mean something of monetary value."

Patrick swivelled in his chair to give Steph a searching look. Jacob and Grace looked blank. Sue and Iain looked mystified.

"I'm not sure what you mean," Sue said. "Max was working under our supervision. He automatically showed anything he found to me or Iain."

"Why do you ask?" Iain said.

"Just a thought," Steph said, wishing she hadn't asked so clumsily. "Just wondering if it was a possibility."

"Max was totally honest. He would never steal anything from a dig, if that's what you're getting at," Grace said heatedly. "He would have found the idea of stealing our heritage totally repugnant. I-I think it's pretty offensive of you to even suggest such a thing." There were nods around the table.

Steph saw no reason to delay anyone any longer. She told them they could all get on with their work.

Predictably, Patrick Bell hung back after the others had gone outside. "Have you spoken with Maryam?" he asked.

"Yes. Don't worry. Her secret is safe for now."

"Are you going to arrest Harry Scott? Or Jerry Roadknight?"

"If we have reason to do so, in Harry's case. Roadknight has an alibi for the night of Max's murder. Besides, he's a very successful businessman. I doubt he'd lose sleep, let alone commit murder, over a delay to this contract."

Patrick had more questions. "Did Max find something valuable? Is that what you're thinking? That he found something he could sell on the Dark Web to help him raise money to get fake documents for Maryam?"

Steph should have realised that Patrick would get there quickly, given what he knew already. He was intelligent and intuitive. Just like his bloody mother. She hoped, fervently, that he would find a new job, and soon. One that took up every second of his time and left him too tired for other pursuits. Like solving mysteries. She wasn't sure if she could cope with two members of the Bell family interfering in her investigations.

But Patrick didn't have as many pieces of the puzzle as them. He knew nothing of the aureus, which he proved with his next question. "What made you think of that? Is it something you found out, or is it just a theory? If it's a theory, I have to say it's pure genius."

In his enthusiasm, Patrick seemed to have forgotten, or overcome, his hostility towards Steph. "Oh, and what about the assault on Linus Crow? My money's on John Headley, not some random burglar. I can't wait to run all this past Mum."

"Well, don't let us hold you up." Steph rolled her eyes. When she glanced at Elias, she caught a look of amusement. It was like they were all ganging up on her.

Patrick walked across to the door, ducking as he went out. How tall was he exactly? Six three? Six four? And big with it. His father must have been tall, because Patrick's size and height didn't come from his mother. Why did she even care?

Elias echoed Steph's earlier thoughts. "He's clever. Like his mother. You know, it wouldn't have hurt to have told him about the aureus. The goal is to find out who's behind these killings."

He didn't say it, but Steph had a feeling he meant that the bigger picture was more important than her pride. Irritably, she said, "For goodness' sake, Elias. Whose side are you on anyway?"

Steph forced herself to refocus. "The big question remains — was Max killed because he found something of value that he could sell to raise funds for Maryam? And what about Crow? I know what I just told the team, but I'm not wholly convinced, myself, that Max's murder and the assault on Crow are unrelated."

Elias weighed in. "Trying to find a buyer for the coin could have led Max into a criminal underworld that he was too naive to navigate. I can see how that could lead to his being murdered. As for connecting Max's murder to the attack on Crow, it's tempting to link the two, isn't it? Only problem is, I can't come up with a theory to support the connection yet."

"Hmm. Me neither," Steph said. "Are we straying into the realms of fantasy with all this, Elias? Maybe we're allowing ourselves to be hoodwinked by all this talk about a gold aureus, when all we have is John Headley's word for it that the fabled coin ever existed. Headley might have simply made it up to deflect suspicion from himself — to make us think that Crow, not he, himself, was the last person to see Max alive that night. And to get Crow into a spot of bother, of course." Round and round in circles. Again.

Steph helped herself to a couple of biscuits from the plate on the table. Why not? They'd only go stale. After a moment's hesitation, Elias followed her example.

Steph continued. "As stated previously, we can't allow ourselves to be wholly sidelined by any one theory. Let's take things one step at a time. Melnyk and Fairbairn should have checked through a lot of CCTV footage from the streets around Darya Shirvani's house by now. If Harry Scott's been captured on camera anywhere in the vicinity of Maryam's house, we can bring him in for questioning. He's still a viable suspect for Max's murder, especially if we can prove that he'd somehow found out about Maryam's illegal status. Given that we've also got his previous assault on Max, and the girl-friend issues, who knows, maybe we'll even get a confession out of him."

"And if Harry isn't on the footage?"

"We'll bring him in anyway."

CHAPTER TWENTY-FOUR

Harry Scott had been picked up on CCTV near Darya Shirvani's property. Watching the slightly grainy footage, Steph felt unsettled to see, not just Harry Scott, but also the victim, Max Barsby, on the screen. Harry was quite obviously trailing Max, and none too subtly. Lucky for him that Max seemed totally oblivious.

It was always disquieting seeing the dead reanimated in this way. Elias summed it up. "If only real life could be stopped and rewound so easily."

Joey was more pragmatic. "Doesn't change anything though, does it? The footage rewinds, but the same thing just happens again."

"Let's get Harry in and see what he has to say for himself," Steph said, eager to get on with it. We can't change what happened to Max, but maybe we can change the status quo of the present."

Harry Scott was cautioned, arrested and brought into the station that afternoon. When he had been fingerprinted and DNA swabs taken, he was accompanied to an interview room. From where Steph was sitting on the opposite side of the table with Elias, Harry looked a bit dazed and confused.

Steph began by telling him that they had witnessed him following Max Barsby to Darya Shirvani's house. "Why were you following Max, Harry?"

Harry had declined legal representation, proclaiming that he wanted to tell the truth. "I wasn't convinced Max had a girlfriend, so I followed him to see if it was true. I admit now that it was a weird thing to do, but I was crazy about Sophie at the time." He shook his head. "Love makes you do mad, crazy things—"

Steph cut him off. "It's called jealousy, Harry, and it can stir up very strong emotions. It can make people commit criminal acts, not just 'mad' or 'crazy for love' things." *Trust me. I know.*

"I didn't kill Max. I would never do something like that. I've already told you I was with my new girlfriend the night he was murdered. She wouldn't lie to the police."

Ignoring his claim, Steph continued. "So, you discovered that Max really did have a girlfriend."

"Yes."

"Why did you return to the address where she was staying, even after you had confirmed that Max was in a relationship with someone who lived there?"

Harry seemed to have developed an itch affecting most of his body. He shifted from side to side, pulled at the sleeves of his jumper and scratched his scalp. "I don't know. That's the truth. One hundred per cent. I'm not sure why I did that. Again, looking back it seems nuts. All I can say is that I wasn't thinking like a normal person at the time."

Steph was becoming impatient with Harry's half-baked defence of temporary insanity. "Come on, Harry. I need a bit more than that."

"I . . . I guess I was hoping to see what she was like. I followed Max there, he went inside and came back out several hours later. Once or twice, I caught a glimpse of him with a dark-haired girl at one of the bedroom windows, but I wanted to see her properly. I kept going back until I did.

It sounds stupid, but I think I was still, at the back of my mind, thinking she might be Sophie. Like they'd rented a place where they could go or something."

"And did you eventually 'see her properly'?'"

"Yes. I saw an older woman coming out of the house and get in a car. A few minutes later Max came out with a girl. He had his arm around her. I could see then that she definitely wasn't Sophie. After that I stopped going there."

Steph pushed him. "Did you really? I think you carried on following Max and his girlfriend."

"No. I swear. Straight up. Seeing him with her, both of them looking so happy, so right for each other, sort of brought me to my senses. I started seeing all sorts of things — like how it wasn't like that between Sophie and me. She'd been telling me that all along, but it was like, suddenly, I got it."

Steph leaned forward. "I don't know, Harry. You're obviously a man whose passions run high. I think that a man like you would want to get your own back on Max for — as you perceived it — coming between you and the love of your life."

Harry looked at Elias, as if expecting him to play good cop. "No. That's not true. I know I pushed him onto that campfire, but I was shocked at what I did. I wouldn't want to hurt anyone. I swear I wasn't thinking when I pushed him."

"That's not what you told us last time. You said Max exaggerated how hard he'd been pushed, that he stumbled backwards onto the fire almost deliberately," Steph said.

"I still think that's partly true," Harry admitted. "But I never meant to hurt him."

"Were you threatening Max over his girlfriend's status? Or threatening his girlfriend directly?" Steph asked, switching topic abruptly.

Harry looked genuinely puzzled. "What do you mean? Threatening to hurt her? Of course not."

"Not hurt her physically, perhaps, but I think you'd found out some information about her."

Now Harry looked bamboozled. "I've no idea what you're on about. What do you think I found out? I only ever saw her from a distance. I never even spoke to her." Again, a glance at Elias, an appeal for clarity, sanity. Was Harry acting, or, as Steph was beginning to believe, telling the truth.

"Straight up. I really, really have no idea what you're talking about." Harry looked ready to burst into tears.

Steph exchanged a look with Elias, reading in his eyes that, like her, he was leaning on the side of believing that Harry was genuinely confused.

Meanwhile, Harry mithered on. "I wish I'd never followed Max. I swear. I'm sorry I did. This is a nightmare. It's like one of those movies you see where people get accused of something they didn't do, and nobody believes them, and they end up getting put in prison, and getting beaten up, and forgotten about and—" Harry was in danger of hyperventilating.

Steph held up a hand. She ended the interview, with a few brusque words for the tape.

"Think he was telling the truth?" Elias said after Harry had been removed from the room. "He was convincing, especially when you asked what he knew about Max's girlfriend. He didn't seem to have a clue about Maryam or her secret."

With a sigh, Steph agreed. The decision whether to hold Harry for longer, until further evidence against him could be found, was hers to make. It was a no-brainer. Everything they had was circumstantial at best. For the time being, Harry Scott was free to leave the station, released under investigation pending further enquiries.

CHAPTER TWENTY-FIVE

Jane's mobile rang. Patrick. She listened as her son told her about Linus Crow being assaulted, and about DI Warwick's visit to the dig that morning.

"I wouldn't like to be John Headley right now," Patrick said. "DI Warwick is bound to be gunning for him for the assault on Crow. It's what I'd be doing."

Jane wasn't so sure. "Headley strikes me as having a bark worse than his bite. I can't see him being physically violent towards anyone."

Jane was fascinated by the other nugget of information Patrick now shared.

"Warwick asked us if Max had mentioned finding something valuable on the dig."

"More details," Jane said. This was intriguing.

"I've told you everything, Mum. She asked us if Max had mentioned finding something of 'monetary' value, as she put it. Sue pointed out that she and Iain would have been aware of anything Max found. Grace was pretty angry at what she interpreted as a slight on Max's good character."

"How realistic is it that Sue or Iain would have been aware of Max finding something and not disclosing it? I mean, does everyone work in very close proximity to everyone else?"

"Pretty much," Patrick said. "Although not exactly on top of one another. I expect someone could pocket an object as long as it wasn't too big."

Jane frowned. "Hmm. It must have annoyed Warwick no end that you made the connection straight away about Max needing to raise cash to obtain fake documents for Maryam. Before I learned about Maryam, I would have said Max would be the last person to ever contemplate stealing an artefact, but love can drive people to desperate measures."

"The things we do for love," Patrick said. "For the sake of Max's parents, I hope he didn't get mixed up in anything criminal. It would break their hearts to learn that he'd been so desperate, and they didn't know."

"Yes. You're right."

"It's driving you nuts, isn't it?"

Jane gave a grim smile. "Not knowing what it was that Warwick was alluding to? Of course it is. That was no throw-away question she asked, although it sounds like she tried to pass it off that way. She must have had a good reason for mentioning it. Which, to me, suggests she strongly suspects that Max did find something, and he didn't tell anyone on the dig about it. How would Warwick have come by such information? John Headley? Linus Crow? Someone else on the dig?"

"Or maybe she was just fishing?" Patrick suggested.

"It's possible she was just trying to think of ways that Max could have raised some cash and hit on that idea. Still . . ."

"Buried treasure is a great idea, if a bit far-fetched," Patrick said.

"Never say never. I've been reading up on Roman Lincoln in the past couple of days. Lincolnshire's littered with remains. It's possible that there was a mint here. Mints make coins. What if Max stumbled on something like that?"

"Just when he needed it most? Come on, Mum. What are the chances?"

The conversation ended there, but Jane couldn't stop thinking about it. In the end, she hit on the idea that if Max had confided in anyone about his find, it was most likely to have been John Headley. He wouldn't have approached Crow, his boyhood hero, because Crow was in charge of the dig. Perhaps John Headley had been the source of Warwick's information. With this in mind, Jane decided to pay Headley another visit.

This time, she'd call on him at the bookshop where he worked part-time. She would tell him he'd sparked her interest in all things Roman and ask if he could direct her to some interesting reading material.

Headley had told her that he worked at the shop on Monday afternoons and Wednesday mornings, so there was a good chance she'd catch him there. The bookshop was located near Newport Arch, an easy walk from Jane's house. She set off after lunch.

When Jane arrived at the shop, John Headley was perched on a stool behind the counter, reading a book with a tattered dust cover. He didn't seem to hear her arrive. There appeared to be no other customers, although Jane couldn't see into all the nooks and crannies — Second Readings was one of those second-hand bookshops where you could get lost among the labyrinthine stacks, not to mention the cavernous basement.

Headley only looked up when Jane approached the counter. "Hello again, Mr Headley."

Headley removed his glasses and replaced them with a different pair. "Jane Bell. Have you heard something about Max?"

"I'm sorry, no. The investigation is still ongoing."

"Well, there's nothing else I can tell you that I haven't already mentioned to you, or the detectives who visited me."

"That's all right. I'm not here to ask you more questions. Well, not about Max anyway. I was hoping you could recommend some books to me. I was really interested in some of the things you talked about last time we met. I'd like to learn more about archaeology, and Roman Lincoln."

"Ah. Well. You've come to the right place. We have a very well-stocked section on archaeology and ancient history.

It's down in the basement, so I can't come down with you — got to mind the till — but I'll write down the names of some books I know we've got in stock to get you started, if you like."

"Yes, please."

Headley tore a page from a notebook and began searching around the counter for something. Jane spotted a pen half covered by the book he'd been reading. "Is this what you're looking for?"

"Ah, yes. Knew it was here somewhere. Thank you."

"How are you feeling?" Jane asked. "I know you must still be sad about Max. Are you doing anything at Christmas? I hope you won't be spending it alone."

"Er, yes. I'll be spending Christmas with family. I'm afraid Max's murder has rather taken the shine off it all for me this year. I curse the day he ever got involved with that dig."

"You still think Linus Crow was responsible?" Jane said.

"I do. And I told those detectives why, but they've done nothing about it."

Jane's heart beat a little faster. She'd told Headley she hadn't come to ask questions, and she had no wish to seem pushy. Then again, what was the point of being here if not to find out what she could? So, she decided to come right out with it. "When my son and I visited you that day, was there something you didn't tell us about? Something that might help explain why Max was murdered?"

Headley put down his pen and looked at Jane, his eyes alert with suspicion. Then, he gave a long sigh and seemed to come to a decision. "I suppose it doesn't matter now. I was afraid of mentioning it to you initially, in case I became a suspect. And that's exactly what I became the moment I told that DI about it."

"What did you tell her?"

"That I saw Max the day he was murdered. He came to me in the evening to show me a coin he'd found at the dig. I have to say I was rather shocked that he'd removed an artefact without telling anyone. I can only think it was because of our friendship, and because he wanted to know if I agreed it was what he hoped it was. All the same, I don't condone what he did, and I told him so. Still—"

"You were touched that Max thought of you," Jane said. And flattered, no doubt. That Max had chosen to show the coin to him first, and not Linus Crow.

"Max did say that he wanted my opinion. He was quite excited about the coin, and with good reason. It was a gold aureus — a rare and valuable Roman coin."

"Aren't Roman coins pretty common around these parts?"

"Yes, and, as I explained to DI Warwick, the aureus was mass-produced from around the time of Julius Caesar. But the earlier coins, particularly those from the time of the Julio-Claudian emperors, are much rarer and therefore much more valuable. Those emperors — Augustus, Tiberius, Caligula, Claudius and Nero — were principal historical protagonists. Max's coin bore an imprint of the head of Caligula."

The zealous gleam in Headley's eyes when he spoke of the aureus gave Jane some idea of how he must have felt when he held the coin. "And you were certain that the coin was one of those rare ones?"

Headley looked displeased that Jane would doubt his expertise. His gaze hardened. "Quite sure. But I can't prove it, because Crow must have got his thieving hands on it. I always thought he was nothing more than a low-life tomb-raiding crook."

Jane pressed on. "That's why you were in Crow's house that day. You were looking for the coin. You believed Crow murdered Max after Max showed it to him."

"I don't just believe it. I know it. I was the one who told Max to take the blasted coin straight to Crow."

"Mr Headley, Linus Crow was attacked at the weekend. He was taken to the hospital."

The colour drained from Headley's face. "Well," he said at last, "I'm surprised the police haven't been banging on my door. I must be number one on their most-wanted list." He looked at Jane with suspicion again. "Or is that why you're really here? Have you come to arrest me?"

Jane protested. "No. Not at all, but I expect you'll be questioned again. They'll probably want to know your whereabouts over the weekend."

"I was in London with my daughter. We left on Friday morning and didn't get back until late last night. She'd got tickets for the theatre and afternoon tea at the Ritz as an early Christmas present for me, and we made a weekend of it. I was at the British Museum all day Sunday. Best time of the year to visit — no crowds. We ate at an Italian restaurant near our hotel, then took a taxi to Kings Cross and caught a train home around nine in the evening."

"Then you shouldn't have anything to worry about," Jane said.

Headley picked up his pen again. He looked slightly rattled. There was a long silence as he scribbled on the notepaper. Then, without looking up, he said, "Whatever you might think, I am sorry to hear about this assault on Crow. We were actually good friends once. Will he be all right?"

There was an awkward silence. Headley had clearly been reflecting on the past as he wrote. He had not, previously, enquired as to the severity of the attack on Crow, or asked whether he would even recover.

"He took a blow to the head and had a slight concussion, but I've heard that he's recovering well," Jane said.

Headley cleared his throat. "Right. Now, about those books. I've got five or six written down for you to choose from." He handed over his list. "Turn left at the bottom of the stairs and it's the third bookcase along."

Jane had the information she'd come for, but she supposed she'd better buy a couple of the books for the sake of her cover. She spent the next hour browsing in the basement — because once down there it was impossible to leave without a good look around. When she came back upstairs — carrying five hefty volumes — Headley was holding a book, the cover of which looked familiar. It was Linus Crow's children's book, *The Magic Ring*. Seeing Jane, he laid it aside.

"There was a copy in the children's section. Probably been there for donkey's years. Not the sort of thing kids read these days. Probably wouldn't be considered suitable, or woke enough. It's not a bad yarn. Quite entertaining in some parts. Highly derivative, of course. I wouldn't be surprised if he got the idea from me — a casual remark I once made about a lad finding buried treasure."

It struck Jane as sad that Headley's unremitting resentment and jealousy of Crow's success had sullied what had once been a genuine friendship. Maybe Headley felt it too after hearing about the assault. Would he seek to make amends? Was it just wishful thinking that caused Jane to see a look of regret in Headley's eyes as he laid the volume aside to take her payment?

Would he return the book to the shelf where it had lain, unnoticed for years? Or would he take it with him at the end of the day and find a place for it on one of his own bookcases at home?

Ever the optimist, Jane didn't wait to find out.

* * *

As soon as she could, Jane relayed what she'd learned to Patrick. "So," she said when she'd finished bringing him up to speed, "now we know why Warwick asked that question about whether Max had mentioned finding something valuable at the dig. Headley had told her about the gold coin."

"And you're sure Headley said he advised Max to show it to Dr Crow straightaway?" Patrick said.

Jane nodded, knowing Patrick didn't doubt what she'd said. He was creating some thinking time.

"So the theory about Max finding buried treasure might not have been so far-fetched after all," Patrick said at last. "Think Headley was telling the truth? About any of it, I mean?"

Jane shrugged. "Who knows? And if the story about the coin was true, where is it now? Warwick must have asked Crow whether Max showed it to him. I'd love to know what Crow told her. Did he deny that Max came to him that night? I think he must have done, or Warwick wouldn't still be asking about it."

"My guess would be that Max never went to see Crow. I think he knew how much the coin was worth, but he went to see Headley for a second opinion. Grace claims she saw Max with a woman in that bar on the Brayford. Was the woman some sort of contact, maybe? A buyer for the aureus, or someone he hoped could help him obtain fake documents for Maryam?" Patrick frowned. "And where does Harry Scott fit in? Did Max run into him before he could arrange anything at all?"

Jane sighed. "It's deeply frustrating that all we can do is speculate. I definitely think you should keep quiet about this gold aureus next time you're at the dig, Patrick. If Warwick had wanted people to know about it, she would have mentioned it directly. It could be a key piece of information that the police are holding back for now." To her relief, Patrick agreed. She must have looked downhearted, for Patrick asked if she was feeling all right.

"It's just, I feel we've reached a sort of impasse as far as our investigations go. I feel so sorry for Max's family. For letting them down."

Patrick squeezed her shoulder. "Don't be silly, Mum. Max's family know we're doing the best we can."

"Maybe we should just bow out of this case, leave it to the professionals."

"Let's not give up on Bell and Son quite so soon," Patrick said. "I'm back at the dig tomorrow. Who knows what I might find out?"

Jane appreciated Patrick's optimism, and his support. "Just . . . be careful is all, Patrick."

"I'm an accountant, Mum. We're not known for getting ourselves into dangerous situations. In fact, a little excitement wouldn't do me any harm."

Jane was about to say 'be careful what you wish for', but Patrick was trying to cheer her up and reassure her at the same time. Sometimes, she did know when it was best to keep her mouth shut.

CHAPTER TWENTY-SIX

After the interview with Harry Scott, Steph's mood was in need of a boost. Food wasn't the answer, but she'd skimped on breakfast, and so suggested to Elias that they decamp to a café near the station for a late lunch.

"Even the tech is proving frustrating on this one," she moaned to Elias. She was referring to Max's burner phone, the one that Maryam had given them, and which had been checked by the Digital Forensics Unit more speedily than usual, presumably because of its lack of content. As Maryam had told them, the phone had not been used.

Steph was also referring to the lack of a result from close scrutiny of CCTV footage of Max and the mystery woman in the Brayford bar on the night Max was murdered. Joey Fairbairn had pinpointed the time and place of the meeting, but they had been too far from the camera for the image to be useful, even when enhanced.

Joey had done his best, peering at hours of footage, trying to pick the woman up on other cameras nearby, and from other angles, but she had been wearing a loose, dark jacket with the collar turned up, and a scarf concealed the lower half of her face. The same problem of distance had prevented him from obtaining more than a grainy impression of a woman of indeterminate age. The moment when she and Max had parted — if they had parted — had been missed amid crowd confusion, which had also prevented the pair from being picked up again.

Elias speared a slice of halloumi with his fork. "She could have been one of the last people to see Max alive."

"So, who was she? Are we back to speculating that she was a contact with whom he hoped to do some sort of shady deal? If she wasn't a stranger, who else might she have been? Max didn't know that many women, and none of them seem likely suspects."

Elias ticked them off on his fingers. "Excluding family members: Sophie Egan, Maryam Bandari and Darya Shirvani, Grace Toyne, Sue Sellars." He frowned, then added another name to the list. "His personal tutor, Dr Carr, maybe."

"What do we know about Dr Carr?"

"As you know, she was checked out by PCs Melnyk and Fairbairn, along with the other staff who'd had contact with Max at the university, and the students in his archaeology year group. Thirty-one years old. She's a third-year research fellow."

Steph was surprised. "She's a student?"

"No. Research fellows are members of staff — for the duration of their fellowship."

"What happens after that? Does she get a permanent job?"

Elias shook his head. "Don't think it works like that in universities these days. Most staff are on short-term contracts, and there's fierce competition for posts. Academia is not for the faint-hearted."

"Not many jobs are for life these days though, are they? Maybe being a copper is, but who'd want to do it?" Steph was amused to see Elias's look of surprise, his mug of tea paused en route to his mouth. "What? You think the only way I'll leave this job is in a box?"

"Pretty much."

Steph smiled. "Yeah. You're probably right."

"Dr Carr has dark hair," Elias pointed out.

Steph grunted. "So do all the others. Shades of, at any rate. Remind me which of them had sound alibis?"

"None of them are watertight. Sue Sellars said she was alone in her rented flat all evening. Carr claimed she was at home marking undergraduate essays. Grace was meeting a friend for drinks at a bar on the Brayford — hence her sighting of Max. Darya and Maryam claimed to be together at Darya's house, and Sophie Egan was at home with her family, although after meeting Sophie's mother, I'd say she'd alibi her daughter for mass murder, even if she'd witnessed her spraying bullets into a crowd of people."

Steph topped up her teapot with hot water. "Do you think Max might have told any of these women about Maryam?"

Elias seemed unconvinced. "I doubt it. He only told Seth because Seth saw him and Maryam together."

Did anyone follow up on the friend Toyne alleged she'd been meeting that evening?"

"I think so, but I'll double-check with PCs Fairbairn and Melnyk," Elias said.

Steph folded her napkin and set it aside. "Maybe we need to take a closer look at all of these women. Sue Sellars claims that Max didn't say much to her about his personal life, but Max did tell her he had a girlfriend called Mary-Ann. Not a stretch to see Mary-Ann as Maryam, is it? Perhaps Sellars knows more than she's telling."

Steph picked at the remains of the salad that had accompanied her brie and cranberry ciabatta. "Take a deeper delve into Dr Carr's background and check whether she ever had any connection to Linus Crow, or anyone connected with Max or the dig. Likewise, Sophie Egan. See if her family crack when pressured to corroborate her alibi. I know we're going over old ground, but how many times on an investigation have we asked the same or similar questions, only to be given different answers, or to be told something new? This mystery woman might know something about Max's movements on the night of his murder. It's important that we find her and speak with her."

Elias nodded. "I'll get the team on it. I'll also make sure the other workers on the dig get a second glance, although we didn't find anything on them first time around." He stacked his cup and saucer on top of his empty plate and brushed some stray crumbs into a tidy heap.

Steph frowned. "Despite what we said to Crow and the team at the dig, we know it's unlikely that it was a burglar who assaulted Crow. But it's also unlikely to be the same person who murdered Max — otherwise, I doubt Crow would still be with us. I'm inclined to think that Crow disturbed someone who was up to no good. Just maybe not the killer."

"Roadknight?" Elias said.

Steph pushed her plate aside, having given up on the salad that was smeared in some kind of unpalatable dressing.

"Melnyk checked him out. He's a reputable businessman. Even pays his taxes, and he's worked with Crow before. His company is doing well enough that it can afford to take a hit on this project. The discussion between him and Crow was probably just Roadknight reminding Crow of the need to stick to schedules as far as possible. Still, we can't discount him. At least we've now established that Headley has an alibi for the assault on Crow, so we can cross him off the list." Steph had had Headley checked out first thing on Monday morning.

"Ready to go?" Steph asked Elias. She noticed he looked tired. They had all been putting in extra hours on this case, as though Christmas being only a few days away represented some kind of deadline for the investigation to be wrapped up like a gift and presented to Max Barsby's family. As compensation for the loss of their loved one.

"Take the rest of the day off," Steph said. "You must have stuff to do for Christmas."

"Christmas is cancelled, bar a miracle, remember?" Elias said gloomily.

CHAPTER TWENTY-SEVEN

Despite his mother's fears about them not being able to add much value to the investigation into Max's death, Patrick resolved to carry on working at the dig. Maybe there was more to be learned there, and besides, they were short-handed with Linus likely to be out of action until the New Year.

Grace and Jacob were already labouring away when Patrick arrived at the site. Both gave him a cheery greeting when he joined them. It appeared that they were planning a meet-up on New Year's Eve, to which Patrick was invited, if he did not already have other plans. Their thoughtfulness only added to Patrick's sense of guilt at deceiving them. At some point, he would have to reveal that he had no intention of studying archaeology, that he was, in fact, an imposter.

"Is there any more news about Linus?" Patrick asked.

"He won't be back at work until the New Year at the earliest," Sue Sellars said.

The mention of Linus's name seemed to cast a shadow over everyone. A subdued atmosphere prevailed as they worked alongside each other in virtual silence for a couple of hours.

Around eleven thirty, Sue made a suggestion. "Look, I can tell your hearts aren't in it today. We've all been shaken up by recent events. We were planning to finish up at lunchtime tomorrow until after Christmas. Why don't we bring that forward a day? Wind down now and go to the pub for a bit of lunch and a drink to cheer ourselves up? I think we could all do with putting a bit of distance between what's been happening here and Christmas. Otherwise, we'll all be thoroughly miserable when the day arrives."

Patrick was relieved to hear the suggestion, and from the looks on the faces of his colleagues, he could see he wasn't the only one.

Iain backed Sue up. "All right with me. The mood here has been gloomy as hell since Max's death and it's only worsened with the attack on Linus." That coming from Iain, who wasn't the cheeriest individual at the best of times, seemed to settle the matter.

Sue suggested a pub at the top end of the high street. Everyone bundled into their cars. Patrick, who'd driven to work in his mother's car, gave Jacob and Grace a lift. He parked the car at home, and the three of them walked the short distance to the pub to meet up with the others.

As soon as they'd entered and Patrick heard one of his favourite Christmas songs playing in the background, his mood brightened.

Sue had called ahead to make sure they would have a table at such short notice. This close to Christmas it was busy, but they were lucky — a noon reservation had been cancelled last minute. A waiter took their orders, warning them they might have a bit of a wait before their food arrived.

"No problem," Sue said. "Let's get some drinks in."

Patrick was finishing his second pint of ale by the time his steak and chips arrived. Beside him, Grace sipped her wine slowly and picked at her turkey salad, making him feel guilty for having a hearty appetite.

Iain must have noticed his empty glass. "I'll get you another." He got up, ignoring Patrick's protests.

Despite everyone trying their best to avoid talking about recent upsetting events, the conversation kept drifting back to Max's murder and the attack on Linus. Then, someone would make a timely comment, leading them on to lighter topics.

"This is nice," Grace said. "I finally feel relaxed after all that's happened. It really did feel like we were starting to be picked off one by one."

"Do you feel unsafe at the dig?" Sue asked.

"Kind of." Grace shuddered. "It does make you wonder. What reason would anyone have to kill Max, or attack Linus?"

"I guess people's lives are often more complex than we know." Patrick was thinking of Max and his secret. He changed the subject, lest the alcohol loosen his tongue. "What will you all do when the dig is over?"

Sue looked at Iain. "We'll be working another dig. Down south this time. Linus has the contract for a site in Oxfordshire."

Iain nodded. He looked lost in his pint of lager. When he'd finished, he announced he was leaving. There were protests all around, but Iain was insistent. "I'm going to my sister and her family for Christmas. I was planning to get a train tomorrow, but I might as well go today. She won't mind if I arrive a day early."

After he'd gone, Patrick realised that he knew very little about Iain's personal life. Sue offered an insight. "I feel sorry for Iain. He recently got divorced. His wife's family is loaded. Her parents bought them a house when they got married, but it was in his wife, Isabel's, name. Seems they never took to Iain, so he's come out of the marriage with nothing. At least there are no kids involved."

"That's rough," Patrick said.

"That's life," Sue said. Sue had previously mentioned that she lived with her partner in Oxfordshire and that she was travelling back on Christmas Eve. "I'll stick to my plan," she said. "Otherwise, I'll just get in the way of Dana's last-minute preparations for the big day." She changed the subject. "I hope your experience of working on the dig hasn't put you off studying archaeology, Patrick."

Patrick avoided the question by taking a long drink from his glass. Then, as everyone still seemed to be awaiting his response, he muttered, "Oh no. Not at all."

No one seemed to be in a rush to get away. Patrick had a few more pints. He wasn't normally a big drinker, so by the time they left the pub, he was feeling tipsy, not to mention sluggish after his large steak and chips, which had arrived with two fried eggs and a large helping of onion rings. He'd rounded it all off with a double helping of Christmas pudding and brandy butter — Sue had ordered some and then decided she couldn't manage it, so Patrick had felt obliged to step up and help her out. Outside, the sudden daylight was dazzling, and everything about Patrick glowed with a boozy aura.

They parted company in the Bailgate, all going their separate ways. Jacob and Grace both lived in Nottingham and had decided to travel back together that evening. They mentioned the drinks meet-up at New Year again, and Patrick promised to get in touch.

Norah was at the cottage when Patrick got back. She looked up from her book when he walked into the sitting room. "Look at the state of you."

"I'm going upstairs for a bit of shut-eye," Patrick said, yawning. "Wake me up in a couple of hours."

"Can't. I'm going out soon," Norah said. "Meeting a friend for a catch-up. I'll let Mum know, if she gets back before I go, but she's out doing a bit of shopping, so she could be a while."

Patrick went upstairs and stretched out on his bed. He was asleep within seconds.

Some time later, he woke with a start, feeling a lot better, and blissfully headache free. Just as well he hadn't had one more pint for the road. In the bathroom, he splashed cold water over his face and felt reinvigorated.

The house was empty. Norah was long gone, judging by the chill in the air. She would have had the heating on until she left. That morning, his mother had mentioned something about going shopping. She must still be out.

It was four thirty in the afternoon. Already almost dark outside. Patrick felt restless and in need of some fresh air. He put his coat on and walked up to the Bailgate. He ended up standing before the imposing west front of the cathedral. Patrick walked over to the Christmas tree and searched, again, for the label that his mum and Norah had tied there in memory of his dad. A light breeze stirred the branches of the tree, causing its silvery lights to shimmer magically in the twilight.

Patrick closed his eyes, his mind suddenly flushed with memories of the many happy Christmases he'd spent with his family. Then, a starker memory intruded, of the first Christmas after his father's death — the grim, subdued atmosphere and lack of merriment. That was how it would be for Max's family this year. If only he could offer them some sort of peace by bringing their son's murderer to justice.

"Happy Christmas, Dad," he whispered, letting go of the label, and stepping back from the tree. Well, he was in a melancholy mood now, all right.

He walked back through the fourteenth-century Exchequer Gate onto Castle Square and was just about to turn onto Steep Hill when a friendly voice hailed him from behind. "Hey, Patrick. Have you sobered up already?" It was Grace Toyne.

"Hi, Grace. I'm good. Takes a lot to incapacitate me. Hey, I thought you'd be halfway to Nottingham with Jacob by now."

"We're catching a train around seven. I walked up here to buy a last-minute present for my sister. It was a nice lunch, wasn't it? I definitely feel better for it. Whoever said we needed some space to separate recent events from Christmas was spot on."

Patrick agreed. "That was Sue, I think. You know, I did feel kind of sorry for Iain, after what she said about his divorce."

Grace grinned and gave a knowing wink. "Well, I wouldn't feel too sorry for him. I didn't want to say anything in front of Sue, but I saw him recently with Dr Carr, one of my tutors at the university. Looked like they were *pretty* close." Grace left Patrick in no doubt what she meant.

"Bianca Carr?" Patrick said, surprised.

"Yes. Do you know her?"

"No. Just recognised her name from when I was research-ing courses at the university. And she spoke at the vigil held for Max, remember? So, you reckon she and Iain are together, then?"

"Looked that way to me."

They spoke for a few minutes more, before wishing each other a happy Christmas and going their separate ways.

Patrick's mind began to whir. There were plenty of reasons why Iain MacDonald and Bianca Carr might have known one another. They were both archaeologists, so they probably moved in similar circles. It was just that they had both also known Max Barsby. Again, why wouldn't they? Max was studying archaeology. He'd had links with the uni-versity, and the dig.

It was just that . . . something about this connection was making Patrick feel tingly. Bianca Carr had seemed to have a close relationship with Max, and he, in turn, had trusted her. Enough to have confided in her about Maryam? If Max had confided in Carr concerning Maryam, Carr might have told Iain MacDonald. But what conclusion could be drawn from that?

And, if Max trusted Bianca enough to tell her about Maryam, maybe he had also confided in her about the gold coin. What would Carr have advised him to do? Had she told MacDonald about the coin and, if so, had MacDonald passed the information on to Crow? Had MacDonald and Carr been on Warwick's radar?

The possibilities seemed endless and impossible to untan-gle. How did detectives like DI Warwick ever join the dots?

Preoccupied by his blizzard of thoughts, Patrick realised that he had walked all the way down the hill to the high street. He glanced up at the clock above the Stonebow: four forty-five. Was there any chance Bianca Carr might still be at the university? If so, he could ask her some questions, perhaps find out if she knew about Maryam, maybe even ask if Max had shown her the aureus. The students had mostly all gone home for the holidays, but academics were notorious for working long hours. In the hope that he might catch her at work, he took a short cut straight through Marks and Spencer and out the back door. Once outside, he hurried across the road without waiting for the lights to change, then cut down the side of an office block. From there, it was a short walk along Brayford Wharf and across a footbridge over the River Witham to the university campus.

A helpful student directed Patrick to the archaeology department on the western fringe of the campus. Carr's office was on the fifth floor. Patrick took the lift. The sequencing of door numbers in the long corridor leading to Carr's office seemed a little haphazard, but he located the office he was seeking at last and was about to knock on the door when he noticed that it was slightly ajar. From within came the sound of Carr's voice. It was a one-way conversation. Carr must be speaking on her phone.

"Yes. I've just received confirmation that we have a potential buyer for the coins in the States. A collector in Boston. No. Just the coins, but I've been assured there's a lot of interest in the other items. I'm confident it won't take long. Oh, Iain. Just think. No more slogging away in academia, competing for an ever-dwindling number of posts for me, and no more thankless digging for you. We'll have financial security for the rest of our lives." A pause. "Now? At the dig? Is it safe to move it so soon? I thought we agreed yesterday that . . . Yes. I know. All right. I can be there in twenty minutes. I love you too."

Patrick's mind reeled. He sank back against the wall, as the full impact of what he had just heard struck home. Boom! A thought hit him. Carr had dark hair. Could she be the dark-haired woman Grace had seen with Max on the Brayford the night he died? It seemed clear that Carr and MacDonald were mixed up in something underhand. It no longer seemed a good idea to question Carr. At least not until he had time to gather his thoughts.

He could hear Carr moving about her office, and if he didn't want to be discovered with his ear to her door, he'd better leg it — and fast. He ran, light-footed, back down the corridor, fearing that the lift might have been called to a lower floor, leaving him stranded.

Fortunately, the lift was waiting for him. Patrick was nervous when he stepped out on the ground floor, even though there was no way Carr could have got there first if she'd opted to use the stairs. The lift doors closed behind him. Carr summoning the carriage back to the fifth floor? Patrick retreated to a place under the stairs and waited until she emerged from the lift a few moments later.

When Carr exited through the main sliding glass doors, Patrick left his hiding place and hurried over to the exit, hoping to spot her outside. Bingo! There she was, striding off in the direction of the car park.

Patrick whipped out his phone and called an Uber. There was a ten-minute wait. By the time his lift arrived, Carr would be well on her way to the dig for her rendezvous with MacDonald. To be on the safe side — Patrick did not wish to be seen arriving there — he instructed the driver to drop him halfway along the single-track road leading to the field where the dig was located.

If the driver thought there was something odd about dumping his passenger in the middle of nowhere, he didn't comment.

The darkness took Patrick by surprise. He waited a few moments for his eyes to adjust. It was less than five minutes' walk to the dig, but it was so still and quiet that he could have been miles from anywhere.

Tall, thick hedgerows fringing the field provided good cover on the approach to the site. Patrick also hoped that the darkness would be his friend if he needed to get nearer to the portacabin, which he could now just make out through the tangled branches.

A dim light flickered behind the blinds of the portacabin. Patrick played it safe, waiting and watching the door with a keen eye, until, after a tense and chilly quarter of an hour, his patience was rewarded. The door swung outwards revealing Carr, closely followed by MacDonald, silhouetted against a rectangle of light. The light was soon extinguished and replaced by the glow of two portable lanterns. Patrick squinted. As well as the lanterns, the pair were carrying spades. MacDonald also had what looked like a short plank of wood tucked under his arm. *What was that all about?*

To follow or not to follow? Patrick took stock. MacDonald and Carr were heading into the open field. It was dark, but there would be no other cover. The slightest sound might betray his presence, but if he stayed out of range of their lamps, he might be okay. *Follow, then.*

To his surprise, Carr and MacDonald walked past the main area of the dig, right to the perimeter of the site. They didn't stop until they reached a narrow watercourse. The purpose of the plank was now revealed. MacDonald laid it across the catchwater, tested it against his weight, then walked across. Safely on the other side, he waited, shining his lantern on the plank to light Carr's way until she joined him.

Fortunately, they left the plank in place. Patrick let several moments pass before shining the screen of his phone over the makeshift bridge, taking care to shield the light with the palm of his hand. The plank felt springy under his considerable weight. He was nearly across — one foot on the bank, one still on the plank — when his balance started to go. One dangerous wobble and he lost it completely. Patrick fell backwards into the catchwater, landing on his backside with a loud splash.

A startled wildfowl took to the air in a noisy beating of wings. Patrick lay frozen, in more ways than one, in the icy water, worried that at any moment he'd be blinded by the beam of a lantern, and the game would be up. Several minutes passed. Had he got away with it? He waited, holding his breath until, at last, he let it go in blessed relief. Saved by a duck.

Patrick got to his feet slowly, legs numb and leaden with cold, feet squelching inside sodden boots. He raised his hands to his midriff to wipe them and realised his jacket was soaked through. With this realisation, he began to shiver. The sensible course of action would be to turn back and call the police. Well, he wasn't going to turn back before he had some idea of what MacDonald and Carr were up to, but he would make the call.

Patrick reached for the phone in his pocket. Finding nothing, he searched the other pocket. With a feeling of dismay, he realised that it must have slipped out when he fell. The realisation was accompanied by a momentary panic.

Okay, Patrick, old man, worst case scenario, it's in the water. And that's where he felt it moments later, after groping around up to his elbows in mud and freezing water — a rectangle of cold plastic, and from the feel of it, lying face down in the sludge. Ever the optimist, Patrick pressed the button. The screen didn't change. The situation warranted a few silent expletives. He shook his phone, jabbed at the empty screen, but there was no sign of life.

He was still in the water, which wasn't helping with the intense cold that he could feel seeping into his bones. He slipped and slid his way up the muddy bank, groping with frozen fingers to find purchase, until at last, he reached level ground.

Casting a malevolent look back at the plank of wood, which he couldn't even see against the dark water, Patrick cursed it for being so bouncy. He straightened up to take stock of his surroundings. A pale moon peeked shyly through a veil of cloud. It was enough to allow him to get his bearings. He was still in the same field, but almost at the boundary. There was a sparse hedgerow ahead, beyond which lay another field, in which, if he was not mistaken, he could make out the eerie flickering of lamplight.

Now that he was soaked to the skin and shaking with cold, good sense dictated that it was time to go back. There was a landline in the portacabin. But, although Patrick

202

wouldn't say he was enjoying himself, there was an element of novelty, not to mention thrill, about his present predicament that you didn't get from pouring over spreadsheets and preparing financial reports. It wasn't every day that an accountant got this much excitement.

So, setting aside some concerns about how to tell when the balance had tipped from merely being cold to developing hypothermia, Patrick advanced to the hedgerow, keeping as low a profile as his bulky frame would permit.

Shielded by the hedge, Patrick looked into the field. The lantern lights were still, suggesting that MacDonald and Carr had reached their destination. Patrick squatted on his hunkers, uncomfortably, to observe what they were up to.

They were digging. Okay, so that's what archaeologists did, wasn't it? Only they didn't usually do it under a cloak of darkness. Unless they were up to no good.

It wasn't that difficult to work it out from the snatches of one-sided conversation that he had overheard outside Bianca Carr's office. Carr had mentioned coins and 'other items'. MacDonald and Carr were stealing from the dig.

Except this wasn't anywhere near the dig site. The pair must have stolen artefacts from the dig site and reburied them, right here in this field, where — from what he'd heard Carr say earlier — they'd intended to leave them for a while. What had changed their minds? This was a question for another time.

MacDonald and Carr worked in silence for a seemingly interminable time, while Patrick remained in his crouched position, aching with cold. Then, at last, a jubilant cry rent the bitter night air. Carr's voice. "Eureka!"

Patrick watched as MacDonald dragged something from the earth. Frustratingly, it was too dark to see what it was until Carr, obligingly, picked up her lantern and held it aloft. The light revealed MacDonald holding a large, bulky rucksack. Bulky with stolen treasure, Patrick was now sure. He deeply regretted the loss of his phone. DI Warwick needed to hear about this before Carr and MacDonald could make off with their loot.

More pressingly, Patrick was now convinced he was look-ing at a pair of ruthless and dangerous individuals. There was a very distinct possibility that MacDonald and Carr had mur-dered Max and injured Linus Crow. Patrick had no desire to become their third victim. He could not remain where he was. The villainous pair would be heading back to their cars soon, and there was every chance they would stumble into him.

They were using their spades again now, presumably to fill in the hole. Time to move. But as he made to unfold himself from his crouched position, Patrick felt a sudden cramp seize his calf. He grabbed his foot to turn up his toes, and as he did so, he lost his balance for the second time that night. This time, he fell awkwardly, landing on his shoulder. There was an agonising pop. Patrick let out an involuntary yelp of pain. The sound of digging ceased abruptly and was replaced by a roaring silence.

"Who's there?" MacDonald's voice boomed out of the darkness. No startled bird or animal came to Patrick's aid this time.

"Show yourself!" the voice boomed again.

No chance. Patrick scrambled to his feet. He sprinted along the side of the hedgerow, hoping for enough cover to prevent him from being seen. If MacDonald or Carr got a look at him, they'd guess who he was immediately by his height. How many other six-foot-four individuals would be on their radar?

And now, unluckily, the previously timid moon was shining brazenly. Having cast off its cloudy veil, it was now a searchlight, setting the field ablaze with incandescent light — or so it seemed to Patrick in his state of heightened panic.

And if the moon didn't do it for him, there was MacDonald crashing through a gap in the hedgerow, lan-tern discarded, armed now with a powerful torch. A ditch lay ahead. Patrick took a dive, screaming silently as his injured shoulder took further punishment on landing, and his ankle turned at an awkward angle.

Had MacDonald spotted him? Or had Patrick's dive into the depths of the ditch saved him from detection? Patrick's teeth chattered, but he suppressed a hysterical giggle at the alliteration in his most recent thought.

He lay in the ditch, fearing that the beam of light from MacDonald's torch would pick him out any second. It was so quiet he could hear his own heartbeat.

MacDonald was drawing perilously close now, the beam of light from his torch sweeping the area in wide arcs. Patrick felt something press against his calf. He gave his leg a shake, moved his hand down, and felt something wet and slithering slip through his fingers — a rat's tail. He fought down an urge to cry out, jump to his feet. Then, a soft plonking sound, as of something dropping into water, and the creature was gone.

But the relentless searching sweep of MacDonald's torch continued. Any moment now, it would pass over the ditch and the game would be up for Patrick.

"Iain? What was it? Did you see anything?" Carr's voice. "A fox or something, maybe?"

The torch beam jerked away abruptly, and MacDonald replied in a harsh voice, loaded with suspicion. "Don't know. I didn't see anything, but it's too dark to make much out."

"Whatever it was, it's gone now. Come on. Let's get out of here." Carr again, her tone urgent.

To Patrick's relief, the beam of the torchlight switched direction. He listened to the sound of MacDonald's and Carr's voices grow fainter and fainter, until they ceased altogether. Nevertheless, he lay where he was, too exhausted to move. Looking again at the moon, he could see that it was not as bright as he'd previously believed. It had been his own fear making it seem so.

The ditch was deeper than he'd thought, and he'd just realised that it was waterlogged. Minutes ticked past. Patrick supposed he should move soon, make his way out of his hidey-hole and get back to civilisation. But, oddly, the longer he put it off, the less uncomfortable he felt. Even his shoulder, which had exploded with pain when he landed in the ditch, seemed more bearable now. The constant throbbing of his ankle seemed as comforting as a heartbeat.

In fact, it was really quite cosy in the ditch. Yes, he was comfortable. And numb. There was a song in there, somewhere, one of his mum's favourites if he wasn't mistaken. Patrick felt drowsy. Maybe he'd just close his eyes for a bit. It couldn't do any harm, could it?

CHAPTER TWENTY-EIGHT

Jane woke with a start at the sound of her phone vibrating noisily against the wooden surface of her bedside table. She'd set it to go off at seven.

The house was quiet. The kids wouldn't surface until at least eight, meaning Jane had first dibs on the shower. She'd gone to bed early with a bit of a headache the previous night. Norah had been watching TV. Patrick was out, surprisingly, after what Norah had told her about him rolling home half-cut in the middle of the afternoon. Unusually, he hadn't texted to say where he was.

Jane had arranged to call on her friend Allie mid-morning. As she was up and dressed early, she decided to make some mince pies. Norah and Patrick loved her homemade ones, and she could take some to Allie's later. She set to work, humming along to Christmas tunes on the radio. The first batch was already in the oven when Norah came downstairs, still in her pyjamas.

"Is that mince pies I smell? Great. I'll have some for breakfast. Then, you'd better hide them from Patrick."

"What time did he get home last night?" Jane asked.

Norah yawned. "No idea. I went to bed at eleven thirty. He wasn't back by then."

After breakfast — porridge for Jane, and two mince pies mashed up with cream for Norah — Jane made another batch and cleared up the kitchen. As soon as she'd finished, it was time to go.

Allie appeared as Jane descended the steps leading down to her front door. "Knew you'd be dead on time. Coffee's ready."

Jane handed over her bag of mince pies. Allie's dog, Dudgeon, gave Jane his usual enthusiastic welcome. He was sporting a Christmas bandana — a red kerchief dotted with Santa heads.

Jane followed Allie into the sitting room, a mirror of hers except for the furnishings, which were more modern and less colourful. It was probably cleaner too, although Jane didn't dwell on that. Allie placed a plate laden with mince pies, Christmas cake and chocolate fudge on the coffee table, saying, "Help yourself." She glared at the dog. "Not you." Dudgeon kept a hopeful eye on the goodies until Allie fed him some dog biscuits.

"This used to be such a hectic time of year, when the kids were little," Allie said. "Now look at the pair of us putting our feet up and having a chat two days before Christmas."

"I feel a bit guilty not going to Ed's to help with the preparations, but he's asked us not to arrive until tomorrow. He's got an order to finish and deliver in time for Christmas. And he's assured me he's got all the preparations under control. I'm looking forward to this Christmas, and it's lovely to think that Patrick won't be rushing back to London the day after Boxing Day."

Jane spent a pleasant hour and a half with her closest friend. They exchanged gifts and hugged before Jane returned to her own house, only two doors down from Allie's. Norah was busy doing some ironing. Jane looked around for Patrick.

"Still snoozing," Norah said. "Can't believe he didn't get up as soon as he caught a whiff of the mince pies."

"I'll just pop my head around his door. Make sure he's all right," Jane said. Upstairs, she knocked lightly on Patrick's door. Not so much as a groan in response. She opened the door and peeked inside. It was immediately obvious that Patrick wasn't there. His curtains were open. His pyjamas lay neatly folded on the end of his bed. "Patrick?" Jane whispered to the empty room, as if he might be hiding under the bed, a ludicrous supposition, given his size. There'd be limbs poking out all over the place.

Next, Jane checked the bathroom. Not finding him there, she checked her own room and then Norah's. She went back downstairs, reminding herself that Patrick was a grown man, and that if he hadn't come home the previous night, it was possible he'd met someone and gone home with them.

"Has he sent you downstairs for some hangover pills?" Norah said, looking up from her ironing.

"He's not here," Jane said, voice flat and tinged with concern.

"Oh," Norah said, her brows raised. It was telling that she didn't make some sharp-witted comment about Patrick getting lucky. Instead, she put down the iron and picked up her phone. "He hasn't texted me," she said. "How about you?"

Jane checked her phone. She shook her head. A sense of unease began to take hold.

"It's nearly noon. He would have been in touch by now if he was okay," Norah said, putting into words what Jane hadn't wanted to say for fear of communicating her incipient panic. "Mum?"

"What? You're right." Jane rang Patrick's number. "Nothing."

Norah did the same. "Straight to voicemail. Maybe his phone's out of power." She took charge. "I'll call all of his friends I can think of."

Jane nodded. Norah's words were like a call to action, blunting Jane's creeping panic and propelling her into cop mode. "Write their contact details down. We'll each take a few and call them. Text if you don't get a response."

Mother and daughter worked together to contact everyone they could think of that Patrick might have spent the night with. No one had seen or heard from him in the past twenty-four hours. "I'm calling the hospital," Jane said. "He might have had an accident."

Far from alarming Norah, this seemed to rally her. "Yes. He probably just got really drunk and fell over or something."

Patrick wasn't at the hospital.

Alarm bells were ringing loud and clear inside Jane's head now. A worrying possibility had occurred to her. What if Patrick's sudden disappearance had something to do with the murder of Max Barsby? "I'm going to contact DI Warwick," she said, hoping that her relationship with the DI, however odd and tentative, might count for something in an emergency.

Warwick sounded impatient. "Yes, SC Bell? Calling to wish me a Merry Christmas?"

Jane was gripped by her usual nervousness when conversing with Warwick. "Er . . . no, ma'am. It's my son, Patrick. He's disappeared."

"Details?" Warwick's voice was brisk, but not hostile.

"He went out some time yesterday and he hasn't returned. My daughter, Norah, last saw him around half past two in the afternoon. I got home around five thirty yesterday and he'd already gone out. I've just checked his bedroom because he wasn't up. His bed hadn't been slept in. Norah and I have rung round his friends. No one's seen him or heard from him. I've checked with the hospital—"

Warwick interrupted. "Give me ten minutes to make some enquiries." When Jane didn't answer immediately, Warwick repeated, "Ten minutes, okay? And try not to panic. You know as well as I do that most mispers turn up safe and well."

"Yes, ma'am. Thank you."

Twenty minutes passed. Jane was on the point of calling Warwick again when there was a knock at the door. Mother and daughter leaped up, simultaneously exclaiming, "Patrick!"

Instead, it was DI Warwick and DS Harper. Jane clutched her throat in alarm.

Warwick reassured her immediately. "It's not bad news. It's not any sort of news. Can we come in?"

Everyone sat down in Jane's small living room. Warwick spoke with calm efficiency, while Elias sat next to her, emanating sympathy. "I've had an incident log created, and the standard checks for a missing person will be instigated immediately. We just need to know what else you can tell us — anything that might be relevant to Patrick's disappearance."

"He wouldn't stay away this long without getting in touch," Jane said, aware she was repeating herself. *Is this how it had all begun for Max's parents?*

Warwick looked at Norah. "How did Patrick seem when you last saw him?"

"He'd been drinking," Norah said. Like Jane, she was probably worried that this would make Patrick's disappearance seem less urgent. "With his colleagues from the dig. They'd finished work early and gone out for a meal together. He was . . . a bit tired when he came in, so he went upstairs to have a nap. Except for being a bit tipsy, not actually drunk, he was fine. I went out soon after that. I looked in on him before I left. He was fast asleep."

Warwick looked at Jane. "You came home around five thirty, and he'd gone out again?"

"Yes." Jane anticipated Warwick's next question.

"Any idea where he might have gone?"

"Naturally, at first, I thought he might have gone out with friends and stayed over at one of theirs, but, as I said, we've checked with all his mates. Other than that, I don't know where he might have gone." After a pause, Jane added, "I've also been wondering if something's happened to him as a result of looking into Max's murder. Maybe he stumbled on some information that led to him . . ." Jane's voice trailed off. Beside her, Norah gave a gasp.

"Let's not jump the gun," Steph said.

"I went to see John Headley again," Jane blurted out. "Patrick told me you'd been asking at the dig about whether anyone knew if Max had found something of value. John

Headley told me about the coin — the aureus — yesterday, and I told Patrick. Max had been looking into how to raise money to buy fake documents for Maryam. What if he got mixed up with some criminal gang that's now got hold of Patrick?"

Norah gasped again. "What are you talking about, Mum?"

Jane felt ashamed for articulating her worst fears in front of her daughter. The last thing she wanted was to upset Norah, who had had a difficult time after her father's death. She took Norah's hand and squeezed it. "I—"

Warwick stepped in. "Again, let's not get ahead of ourselves. We need to stick to the facts. We have it from Maryam that Max did not contact anyone about obtaining fake documents."

Jane knew that Warwick was trying to offer reassurance. Of course, Warwick couldn't possibly know whether Maryam had been telling the truth, or whether Max had concealed the truth from Maryam. Her words offered Jane little comfort, but at least Norah seemed calmer.

"What now?" Jane said. "I can't just sit here waiting for news."

"That is exactly what you are going to do," Warwick said, looking from Jane to Norah and back. "Leave this with us."

"Do you have any ideas?" Jane said, exasperated.

"We'll do everything necessary to find your son."

Then, to Jane's astonishment, Steph stood up and crossed the room to kneel before them. "We will find Patrick. Please . . . just . . . wait, and put your trust in us." Jane looked at Warwick, open-mouthed, overcome by the apparent kindness and concern in the DI's eyes. Reluctantly, she nodded.

"Good," Warwick said, her manner brisk again. "We'll be in touch. Don't get up. Elias and I have been here often enough now to know where the door is."

When the door closed behind them, Norah turned to Jane. "Whatever happened to DI Bitchy McBitchface?"

"I have no idea," Jane said. She shook her head. "I just hope this new version of DI Warwick is as efficient as the old one."

CHAPTER TWENTY-NINE

"So, what do you think?"

They had barely reached the top of the steps leading to the pavement above Bell's front door when Elias asked the question.

"Worst case scenario? Bell's hunch is right and Patrick's got himself in over his head. He disappeared after lunch with his colleagues. We should speak with them first."

Immediately upon their arrival at the station, Steph called PCs Joey Fairbairn and Olena Melnyk to her office. After briefing them on Patrick Bell's disappearance, she tasked them with contacting Sue Sellars, Iain MacDonald, Jacob Abbot and Grace Toyne. "Ask them about Patrick's frame of mind at the meal, how much he had to drink, who was last to leave the pub. Did he say where he was going afterwards? Did he talk about Max or mention anything about the investigation into his murder? Anything that might help us work out where he might have gone when he left home later that evening."

PC Fairbairn was the first to report back. He had spoken with Jacob Abbot and Sue Sellars. "They both gave similar accounts, ma'am. The mood all round had been gloomy beforehand. Once at the pub, everyone was trying to make an effort to get in the Christmas spirit. They tried to avoid dwelling on Max Barsby's murder, and the assault on Dr Crow, but the topics were touched on from time to time. Iain MacDonald left earlier than the others, who all left at the same time, around two o'clock. Patrick said he was going home. Sellars described him as being tipsy, but not drunk."

Melnyk had something potentially more useful to report. "Grace Toyne bumped into Patrick on Castle Square at around four thirty to four forty-five yesterday. They didn't speak for long, but when I pressed Grace to remember what they talked about, she said Patrick had mentioned that he felt sorry for Iain MacDonald. Apparently, after Iain left the pub, Sue Sellars had told them all that Iain had recently come out of a messy divorce with nothing much to show for it.

"Grace told him not to feel too sorry for Iain because she'd seen him with Dr Bianca Carr and was sure they were an item. Patrick seemed very interested to hear the news. Grace reckoned he hurried off down Steep Hill as if on a mission."

"Bianca Carr," Steph said. "She was Max Barsby's personal tutor at the university. I can see why Patrick would have found Toyne's news every bit as interesting as I do. What did you get from MacDonald?"

"MacDonald didn't answer his phone," Melnyk said. "According to Grace, he was intending to catch a train to his sister's that evening."

"Where does his sister live?" Steph asked.

Melnyk looked shamefaced. "Sorry, ma'am. I didn't ask."

"Call Sue Sellars immediately and ask her if she knows the sister's name and contact details. If she doesn't know, see if you can find out. Call MacDonald's ex-wife if you have to."

"Yes, ma'am." Melnyk went off to do Steph's bidding.

Steph thought aloud. "Patrick didn't go back to Danesgate after he spoke with Toyne. Where did he go? He'd just heard that Iain MacDonald and Bianca Carr were an item, and that interested him, as well it might."

"This means that Carr is connected with the dig through her relationship with MacDonald," Elias said. "When we interviewed Carr the day after Max was murdered, she didn't mention that Max was volunteering at the dig, yet there's a good chance she knew. You have to wonder why she kept quiet about it. Do you think Patrick might have gone to the university to ask Carr some questions?"

"He's an idiot if he did. He should have come to us first," Steph said. She checked herself. Patrick Bell was missing. If he'd done something foolish and put himself in danger, that was irrelevant now.

Melnyk came back to them with the news that Sue Sellars couldn't help with any details about MacDonald's sister. "Sorry ma'am. Do you want me to keep digging?"

"Yes," Steph said. And, to Joey Fairbairn, "See what else you can uncover about MacDonald and Carr." And then to Elias, "Let's see if we can catch Carr at the university."

A short drive later and Steph and Elias arrived at Carr's place of work. Unfortunately, Carr was not at her office, but the visit was not wasted. Steph tracked down the security team responsible for the building where Carr worked and asked to look at CCTV footage for the previous day. She wanted to know if her hunch about Patrick going to see Carr had been correct.

"Slow it down," she said, when the guard assisting them located the approximate time of Patrick's arrival, which Steph had calculated based on how long it would have taken him to walk to the university after leaving Grace Toyne on Castle Square. "There he is. He's entering the lift. Can we switch the view to the fifth floor?"

It took a bit of fiddling, but the security guard was able to locate Patrick striding down the corridor to Carr's office. Outside, Patrick stopped and leaned in towards the door.

"The door's slightly ajar, can you see?" Elias said. "He's listening."

All three watched as Patrick stood motionless for a few moments, then turned on his heel and hurried back down the corridor towards the lift.

"Want me to switch to the ground floor again?" the guard asked.

"No, wait a minute," Steph said. Soon, a dark-haired woman left the office and made for the lift. "That's Carr. Now take us downstairs."

With the view focussed again on the ground floor, they watched Carr emerge from the lift and leave the building. She headed off in the direction of the car park. Immediately, Patrick Bell appeared, as if from nowhere.

"Must have been hiding under the stairs," the guard said. "Out of view of the doors, and the lift."

They watched as Patrick also left the building, mobile phone in his hand. His fingers moved over the screen before he slipped the phone back in his trouser pocket. The security officer swapped to a view of the outside.

"What's he waiting for?" the guard said after a few moments of inaction on Patrick's part.

"I think he's just called an Uber," Elias said.

"Let's find out," Steph said. "Wind it on."

Elias was right. A car pulled up outside the building, an Uber sticker plainly visible on its side, and Patrick got in. As soon as the car began to pull away, Steph snapped at the security guard. "Zoom in on the registration number."

"Got it," Elias said.

Steph thanked the guard for his assistance, and she and Elias hurried back to their car. Within minutes of contacting the station and asking Joey to check the PNC for the registered keeper of the vehicle, they had the driver's details.

A quick check of the intelligence database gave them a contact phone number. Steph pulled out her phone. The driver remembered picking Patrick up. "Big lad. Yes. Where did I drop him? In the middle of nowhere." The middle of nowhere turned out to be a farm track within a few minutes' walk of the dig. "He must have overheard Carr talking on the phone and mentioning that she was going there," Steph said. "Was she meeting Iain MacDonald there, I wonder?"

"Where now?" Elias said. Steph knew what he was asking. Carr and MacDonald were now suspects for the murder of Max Barsby. They needed to be apprehended as soon as possible. But Patrick Bell was missing and might be injured, or worse.

"The dig," she said without hesitating. On the way, she called the station and arranged for both names to be circulated as wanted on the PNC, and requested that efforts be made to arrest MacDonald and Carr as soon as possible.

"Should we let Jane know?" Elias said.

Grim-faced, Steph caught his eye. "Not until we know the worst."

CHAPTER THIRTY

Jerry Roadknight was waiting to open the gates when they arrived at the dig. With Linus Crow still recovering in hospital, he had been contacted regarding access. "What's going on?" he asked as Steph got out of the car. "Is it something to do with the assault on Linus?"

"No," Steph snapped. "A young man is missing. Patrick Bell, one of the volunteers on the dig. We need to search the site."

Roadknight looked perplexed. "But why would he be here? Everyone finished work yesterday for the holiday."

Steph ignored Roadknight's question and addressed the four PCs who had just arrived and stepped out of their two separate vehicles. "We are looking for a white male, six foot four. His name is Patrick Bell. He might be injured or incapacitated in some way. Spread out and search the dig site and the adjoining fields. Stay in contact and, if you find him, alert me or my sergeant immediately."

The PCs dispersed in a chorus of 'Yes, ma'ams'.

Roadknight let Steph and Elias into the portacabin. Unsurprisingly, Patrick wasn't there. As they stepped back outside, another response car pulled up. Steph directed the latest recruits to the field west of the dig.

She took a moment to survey the wide, flat expanse of open fields, her eyes coming to rest on the wooded area over to the east of the dig — Boultham Mere nature reserve, a sanctuary for birds and other wildlife, with a large, secluded lake. Elias must have caught the direction of her gaze.

"You're thinking he might be in the woods over there?"

"Let's hope not," Steph said. "I'm hoping that if he's here at all, he'll be easy to find on this flat terrain. It would take hours and far more resources to search the woods." She deliberately avoided mentioning the lake, though she knew it would be in Elias's mind as it was in hers.

Steph was aware of all the resources she could summon to assist her in the search for Patrick. If need be, she would contact PolSA to ask a police search adviser for advice. She could also request a drone to search for any heat sources in the area, but she held back for now, hoping that Patrick would be found quickly.

The sound of a vehicle approaching caught her attention, and, turning back to the portacabin, she was relieved to see another response vehicle pull up. *Good. The more the better.*

There were now ten people searching, fanning out to cover the area. Even so, it would take time to comb the fields. Flat as the landscape appeared, and although there were no tall crops growing at this time of year, there were ditches and hidden dips where an injured person might lie unseen until you were up close.

The weather wasn't helping either. It was a miserable day for searching outdoors. Heavy rain had fallen in the night, and still persisted, not heavy now, but dogged, driven by a cutting wind blowing unchecked over the open fields. At least it was milder than it had been the previous day, and overnight.

After twenty minutes, Steph's radio crackled.

"PC Niall Stone here, ma'am. We've come across some disturbed ground. Looks like someone's been digging here recently."

Steph's heart lurched. A scene played out in her head in which she informed Jane Bell that her son's body had been discovered, freshly buried in a desolate field. She dispelled it immediately. All the same, her whole body sang with relief at PC Stone's next words.

"It doesn't look like a grave, ma'am. Too shallow."

"Where are you?" Steph said.

PC Stone shared his location, one field over from where she and Elias were searching. If it hadn't been for a prickly looking hedgerow, they might have been able to see him. They walked as fast as conditions would allow. The field was a quagmire. Mud clung to their boots, turning them into leaden weights, making every step hard won. Steph swore as she slipped, nearly losing her footing.

When, at last, they joined PC Stone and his colleague, Stone showed them the mound of earth that had given rise to his theory that someone had been digging there. They caught another break — despite the rain, footprints were discernible in the churned-up mud around the mound.

"Two sets of footprints, we think, ma'am, and two sets on the other side of the hedge."

Steph nodded. "Show me."

The third set of footprints was larger than the others. "Looks like a giant made these," Stone commented. "This Patrick we're looking for is a big lad, isn't he?" He pointed. "The prints end in a ditch just over there, then start up again on the other side. We found this in the ditch." Stone held out a sodden handkerchief. There was some sort of design in one corner.

Steph rubbed away the mud to reveal an embroidered letter P. He'd been here, then, Patrick. Where was he now? Steph's eyes followed the direction of the footprints heading eastwards to Boultham Mere.

PC Stone saw her look. "That's Ballast Holes over there," he said, giving the wetland its other name. The area had been excavated as a source of ballast for the railway line in the nineteenth century, and the pits created in the process had filled and swollen into a large lake. "I used to fish in there with my dad years ago before they turned it into a nature reserve."

Steph was filled with a sense of dread. With a heavy heart, she gave Elias an instruction. "Put a call in to Force Control Room to contact the underwater search unit supervisor so that the team can be held on standby if we need to search the lake."

CHAPTER THIRTY-ONE

Jane was going out of her mind with worry.

"We can't just sit here," Norah said for the umpteenth time. Her daughter's words were an echo of Jane's own thoughts, but she kept them to herself.

"Why hasn't DI Warwick got back to us yet? It's been over an hour."

Jane was silent. She'd already explained to Norah that Warwick was likely too busy, or had no information for them yet.

"I'm sorry," Norah said. "I know you're upset too. I'm sorry I keep going on."

Jane hugged her daughter tighter. Tired of pacing, they were now sitting on the sofa, huddled together for comfort. When Norah seemed calmer, Jane rose. "I'll make us a cup of tea." She needed to do something. As she waited for the kettle to boil, she considered calling Allie to come over to sit with Norah, so that she could join the search for Patrick. But what would be the point? She had no idea where to start looking.

Jane wished she knew what had prompted Patrick to go out again when he woke from his nap. None of his friends had heard from him, so he hadn't gone out socially.

Think, Jane, think. Patrick must have been following a lead. If only he had said more to Norah when he returned from the pub. Had he discovered something at the dig just before going there? Jane had told him what John Headley said about Max bringing the aureus to him. Patrick had agreed not to mention this to anyone at the dig, but had he changed his mind? It didn't make sense. If Patrick had stumbled upon some new lead, he wouldn't have drunk so much at the pub that he had to come home and sleep for an hour or two before following it up.

"Mum!" Norah's voice, urgent.

"What is it?" Jane hurried into the sitting room.

"Your phone's ringing. Didn't you hear it?"

"The kettle was boiling." Jane snatched her phone from Norah. "Hello?"

Norah grabbed Jane's arm. "Put it on loudspeaker."

"DI Warwick here. We've found something that we think might belong to Patrick. A white handkerchief with an embroidered letter P. Can you confirm that he owned one of these?"

"What? Where? Where did you find it?" Jane couldn't make sense of what Warwick was saying at first. "Yes, yes. Patrick has some monogrammed handkerchiefs. I give him a pack every year at Christmas." Jane's eyes flicked to the Christmas tree, where this year's pack lay wrapped up ready for Christmas. Her eyes blurred. She heard Warwick's calming voice in her ear, as if in a dream.

"Jane, I need you to take a breath. We haven't found Patrick yet. We've been searching some fields near the dig and we've found the handkerchief. We're going to continue searching, and I'll let you know as soon as we find him."

"The dig," Jane said. "Patrick was at the dig last night . . ."

There was the slightest pause. Jane guessed that Warwick had probably not intended to reveal the location.

"Yes. We have some reason to believe that he was here. I need you to stay where you are and wait for news, Jane. Jane? Can you hear me?"

"Yes," Jane said at last. "Stay here and wait for news."

No chance.

"Good," Warwick said. "I'll be in touch."

As soon as the call ended, Jane said, "I'm going to call Allie round to stay with you while I go to the dig."

Norah flashed her a rebellious look. "Oh no you're not. I'm coming with you."

CHAPTER THIRTY-TWO

"How confident are you that she won't be down here within the next ten minutes?" Elias said, when Steph had finished speaking with Jane Bell.

"Not confident at all." Steph sighed. "I need to radio for more assistance to search the nature reserve." For a moment, she was uncertain. "If we don't find Patrick soon, I'll have to call in a diving team."

PC Stone shook his head. "Let's hope it doesn't come to that." There was no need for him to elaborate. The minute Steph called in a diving team, they would be searching for a body.

Stone spoke again. "Not many people come to these woods. They aren't well known, even locally. I walk the dog there sometimes. There's a bird hide overlooking the mere. If he took shelter there, he'd at least have had a bit of protection from the weather overnight."

"Do you know where it is?" When PC Stone answered that he did, she said, "Show us."

Stone led them across the field to the catchwater, which they followed for a short distance before entering the wood. Steph was immediately struck by the sense of quietness and seclusion within. She knew they were only a short distance from the city centre, and that they were close to the railway and the Foss Dyke, Lincoln's ancient canal, but she had never been here before now. She had only ever caught fleeting glimpses of the woods fringing the nature reserve from the windows of a train. She had never given much thought to what lay beyond the dense screen of willow and sallow.

They pressed on, deeper into the wood. The mere, with its beds of reed and sage, soon became visible through the trees. It seemed alive with overwintering wildfowl. Catching sight of the water, Steph asked PC Stone, "Are we nearing the hide now?" She felt as restless and impatient as a child on a long car journey.

Stone pointed. "It's just up ahead."

Steph followed the direction of his pointing finger. Catching sight of it, she felt foolish for having missed the wooden structure straight ahead of her. Now that they were here, she felt a sense of dread. Again, she envisaged having to tell Jane Bell that her son was dead.

"Ma'am?" Stone said.

Steph hadn't even realised that she'd stopped. Stone and Elias were slightly ahead of her on the path. Now they looked back questioningly. Steph took a breath and joined them, but as they approached the hide, she dropped back again to let Stone be the first to enter.

Even before Stone called out, Steph could see that there was someone inside, lying on the floor, covered by some sort of blanket.

"It's him," Stone said. He knelt by the prone figure and reached out to touch Patrick's neck. "He's alive."

A sense of relief swept over Steph. The others felt it too, she could see. While Elias radioed for assistance, Steph stepped inside the hide. She noticed a heap of folded-up clothes on the floor next to Patrick. They looked wet.

"What's his condition?"

"I think he's stable. Maybe mildly hypothermic. I'd say that blanket did him a big favour, kept him warm enough to prevent him deteriorating. And he had the sense to change out of his wet clothes."

At his words, Patrick stirred and opened his eyes. He looked at each of them in turn with an expression of confusion, before focussing on Steph. "MacDonald . . . Carr . . . killed Max for the treasure . . . saw them . . . digging it up—"

"Easy, lad. No need for you to worry about that for now," Stone said. He removed his jacket and placed it over Patrick.

Steph stifled her frustration. She wanted to find out what Patrick knew, but he was in no condition to answer questions. Suddenly, she remembered she had not informed Jane Bell that her son had been found. She took out her phone.

At that moment, she heard a woman's voice calling out loudly, "Elias!" Every bird on the lake took startled flight.

Steph emerged from the hide to see Jane Bell charging along the woodland path towards an equally startled Elias.

"Have you found him. Is he in there?" Bell sounded on the verge of hysteria.

"Yes," Warwick said, stepping out of the hide to make way for Bell, who had now been joined by her daughter. "He's alive. Help is on its way."

Before long, Patrick was being wrapped in a foil blanket, stretchered out of the hide and carried through the woods to a waiting ambulance. Bell and her daughter intended to follow in Bell's car.

"Thank you," Bell said as they all stood in the field on the edge of the wood, watching the ambulance lumber off through the mud to pick up the track for the main road. "Thank you for finding him."

Steph mumbled that she had just been doing her job.

"Oh, for goodness' sake," Bell said, sounding perplexed, and before Steph knew what was happening, Bell had gripped her by the shoulders and pulled her into a tight hug.

Steph was too astonished to react. She stood rigid for as long as the embrace lasted, holding her breath. No one had touched her in a long time. After what seemed like an eternity, Bell released her and turned to Norah, who was standing nearby, talking to Elias. Mother and daughter walked away together.

Watching them depart, Steph muttered. "I swear I have no idea what part of being told to stay at home and wait for news that woman didn't understand."

CHAPTER THIRTY-THREE

Steph pondered over whether Patrick's claim that MacDonald and Carr had murdered Max Barsby 'for the treasure', which he claimed to have seen them digging up, was sufficient grounds for her to arrest the pair. For one thing, it was questionable whether Patrick had been of sound mind when he made his claim. She decided to go ahead — if MacDonald and Carr were digging in an isolated field under cover of darkness, they must have been up to no good.

Her case was strengthened when PC Melnyk reported back to Steph after her attempts to trace Iain MacDonald's sister. MacDonald didn't have a sister, and he wasn't at his rented flat in Lincoln. His present whereabouts were unknown.

After leaving the dig, Steph and Elias drove to Dr Bianca Carr's home, a modest ground-floor flat on West Parade.

"She's at home," Elias remarked, pointing to a brightly lit Christmas tree at the window of the flat. As luck would have it, a postman, carrying a parcel, approached the door of the house just as Steph and Elias got out of their car. Carr would not be suspicious of the postman. They hung back until she opened the door.

Carr's eyes travelled over the postman's shoulder as she accepted her parcel. It was obvious she recognised Steph and

Elias from her previous interview with them. When the postman withdrew, she spoke to them.

"Hello, Inspector Warwick and . . ." She looked at Elias, frowning.

"Sergeant Harper," Elias said.

"Have you come about Max? I hope you have positive news," Carr said.

"May we come in?" Steph asked.

Carr seemed hesitant. "I'm rather busy."

I wasn't really asking your permission. Steph kept her comment to herself. "It won't take long."

Carr moved aside. It was a small flat. She led them into a cramped living room. She placed her parcel on a pine table that was obviously used as a desk and for dining — with the space being roughly divided between the two. At one end was a laptop. At the other end, four round hessian table mats were stacked in a pile, with matching coasters on top. The rest of the space in the room was filled with two small sofas arranged on either side of a pine coffee table, and two bookcases, one in each alcove on either side of the fireplace. A door led through to the kitchen.

Carr seemed a little nervous now. She hesitated, as if unsure whether to ask them to sit down. Then, she sat down on a chair at the table and waved her hands at them to join her.

"I'll get straight to the point," Steph said. "A witness reports seeing you and Iain MacDonald yesterday evening, digging in a field near the site of the archaeological dig that MacDonald is currently working on. The witness saw you pulling what looked like a large, bulging rucksack out of the ground."

Carr swallowed. She stared at her laptop. "What witness?"

"It doesn't matter," Steph said. "Tell us why you were digging up a rucksack after dark when you thought you were unobserved. What was in the rucksack?"

"Your witness must be mistaken," Carr said stiffly. "I was at home all evening, and then I went to bed. Why on earth would I be digging in a field in the middle of nowhere?"

"That's my question," Steph said. She leaned forward. "Look, we know you were there. This is what I think. I think you were digging up artefacts stolen from the dig. What happened, Bianca? Did Max Barsby find out what you were up to? Did he confront you concerning this?" Steph dropped her tone. She laced it with menace. "Did you and MacDonald kill Max to shut him up when he threatened to report you?"

"Kill Max?" Carr looked from Steph to Elias and back again, clearly at a loss for words. She teared up. "I was fond of Max. I would never have done anything to hurt him. How can you say that?"

Putting on a good show? Or is she genuinely shocked? Carr hadn't reacted with anger but disbelief, and what seemed like grief. Steph began to doubt herself. She gave Elias a nod. "Do you give your consent to my sergeant searching your flat?"

Elias stood up. "I'll start in the bedroom."

"No!" Carr cried out. "You need to have a warrant for that, don't you?"

Steph turned to Carr. "Well, I could arrest you first, and then apply for a search warrant."

There was the sound of a door opening and closing. Footsteps in the hall. Elias leaped for the door, followed by Steph. They were just in time to see Iain MacDonald, a large rucksack slung over his shoulder, unlocking the front door to make his escape. Elias moved fast to grab him by the arm. He guided MacDonald into the living room with a light but firm touch. Once inside, he pushed him gently onto one of the sofas.

"Ah," Steph said. "The elusive Dr MacDonald. How's your sister?"

MacDonald's face was thunderous, but his expression softened when he looked at Carr. "I'm sorry, Bianca. You were right. We should have left it in the ground for a bit longer."

Carr made a sobbing sound. "They're accusing us of murdering Max. We need to confess to what we've done, and then they might believe that we had nothing to do with Max's death."

As if spurred on by Carr's tearful plea, MacDonald began to unzip the rucksack.

Steph's eyes widened as MacDonald carefully emptied the contents across the floor in front of him. She heard Carr give a low, pained moan, presumably of regret, as coins — gold, silver, bronze — spilled across the carpet in a seemingly unending stream. Not finished yet, MacDonald then undid the larger compartment of the rucksack and pulled out jewellery and other items — bracelets, brooches by the look of them — all solid gold.

When, at last, the rucksack was empty, MacDonald tossed it onto one of the sofas and went to stand by Carr. She was sobbing openly now. MacDonald pressed her shoulder. Then, he turned a steely eye on Steph. "We're thieves, Inspector, but we're not killers, and we can prove it. You'll have to find someone else to pin Max's murder on."

"How did you conceal your finds from the others on the dig?" Steph asked.

MacDonald answered the question. "I didn't find these things on the dig. I went off across the fields one lunchtime to stretch my legs and tripped over something sticking out of a furrow — a large stone. I'd turned my ankle and I bent down to rub it. And there it was."

MacDonald broke off for a moment as he too gazed, sadly, at the treasure. "A gold bracelet — a torque."

Now MacDonald looked shamefaced as he revealed that he had not informed anyone of his discovery. "I went back to the field that evening with my metal detector. That was when I found" — he spread his arms to encompass the treasure — "all this."

There was a silence as they all gazed upon the wonderful things on the carpet. Steph could only imagine how thrilling it must have felt to find such a hoard. "Go on," she said again.

"I took some of the coins and left the rest in situ."

"Iain brought the coins to me at the university," Carr said. "At the precise moment he took them from his bag to show me, who should knock on the door and walk into my office but Max Barsby? He'd never walked in without waiting for an invitation before. He took one look at Iain and understood exactly what was going on. Max was nothing if not smart. It didn't matter that the coins weren't found on the dig."

"What happened then?" Steph asked.

MacDonald and Carr exchanged a look. Carr spoke. "We had no intention of declaring Iain's find. We had to get Max on our side." Carr paused to take a deep breath. "We made a deal with Max."

Steph thought she could guess what Carr was going to say. She was right.

"You know about Maryam?" Carr asked.

"Max's girlfriend?" Steph said. "Yes. We do."

"Then you are aware of her status?"

"Yes."

"Max told me about her in one of our meetings. I'd noticed that he seemed unhappy, and I asked him if something was wrong. It all came pouring out. He was so desperate to help her."

Steph nodded, feeling angry. "You took advantage of his vulnerability. You threatened to report Maryam to the authorities if Max reported your theft. You promised him your silence in return for his."

Carr looked hurt. "He got more out of it than that. I was sympathetic to the plight of Max and his lover. I—"

Steph understood. "We were told that Max had come into possession of a gold coin. An aureus. You gave it to him as a bribe."

"Not a bribe as such. I genuinely wanted to help Max and Maryam," Carr insisted.

Steph felt a twinge of sadness. She'd hoped that the aureus had been a fable, that John Headley had made it up. If Carr was telling the truth, it meant that Max had been complicit in MacDonald and Carr's crime. It must have broken his heart to betray his ideals. The only consolation was that he'd at least done it out of love, not greed like this pair.

Carr gazed down at the treasure on her carpet, a look of sadness in her eyes. She looked at Steph and Elias. "It's probably worth millions, you know."

Grim-faced, Steph looked at the pair of them. "Yes, well, you two can kiss goodbye to whatever plans you had for selling this loot and living the high life on the proceeds. You'll be facing a fine and a prison sentence instead. That's if you're telling the truth about being able to prove you didn't murder Max Barsby. If not, you'll be facing a murder charge. Not to mention assault. I've been reliably informed that the man who called an ambulance for Linus Crow immediately after he was attacked spoke with a very distinct Scottish accent."

Unsurprisingly, MacDonald declined to comment.

Steph cautioned the pair of them and arrested them.

MacDonald protested. "It's almost Christmas."

Steph gave him a thunderous look. "Christmas is cancelled."

CHAPTER THIRTY-FOUR

It's almost Christmas! Steph was luxuriating in a foaming, scented bath. Soporific music drifted dreamily down from her mobile phone on the window ledge. It was all supposed to be boosting her alpha activity and promoting feelings of deep relaxation and calm for the day ahead, but all Steph could think of was Iain MacDonald and his peevish comment after she arrested him. *The cheek of the man!* As if he had a right to a wonderful Christmas.

Steph had stayed late at the station the previous night, making sure that Bianca Carr and Iain MacDonald were processed and settled into their accommodation. Prior to being locked up, they had been interviewed separately. Each had related the same story of how, after MacDonald had found the treasure, they had agreed to rebury it and wait for a 'safe' time to dig it up again.

Unfortunately, MacDonald had panicked after Max Barsby's body was found and the police started sniffing around the dig. He persuaded Carr of the need to dig the treasure up sooner rather than later. The intention had been to sell the treasure to carefully selected dealers across the world — those who would have no qualms about handling stolen goods. Then, they would use the proceeds of their crime to disappear and live out their lives in luxury abroad, perhaps under assumed identities.

Steph had almost felt sorry about scuppering their dreams. Almost.

For the time being, Carr and MacDonald had been charged with theft. The CPS would authorise other types of charges, as appropriate following a review of the evidence.

Steph was aware that she must now decide whether there was sufficient evidence to charge them with the murder of Max Barsby, but she could put this off until their new alibi had been investigated.

There was motive — Max had discovered their secret, and they stood to lose a fortune unless they silenced him. As for opportunity, neither Carr nor MacDonald had provided a satisfactory alibi for the time of Max's murder. Both had claimed to be at home alone. But they'd changed their stories as soon as they had become credible murder suspects.

Now both contested that, far from being alone on the night of Max Barsby's murder, they had spent that night together at the Petwood Hotel in Woodhall Spa. They had arrived in the early evening and enjoyed a stroll in the grounds before having an intimate dinner to celebrate Iain's birthday. Afterwards, they had sat in the bar emptying a bottle of champagne before retiring to their room around ten thirty. They had not mentioned any of this before, partly because they'd wanted to keep their relationship a secret, and partly because it would allow the police to connect them to each other, and to Max.

A feeling of unease had crept through Steph on hearing their revised account. It would have to be checked out, of course, but it would be so easy to prove false that she was inclined to believe they were telling the truth. If so, Carr and MacDonald would be in the clear, and the investigation into Max's murder would drag on, unresolved, into the New Year.

Steph pulled the plug on her bath, stepped out and reached for her phone to turn off the music. As she donned her bathrobe, she cursed the way the investigation had played out in the early stages. Max's grief-stricken parents had failed to mention details that they had subsequently mentioned to Jane Bell. It had been embarrassing to learn second-hand about Max's friendship with John Headley and about his work at the dig. Not to mention the delays that had been caused by Bell's failing to inform the police about Maryam.

Then there had been the interview with Bianca Carr. Steph worried that she had missed some small detail in what Carr had said, or something telling in her demeanour that might have raised suspicions about her honesty. Carr had deliberately omitted any mention that Max was working on the dig, and she had not told them about Max's relationship with Maryam. On the other hand, she had been quick to mention the notorious Vindolanda incident involving Harry Scott, no doubt to deflect attention from herself.

Still wrapped in her bathrobe, Steph crossed the landing to her bedroom, where she spent ten minutes blow-drying her hair. Afterwards, she threw on a dark teal cashmere jumper and tailored black jacket and trousers. Her make-up routine took minutes. She wasn't in a rush to get to work — it had been gone midnight by the time she got home the night before, so she made sure she had time for breakfast and coffee.

The first thing that caught her eye when she came downstairs to her kitchen was the beautiful bouquet of flowers that her neighbour had left at her back door the previous evening, after sticking a note through her front door to alert her to its presence. It was from the Bells — a thank you for finding Patrick. Elias had texted her to say that he'd received one too. Steph removed the flowers from the bowl in her kitchen sink, arranged them in a vase and moved them into her living room.

When she checked her phone, Steph found a recently sent text from Jane Bell thanking her again. The message ended with a string of seemingly random emojis, followed by a second text apologising for the emojis. Steph simultaneously rolled her eyes and smiled.

She was washing up her breakfast dishes when her phone rang. Elias. "Sorry to bother you at home, boss. I've just had a call from the enquiry office. Darya Shirvani just turned up asking to speak with you. Want me to speak with her? Or would you rather—"

Steph interrupted. "Make her a drink and wait with her. I'll be there in ten."

Now what?

CHAPTER THIRTY-FIVE

Steph was astonished to find not just Darya Shirvani but also Maryam Bandari waiting for her at the station.

Darya began by apologising. "I am so sorry to bother you this close to the holiday."

"Has something happened?" Steph asked.

"I would have just reported it at the desk," Darya began hesitantly. Her gaze flitted to Maryam.

Steph reassured her. "I understand that you would have been reluctant to do that if it involved Maryam."

"We've been receiving notes pushed through my letter-box. Threatening notes saying that Maryam's time in this country is up, and that if she does not declare herself to the authorities, there will be serious consequences."

"Did you keep the notes?" Steph asked.

Darya searched in her handbag and produced three pieces of paper, which she passed to Steph. All three were addressed to '*The illegal alien*'.

As Steph shuffled the notes in her hand, Darya pointed to the order in which they should be read. Steph's frown deepened as she read the third note, which like the others contained a threat of consequences if Maryam did not declare herself to the authorities, but with one crucial escalation in tone — the third note also contained a death threat.

If you do not make yourself known to the authorities by 1 January, you will die.

"This is very — disquieting," Steph said. She sighed, knowing that it would be difficult to provide protection for Maryam without revealing her illegal status. She looked at Maryam. The young woman seemed subdued, as though she'd lost some of her fighting spirit. It saddened Steph to see her like that.

Steph passed the notes to Elias without mentioning to the two women that they would be held for forensic analysis. Then, she made a decision.

"Look, I need to know that the two of you are safe. Is there somewhere you can stay for a few days?"

"Yes," Darya said. "I have a caravan in Mablethorpe. We can go there."

"Good," Steph said. "That will give me a chance to assess the threat to your safety without having to ask you to fill in any official paperwork. But I can't make you any promises. The threat is very specific, and I have to take it seriously. If I'm obliged to obtain the resources necessary for your protection, or if it comes down to taking action against the individual responsible, it might involve having to reveal your status, Maryam."

When Maryam merely shrugged, Darya replied, "We understand. Thank you for your kindness, Inspector Warwick."

Maryam said nothing. She looked at Steph, her eyes empty. It was as though she had already accepted her fate.

Steph hoped that she could find some way of helping Maryam without having to reveal the young woman's secret.

The two women left the station. They would call at Darya's house only long enough to collect what they needed for a few days away, and then drive to the coast.

Steph voiced her thoughts to Elias after they'd gone. "The trouble is, at the moment, I can't see any way of resolving this without revealing Maryam's secret. And, if we manage to catch the perpetrator, they will almost certainly spill the beans about her status. I think Maryam realises this, but she knows that she can't ignore a death threat. Apart from the risk to her own safety, it wouldn't be fair to Darya."

"What if she decides to do a runner?" Elias said. "Move somewhere else and start again?"

"That had occurred to me," Steph admitted. She thought of how Maryam had presented. How quiet and resigned she'd seemed. Would she be able to summon up the energy to run, to start all over again?

"So, want me to trawl through the more recent CCTV footage around Darya's address? Find out if Harry Scott's been back there playing postman?" Elias asked.

There was no one else to assign the job to — the fewer people who knew about this the better.

Steph nodded. "Thanks, Elias. Check some of the previous footage too. It's unlikely, but Joey might have missed something."

While Elias set to work, Steph busied herself with paperwork relating to the arrest of Bianca Carr and Iain MacDonald. A few hours later, there was a tap on her door. She looked up to see Elias standing in her doorway. "Have you found something?"

Elias nodded. "Joey missed something. Someone else was following Max. A woman with dark hair."

Steph looked at him with a puzzled frown. Then, her eyes widened. "The woman with the dark hair from the Brayford. You've identified her?"

Elias gave a grim smile. "I think so, yes. Let's see if you agree."

"Show me."

To be fair to Joey, it would not have been obvious that the woman was following Max. As she watched, Steph had to concede, grudgingly, that the dark-haired woman's shadowing skills were worthy of a trained spy. She kept just the right distance away, and even walked along looking at her mobile phone. When Max disappeared inside Darya's house, she walked right past Darya's door without a second glance.

Elias had also scrutinised video footage of the days after Harry had been spotted. "This is from a couple of days after Harry followed Max. Joey wouldn't have checked this far on."

It was the same woman again. She was dressed in wide, billowy trousers and a loose-fitting hooded jacket. She approached Darya Shirvani's house, as before. But, this time, she remained on the other side of the street and slipped through the gate of the house opposite Darya's, which had a 'For Sale' sign in the garden.

Steph felt a jolt of recognition. "She's dressed in the same clothes as the woman who met Max in the bar on the Brayford. Are you going to tell me who she is, Elias? You must know by now that patience isn't one of my virtues."

"So," Elias said, drawing it out, "fortunately for us, she forgot to check for surveillance cameras on the empty property. Rookie mistake." The view on the screen shifted to show the woman in the garden. Elias zoomed in on her face.

Steph gasped. "Sophie Egan!"

"Yes." Elias wound the tape on three hours. "Got to hand it to her. She was prepared for a long stake-out."

Steph watched with surprise as Elias zoomed in again to show Sophie pulling a small pair of binoculars from her pocket. She trained them on the upstairs bedroom window of Darya's house.

"Watch this," Elias said. They both watched as Sophie lowered the binoculars. She took a few steps backwards, folded over, as though in pain. Then, straightening up, she threw the binoculars to the ground and kicked them as if in a rage.

"Guess she saw something that upset her," Steph said dryly.

Elias gave a wry smile. "Hmm. What was that, do you think?" There was no need for either of them to state the obvious.

Elias then moved the tape on to the date when, according to Darya, the first threatening note had been received. There was Sophie, caught on camera on the street leading to Darya's. She turned at the corner.

Steph shook her head. "I think we might have found our killer. Max met Sophie in that bar on the Brayford. Did she then lead him to his death? If so, her motive was the oldest in the world, and the same one that propelled Harry Scott to push Max onto the campfire at Vindolanda."

Elias nodded. "Jealousy."

CHAPTER THIRTY-SIX

When Elias turned off the footage, Steph's mood darkened. "It seems that killing Max didn't satisfy Sophie. She's going after Maryam now. Beatrice Egan gave her daughter an alibi. Either she was deceived in some way, or she lied. We need to get her to talk."

Steph arranged for a response vehicle to meet them outside the Egans' house in Hull. She was keen to make an arrest that afternoon, whether or not Beatrice Egan changed her story about her daughter's whereabouts on the night of Max Barsby's murder.

The drive from Lincoln to Hull seemed endless. Steph fidgeted constantly. To have made a major breakthrough in the investigation and then have to sit through a long and tedious car journey before being able to act on it was unbearable. Elias didn't seem similarly afflicted.

"Wish I'd remembered to eat something earlier. Should have grabbed my turkey and cranberry sandwiches from the fridge at work."

"I would have thought the adrenalin would take the edge off your hunger," Steph remarked.

Elias didn't reply. His stomach rumbled.

At last, the Humber Bridge loomed up in front of them and they sailed across, surprisingly unhindered by traffic. From there, time seemed to speed up.

The patrol car was already parked around the corner from the Egans' house when they arrived at their destination. Steph asked the two PCs to be on standby. Then, she and Elias approached the house.

There were four cars on the drive. "Full house," Steph said. "Seems a shame to spoil a happy family gathering, if that's what's going on." Elias gave her an admonishing look. "I'm not being wholly sarcastic, Elias," she reassured him.

The man who answered their ring gazed at them without recognition.

Steph introduced herself and Elias before asking, "Are you Mr Egan? Sophie Egan's father?"

From somewhere within the house came the sound of laughter. The man cast a look over his shoulder. He stepped forward, pulling the door behind him.

"What's this about?" he asked, with a look that was half anxious, half suspicious.

"We're investigating the murder of a young man who was a friend of Sophie's. His name was Max Barsby. We've been here before to interview your daughter, Sophie. Your wife, Beatrice, was present. Did she mention it to you?"

The suspicion in Mr Egan's face morphed into anger. "Can't this wait? We've got friends visiting."

"I'm afraid it can't wait, Mr Egan. We need to speak with your wife and daughter urgently."

At that moment, Beatrice Egan's voice called from the hallway. "Who is it, Clive? We're about to start another game of charades."

Clive Egan opened the door so that his wife could see who was on the doorstep.

Beatrice's face fell. "Oh. It's you again. What on earth are you doing here two days before Christmas? We've got friends round."

"It's about that murder again. The young lad Sophie knew at the university in Lincoln," Clive said.

Steph repeated her request to speak with Beatrice and Sophie, this time injecting her voice with a tone of authority.

"This is most inconvenient," Beatrice said. "Come in if you really must, but I hope it won't take long. Take them to the dining room, Clive. Sophie and I will join you in a minute. I just need to tell everyone what's going on." With an accusatory glare at Steph and Elias, she turned back into the hallway.

"Go with her, Sergeant," Steph said to Elias. "Make sure she brings Sophie with her."

Clive began to protest. "Now, hang on a minute. You can't just—"

Steph was losing her patience. "Yes. We can."

The dining room table was laid with what looked like the remnants of a festive buffet. You'd have thought it was Christmas already. The non-perishable leftovers — crisps and savoury bites, crackers, half a chocolate cake, and an assortment of other party staples — had been covered over with cling film. Streamers from party poppers littered the spaces between the plates. An empty magnum of champagne stood sentinel over the remains, reminding Steph of the celebration she was disrupting.

Elias returned with a stone-faced Beatrice, and Sophie, whose cheeks looked flushed. Her gait was slightly unsteady, causing Steph to wonder how much of that magnum Sophie had put away. Steph brushed some streamers from the seat nearest to her. "Shall we all sit down?"

Sophie reached for a plate of crisps and peeled off the cling film before helping herself to a handful. "Have you caught Max's killer, then?" she asked.

Steph ignored the question. "Where were you really on the night of the eighth of December, the night Max was murdered, Sophie? Please think carefully before you lie to us again."

Predictably, Beatrice leaped to her daughter's defence. "Are you calling my daughter a liar? Not to mention me. I told you Sophie was at home with us that night." Her gaze strayed momentarily to her husband's face. He frowned.

Was that a tell? Steph wondered. "Can you confirm what your wife just said, Mr Egan?"

When Clive seemed to hesitate, Beatrice prompted him. "Surely you don't even have to think about it, Clive? It's not as if Sophie's here that much during term time, is it? She was here because it was little Ferdy's birthday, and we were celebrating. Don't you remember?"

Steph remembered seeing Ferdy the French bulldog on their previous visit. She couldn't recall any mention of the dog's birthday. It was obvious that all this was news to Clive too, but he rallied and backed his wife up, if without any great sense of conviction. "I'm sure you're right, Bea."

"You know we can easily check the dog's birth date, right? He's a pedigree, isn't he? You mentioned taking him to Crufts a few years ago." Steph was blagging a bit, but she thought she recalled Jane Bell telling her that her friend's dog, Dudgeon, had a birth certificate.

Beatrice revealed a talent for thinking on her feet. "It wasn't his *actual* birthday we were celebrating. It was the day he entered our lives. The day he came to live with us. More an anniversary than a birthday, really."

Steph was growing tired of the charade. She turned to Sophie. "Let's try a different question. We have you on camera watching the home of Maryam Bandari and posting a threatening note through her letterbox. Care to comment?"

No response. Steph twisted the knife. "Maryam Bandari. Max's girlfriend. The woman he adored and loved."

Sophie started. Her fist clenched around the second handful of crisps to which she'd just helped herself, pulverising them. "That foreign bitch?" she hissed in a venomous tone.

"Sophie!" Beatrice said in a mildly reproachful voice. "Have you had too much champagne?"

"Oh, so you know who I'm talking about," Steph said. "I'm slightly puzzled, though. Harry didn't know about Maryam's illegal status. How did you find out?"

To Steph's intense annoyance, Beatrice butted in again. "All right. That's enough. I can tell you where Sophie really was that night. The eighth of December. She swore me to secrecy, but as things seem to be getting out of control here . . ." She looked at her daughter. "Sorry, Sophie, darling, but I think we need to be up front about it now that they're practically accusing you of murdering Max."

"No!" Sophie cried, but her mother got in before she could say any more.

"Sophie was with my husband's best friend, Dave Fairley. They were having an affair, and Sophie didn't want her dad to know. She only told me because she knew the police would be round asking about the boy's murder, and she was afraid Clive would get to hear about it, so I agreed we'd say Sophie was at home that night." She looked at her husband. "You were away on business that week, remember?"

Steph glanced at Clive Egan. He looked confused. "What the hell, Beatrice? Sophie and Dave? That's ridiculous. Dave's my age." He looked at his daughter. "Sophie?"

An urgent, staccato-like knocking at the kitchen door interrupted the proceedings. All eyes turned to look as a red-faced, middle-aged man strode into the room, a slightly shocked-looking woman by his side. Both were wearing party hats.

"I'm Dave Fairley," the man said. He pointed at Sophie. "And I categorically deny that I've ever had an affair with that young woman."

For a few moments no one said anything. Then, Beatrice spoke. "You've been listening at the door. How rude!"

Steph pushed back her chair and stood up. "All right, Mr Fairley. Thank you for letting us know. Now, Mr and Mrs Egan and Sophie are going to be with us for some time, so may I suggest that you and Mrs Fairley — and any other guests still in the other room — leave us to it?"

Mr Fairley nodded vigorously. "Too right. We're going. Come on, Rosemary." The couple began to back out of the room.

"I'll see you to the door," Beatrice said, making a move to get up.

"No need," Dave Fairley said decisively.

Steph addressed the Egans. "I said we were going to be here for some time, but you know what? There's really no need. Let's bring an end to this farce right now." She signalled to Elias, who got up and reached inside his jacket, from where he produced a pair of handcuffs. Beatrice gasped loudly as he cautioned her daughter.

Sophie shot a poisonous look at her mother. "You moron. All you needed to say was the same as we told Dad — that I was here all that evening, and that I stayed overnight. Only an idiot like you would believe I was having an affair with an ugly old fart like Dave Fairley."

Steph glanced at Beatrice. She looked confused and hurt. She really didn't get it. Sophie could have told her anything, and she would have believed it.

CHAPTER THIRTY-SEVEN

The year was drawing to a close when Jane and Patrick, at last, heard the full story behind the arrest of Sophie Egan for Max Barsby's murder.

It was New Year's Eve. Jane and Patrick, along with Norah, Ed and their usual group of friends, were at Veganbites for a private party hosted by Frieda and Karun Arya. Mostly everyone had arrived, except for DI Steph Warwick and DS Elias Harper. Elias had already filled Jane and Patrick in on some of the details of what had occurred since the arrest. In his most recent call, he had also thrown out some hints that Warwick would give them a fuller debriefing at the party. Jane was on tenterhooks.

There was a blast of cold air from the door. The late-comers had arrived. Warwick was wearing a plain black shift dress and sparkly earrings, and looked rather stunning. She was one of those deceptively plain people who scrubbed up astonishingly well. Elias looked smart in a pair of beige chinos and a white shirt, open at the neck. Jane noted Patrick's wistful sigh as he caught sight of Elias. Elias was straight, and besides, Patrick must have noticed the way the sergeant looked at his sister, Norah.

At a certain point in the course of the evening, the four managed to form a little huddle away from the others in the room. Patrick gave Warwick an old-fashioned bow and thanked her again for coming to his rescue.

"I trust you have thoroughly defrosted," Warwick said.

"Yes, and as much as that bird hide and the blankets left in there probably saved my bacon, I'm not becoming a twitcher any time soon. Or an archaeologist for that matter, although I might hang on to the fedora."

"Good to see you looking well," Elias said.

Patrick had already filled everyone in on how he had fallen into the catchwater, then into a ditch, turned his ankle and dislocated his shoulder. He'd dragged himself out of the ditch when he realised he was getting drowsy, and feared hypothermia might set in. Somehow, he'd made it to the woods before the pain in his ankle forced him to rest. By sheer luck, he'd stumbled on the bird hide and the blankets. He'd reasoned that he would stand a better chance of finding his way through the woods in the daylight.

"Did you both have a nice Christmas?" Jane asked, addressing Warwick and Elias.

Elias replied first, his voice full of warmth. "Lovely, thanks. I spent it with family. Ate and drank too much, played silly party games, all the usual stuff. How about you?"

"Same," Jane said, smiling at Patrick. "We were at Ed's house in Doveby. He'd decorated it beautifully, and he cooked an amazing Christmas lunch. We had a long walk over the fields on Boxing Day, followed by lunch with friends in the village pub, then a nice leftovers buffet supper in the evening in front of a cosy log fire. Perfect."

They all looked at Warwick, who cleared her throat and muttered something about having enjoyed a quiet day at home with a nice bottle of scotch.

Jane moved on quickly. "So, can you tell us more about the arrest, or is it still hush hush?"

"Sophie Egan has made a full confession," Warwick said. "The evidence kept mounting up until it became obvious to her legal representative that a confession would be her best option. She told us everything. The case won't go to trial."

"That's wonderful news for Max's family," Jane said.

Warwick agreed. "Yes. I suppose there's no harm in giving you some of the facts. Sophie's alibi was fake. We've now been able to trace more of her movements on CCTV to show that she'd been following Max, and later, Maryam. There were pictures of Max and Maryam on her phone, and we've been able to retrieve the message she sent to Max to arrange the meeting at the bar on the night he was murdered, despite her having deleted it."

"Excellent," Patrick said. "Oops. Sorry for interrupting. Please tell us more."

Steph resumed her account. "Most damningly, a search of Sophie's bedroom at the university uncovered a somewhat surprising murder weapon." Here Steph paused, before revealing what it was. "A solid brass teddy bear."

"A teddy bear?" Jane and Patrick said in unison.

"With a slot on its head to put coins in. Like a piggy bank," Steph said. "Sophie took it with her when she met Max, with the sole purpose of bludgeoning him over the head with it. She figured that if the blow to his head didn't kill him, it would stun him enough that he'd almost certainly drown.

"She didn't dispose of the bear afterwards, because it never occurred to her that anyone would see it as anything other than a child's toy. Clearly, no one ever told her that a detective regards any heavy object as a potential murder weapon. The more unlikely the better.

"There was some etching on the bear to create the appearance of fur. Traces of blood were recovered from grooves in the etching, and swabs taken from inside the slot on the bear's head also contained evidence of contact with Max."

"DNA, right?" Patrick said. Steph gave him an indulgent smile.

"Poor Max," Jane said.

DI Warwick continued. "Sophie Egan was still with Harry Scott when she first met Max Barsby. To begin with, she flirted with Max to make Harry jealous. She was never in love with Harry, and had already told him that she didn't see their relationship the same way he did. It seems that she'd planned to play one off against the other for a while. However, she soon discovered that Max wasn't interested."

"Of course not. He was in love with Maryam," Jane said.

"Poor Harry was convinced that Sophie was 'the one'," Elias commented.

"Messy," Patrick said.

"Yes," Steph agreed. "Well, we all know that Sophie's flirting with Max led to that infamous showdown at Vindolanda."

"How did Sophie trace Maryam and find out that she was in the country illegally?" Jane asked.

"She traced her the same way that Harry did, by following Max."

Jane and Patrick listened as Steph related how Harry had followed Max to find out if he really was seeing someone.

"Sophie believed Max was 'too geeky to have a girl-friend'. But even after she saw Max with Maryam, she didn't regard Maryam as competition. She was convinced Max would choose her, given the opportunity. Sophie has some of the hallmarks of a narcissist, in my opinion."

Steph paused to take a sip of her wine. She signalled to Elias to take over.

"Sophie began stalking Max, hoping to learn more about his relationship with the woman he was seeing. It became an obsession with her, to find out what Max saw in 'that foreign bitch' as she put it.

"One afternoon, Sophie followed them into a café. She sat where she could listen to their conversation without being seen. This was when she learned that Maryam had entered the country illegally, but she also learned that Max was besotted with Maryam, that he loved her and wanted to marry her. In other words, there was no way Sophie stood a chance with him. And that enraged her. All she wanted to do was hurt them both."

Jane shook her head sadly. "What makes a person react like that? Most people would feel sad, accept their lot and get on with it, not go on a murderous rampage."

Steph shrugged. "Like I always say, that stuff's best left for the shrinks to figure out. They'll always come up with some syndrome or other to explain the darker side of human nature. It seems to me that there's not always a lot to figure out. Most murders can be traced back to simple, age-old motives such as rage and jealousy. But what do I know?"

Jane nodded, although she would not be so quick to dismiss the shrinks. Not everyone who experienced anger or jealousy became a killer. There had to be reasons for that.

Steph had paused, perhaps to gauge their reactions. Now, she continued. "Rightly or wrongly, I think that Beatrice and Clive Egan should shoulder some of the blame. Beatrice indulged her daughter and refused to see her faults. Both were willing to cover up when Sophie 'made mistakes'."

"How so?" Jane asked.

"Sophie hurt people before. As a child, a teenager. Clive Egan told us about a few incidents. The worst was when Sophie wounded another teenage girl on the arm with a knife when they fell out over a boy they both liked. Every time an incident occurred, Beatrice and Clive ensured that it was covered up, even to the extent of bribing the victims or their families. The teenage girl was bought off with an iPhone in return for telling her parents she'd accidentally injured herself while cutting up an apple at the Egans' house. Her parents were told the phone was a thank you gift for helping Sophie learn to swim."

"How did Max's final hours play out?" Jane asked, although it filled her with dread to hear the answer.

Elias took over again. "Sophie got in touch with Max and told him that she knew about Maryam and wanted to help. She said she knew someone who could help with obtaining documents. That's why Max met her in the bar on the Brayford.

"I expect he was too desperate to question what Sophie told him, or even how she knew about Maryam. So desperate that he trusted her completely.

"When they left the bar that night, Max thought it was for a meet-up with Sophie's contact, who would be waiting for them in a car parked in a lay-by on Spa Road, next to the River Witham. There was no car.

"Sophie told Max her contact would arrive soon. They stood, close to the river, to wait. Sophie pretended the catch on her bracelet had come undone. That the bracelet had slipped off her wrist. Max bent down to search for it in the long grass growing on the riverbank. That's when Sophie struck."

The background sound of conversation and laughter rippling around the room suddenly seemed louder and more intrusive. Jane wanted to tell everyone to be quiet, to show some respect, but, of course, only they four were absorbed in reliving the last moments of Max Barsby's tragically short life. Everyone else was oblivious.

Elias had finished his account. He reached for his drink and gulped it down. Jane and Patrick exchanged a look. Jane guessed that, like her, Patrick was thinking of Max's parents and their tragic loss. She felt a need to touch her son, feel that he was really there. She pressed his arm.

Steph cleared her throat. "Would you like to hear how we closed in on Sophie Egan?"

Jane and Patrick listened as Steph recounted how Darya and Maryam had appealed to her for help when Maryam received a death threat, and how Elias's diligent, close scrutiny of CCTV footage had revealed Sophie Egan as the person responsible.

"What will happen to Maryam now?" Jane asked.

"I'm afraid it hasn't been possible to conceal Maryam's illegal status. Sophie spoke about it in her confession," Warwick said. "Maryam has decided to appeal for asylum. Elias and I are going to support her in any way we can."

Jane nodded. "So much for Patrick and I helping Max's family by solving his murder. Still, I suppose Patrick's involvement with the dig did help you stop Bianca Carr and Iain MacDonald making off with a hoard of treasure."

Warwick grunted. "Yes, well that's one way of looking at it. Patrick's stunt cost a considerable amount in police time and resources." She opened her mouth as if to say more, but was silenced by a timely interruption from Elias.

"Tell them about the aureus."

"You tell them," Warwick said, sounding sniffy.

Elias gave a sly smile and began. "As I told you in my recent call, Max accepted the aureus from MacDonald and Carr in return for his silence about the hoard. Max must have had some idea of its value, but he showed it to John Headley, partly for a second opinion, but also, we think, because he wanted someone else to be aware of its existence, as a sort of insurance. If anything happened to him, perhaps he hoped that Headley would ask questions about the coin, thereby drawing our attention to the dig."

"Which Headley sort of did," Jane said. "In his own inimitable way — by jumping to the conclusion that his old nemesis, Linus Crow, had murdered Max and stolen the aureus. Then, of course, he broke into Crow's property to look for evidence." She frowned. "But what became of the coin? It wasn't on Max's body when it was discovered, was it?"

"When we mentioned the aureus to Maryam, she immediately disappeared up to her bedroom and returned a few minutes later with a small box. Inside was a coin," Elias said, smiling.

"The aureus," Jane said in wonder. "Did Maryam have any idea what it was?"

"Not a clue. Until we told her," Elias said. "Max gave it to her as a token of his love, until he could afford to buy her a ring. He told her it was a replica, like the ones you can buy at a museum."

"She needn't have given it to you," Jane said. "When you told her about the missing coin, and she suddenly realised it was in her possession, she could have just kept it. No one would have been any the wiser."

"Max would have wanted her to keep it and sell it to help buy her freedom, just as he'd intended to do," Patrick said.

Warwick seemed to have overcome her annoyance. "We're going to make sure that Maryam's part in returning an important piece of English national heritage is highlighted when she makes her application for asylum."

"What about the rest of the hoard?" Patrick asked. "When I saw MacDonald and Carr digging the rucksack up, I assumed that they'd stolen artefacts from the dig and buried them in the adjacent field, but MacDonald didn't find them on the site of the dig, did he?"

"That's correct," Steph said. "I know you've already heard some of the story from Elias. They would probably have left the hoard buried for longer, but MacDonald was getting jittery, what with the police asking questions around the dig." She looked at Patrick. "You happened to be in the right place at the right time to overhear their plans."

"Lucky me," Patrick said, grimacing slightly, no doubt at the memory of his traumatic night in the woods.

"We've been in touch with Linus Crow. He was astonished to hear about Iain MacDonald's treachery, but even more astonished, I think, to hear about the treasure. He had several ideas about why it might have been buried there. One explanation was that it might have been left by some ancient person for safekeeping. They would have intended to dig it up again later to trade for something else."

"Bet they would never have dreamed it would be dug up hundreds of years later by a pair of nighthawks," Patrick said.

Steph frowned and looked to Elias. "What else did he say? I remember him going on about stuff being buried as offerings to gods, or some such. I'm afraid I switched off a bit when he went on and on about it."

Elias took up the tale with enthusiasm. "Yes. Dr Crow said that another explanation for the existence of hoards is that they might have been buried as offerings to deities. Those found in marshy places, or in rivers, might have been intended for water deities, for example, and those found on land, for deities of the underworld."

"Fascinating," Jane said.

Pleased to have at least one interested party, Elias continued. "According to Dr Crow, after the Romans arrived in Britain, the Romano-British people continued to worship their own gods alongside the imported Roman ones.

"The Romano-Britons gave up as offerings what was valuable in their own world — the same object can have different meanings to different cultures. To the Romans, coins meant money, but to the Romano-British people they could become sacred offerings. So, Roman coins were buried alongside other offerings such as gold jewellery and precious metals. The—"

"Thank you, Elias," Warwick interrupted. "You should have seen Crow's face when we told him the gold aureus was for real. He really couldn't believe it. Kept going on about how exceptional it was."

"What will happen to the treasure now?" Patrick asked.

"As you know, the discovery of the hoard is being kept quiet for a bit," Warwick said. "This is partly because of its connection to the murder investigation, and partly to give archaeologists time to assess the area where it was found. Eventually, the landowner will get a share, and because the treasure belongs to the nation, it will ultimately end up somewhere it can be seen and enjoyed by everyone."

"Wouldn't it be great if it ended up in Lincoln?" Patrick said. No one disagreed.

"Have you spoken with John Headley?" Jane asked. Warwick and Elias exchanged a look.

"Yes," Warwick replied. "Given his involvement, I decided that he should be a party to at least some of this information. He knows about the aureus and the treasure and has been sworn to secrecy until it can be made public."

"I've spoken with him too," Jane said. "Just the other day at the bookshop where he works. Did Dr Crow tell you that Headley contacted him?"

Warwick looked surprised. "He didn't mention it. I hope Headley hasn't been harassing him in some way?"

Jane shook her head. "The opposite, actually. Headley got in touch to apologise. They had quite the chat, apparently. Dr Crow even offered to show Headley around the dig in the early New Year."

"Amazing, isn't it?" Patrick said.

"Absolutely," Elias agreed. "Who'd have thought it?"

"Not simply a case of keeping your enemies close?" Warwick said.

There was a silence. Jane exchanged a look with Elias. They shook their heads.

"What?" Warwick said.

"I think they disapprove of you putting a cynical spin on it," Patrick said helpfully.

At that moment, Karun announced, in a booming voice, that it was fast approaching midnight. The huddle of four was drawn back into the party. Everyone in the room began to form a circle, linking arms. Jane found herself linked to Warwick.

Ten, Nine, Eight, Seven, Six . . .

Speaking loudly, to be heard above the noisy countdown, Jane said to Warwick, "If Linus Crow and John Headley can be friends after forty years of feuding, there's hope for us, don't you think?"

. . . Three, two, one . . .

Warwick's answer was lost in the cheering that broke out on the chimes of midnight.

THE END

ACKNOWLEDGEMENTS

It's ten years since my first Merry & Neal novel was published with Joffe Books, so I'd like to say a special thank you to CEO Jasper Joffe for offering me that first ever contract in 2015 and making my dream of becoming a published author come true.

Twelve books, two series and one standalone novel later, I'm still in awe of the hard work, expertise and dedication that the team at Joffe Books puts into preparing my novels for publication — from my publisher and editor Kate Lyall Grant to her colleagues in Marketing and Production. So huge thanks to all of you guys too.

THE JOFFE BOOKS STORY

We began in 2014 when Jasper agreed to publish his mum's much-rejected romance novel and it became a bestseller.

Since then we've grown into the largest independent publisher in the UK. We're extremely proud to publish some of the very best writers in the world, including Joy Ellis, Faith Martin, Caro Ramsay, Helen Forrester, Simon Brett and Robert Goddard. Everyone at Joffe Books loves reading and we never forget that it all begins with the magic of an author telling a story.

We are proud to publish talented first-time authors, as well as established writers whose books we love introducing to a new generation of readers.

We won Trade Publisher of the Year at the Independent Publishing Awards in 2023 and Best Publisher Award in 2024 at the People's Book Prize. We have been shortlisted for Independent Publisher of the Year at the British Book Awards for the last five years, and were shortlisted for the Diversity and Inclusivity Award at the 2022 Independent Publishing Awards. In 2023 we were shortlisted for Publisher of the Year at the RNA Industry Awards, and in 2024 we were shortlisted at the CWA Daggers for the Best Crime and Mystery Publisher.

We built this company with your help, and we love to hear from you, so please email us about absolutely anything bookish at feedback@joffebooks.com.

If you want to receive free books every Friday and hear about all our new releases, join our mailing list here: www.joffebooks.com/freebooks.

And when you tell your friends about us, just remember: it's pronounced Joffe as in coffee or toffee!

www.ingramcontent.com/pod-product-compliance
Ingram Content Group UK Ltd.
Pitfield, Milton Keynes, MK11 3LW, UK
UKHW042301230925
8048UKWH00002B/145